Penny Blood A

The Triskelion Prophecy

A D&D 5e Adventure

The Triskelion Prophecy

Collect All The Penny Blood Adventures

Adventures

- The Dark Nun's Church
- Marie Laveau's Army
- The Werewolves of London
- The Thirteenth Hour
- The Mad Lab
- Krampus
- Midwinter Vampires
- Walk the Plank
- The Leprechaun's Trap
- Mutanti - Whispers of War
- Mutanti - Tears of War
- Mutanti - Lords of War
- The New Dark Age
- Crescent Moon Circus
- Catalyst
- Clockwork Tower
- Gorgon
- The Illustrated Troll
- Witches of the Blood Moon
- The Christmas Chronicles of Winterglen
- The Dragon's Heir
- Pyramids of Power
- Dragon's Rise
- Crypts of the Shadow Court
- Dragon's War
- Battle Cry!
- The Triskelion Prophecy
- Wasteland Chronicles: Beyond The Wall

Compilations

- Gothic Horror - 5 Gothic Horror themed Adventures
- PBA Vol 1 - 4 Adventures
- The Mutanti Cycle
- The Shattering
- Mysteries of Myth and Machine

Supplemental Rules Books

- Arcane Codex
- Creatures of the Realm
- Gourmet Guildmaster
- Breath of the Dragon
- Stories of the Fey
- Pocket Game Master: Magic Items

Credits

Author: M A D (aka, Matthew David)

Editor: Alysson Wyatt

Lead Game Testing: Team Wyatt

Game Testers: All of Team Wyatt's friends - you guys rock!

Artists: Adobe Stock Art, Adobe Firefly, Adobe Photoshop, DALL-E, Midjourney

The Triskelion Prophecy

- Managing Encounters 7
- Starting the Adventure 9
- Act 1 - The Village of Aerilon 11
  - The Village Green 11
  - Blacksmith's Forge 14
  - The Celtic Knot 16
  - Residents 18
  - Eilidh's Grove 21
  - The Battlefield - Gleann na Marbh (Valley of the Dead) 26
  - The Hermit's Hut 31
- Act 2 – The Fey 36
  - Coill Draíochta, the Enchanted Forest 37
  - Edge of the Enchanted Forest 38
  - The Enchanted Forest Clearing 42
  - Center of the Enchanted Forest 43
  - Scaling Coill Draíochta (Enchanted Forest) Encounters 46
  - The Sunset Forest, Coill an Luí na Gréine 48
  - The Center of the Sunset Forest 50
  - The Magic Pond 53
- Act 3 – The Wicked Ones 59
  - Droichead na Carraige (Bridge of the Rock) 59
- Caisleán na Taibhse (Castle of the Ghost) 61
  - Entrance Hall 61
  - Library 62
  - Dining Hall 63
  - Throne Room 64
- Uaimh Chráite (Ghost Cave) 66
  - Entrance Cave 66
  - Bone Chamber 67
  - Summoning Chamber 70
  - Shadow Sanctum 73
- Aillte na nDeor - Cliffs of Tears 75
  - Cliffside Path 75
  - Druidic Stone Circle 76
  - Storm Sanctum 77
- Túr na nScáth (Tower of Shadows) - 81
  - Ground Floor: Entrance Hall 81
  - 2nd Floor: Armory of Corrupted Relics 83
  - 3rd Floor: Chamber of Corrupted Nature 87
  - 4th Floor: Ritual Chamber - Final Confrontation 89
- Denouement 95
- Perform the Purification Ritual with the Unified Triskelion 95
- Conclusions 98
- The Triskelion Restored: A New Dawn for Aerilon 98
- A Pyrrhic Victory: The Shadow of the Triskelion Lingers 98
- The Looming Shadow: Fionnlagh's Enduring Threat 99
- The Fall of Hope: Darkness Triumphant 99
- Embracing the Darkness: Champions of Chaos 100
- Appendix 102

Scaling Monsters ---------------------- 104

Monsters ----------------------------- 106

Animated Spellbook 106

Corrupted Beast 106

Fey Skeleton 107

Lucht Siúil (Traveler) 108

Peist Dhraíochta (Magic Serpent) 109

Saoi na Coille (Sage of the Forest) 110

Scáthannaí (Shadow Walker) 111

Sídhe Sentinel 112

NPCs -------------------------------- 114

Conall 114

Eilidh the Druid 115

Eoghan na Luí (Eoghan of the Sunset) 115

Fionnlagh, the Dark Sorcerer 117

Maolmhuire 118

Ríona na Sí (Ríona of the Fey) 119

Rivac Amretvo, the Storm Herald 120

Róisín 121

Tadhg an Airgid (Tadhg of the Silver) 122

Magic Items -------------------------- 124

The Triskelion 124

Claidheamh Solais (Sword of Light) 124

Brat Draíochta (Cloak of Enchantment) 125

Cruach Draíochta (Cauldron of Magic) 125

Pronunciations ---------------------- 127

Map -------------------------------- 130

Thank You ------------------------- 132

Managing Encounters

Managing Encounters

To help DMs tailor the adventure to the party, each encounter is designed with flexibility in mind. Whether your group consists of fledgling adventurers or seasoned heroes, the provided guidelines will help ensure that the challenges are both fun and fair.

Encounter Structure

Encounter Name: The title of the encounter, usually indicating the primary theme or challenge.

DM Information: A brief summary to give you a clear picture of the encounter's purpose and its role in the overall adventure.

Read Aloud: Descriptive text meant to be read verbatim to the players, setting the scene and atmosphere.

Activity: Detailed guidance, including potential variations, expected player strategies, and potential outcomes.

Lair Actions: Specific actions or effects that occur in certain locations, often benefiting the encounter's primary antagonist.

Scaling the Encounter: Instructions on how to adjust the encounter's difficulty based on player levels:

- **Beginner (Level 1-5)**: Simplified challenges tailored for newer or less powerful characters.
- **Intermediate (Level 6-10)**: Moderate challenges that require a mix of skill, strategy, and teamwork.
- **Advanced (Level 11+)**: Complex and multi-faceted challenges suitable for veteran adventurers.

Monster and/or NPC: Details or references to any creatures or characters the players might interact with during the encounter.

Encounters may reference content found later in the book, such as detailed monster statistics in the Monsters section. Feel free to adapt or replace these elements to better fit your group's preferences or the storyline you're weaving.

Modularity and Flexibility

This adventure, like all Penny Blood Adventures, is modular by design. If a particular monster or challenge doesn't resonate with your campaign's theme, feel free to replace it or adjust as needed. The goal is to provide a rich framework that sparks inspiration, allowing you to craft an unforgettable journey for your players.

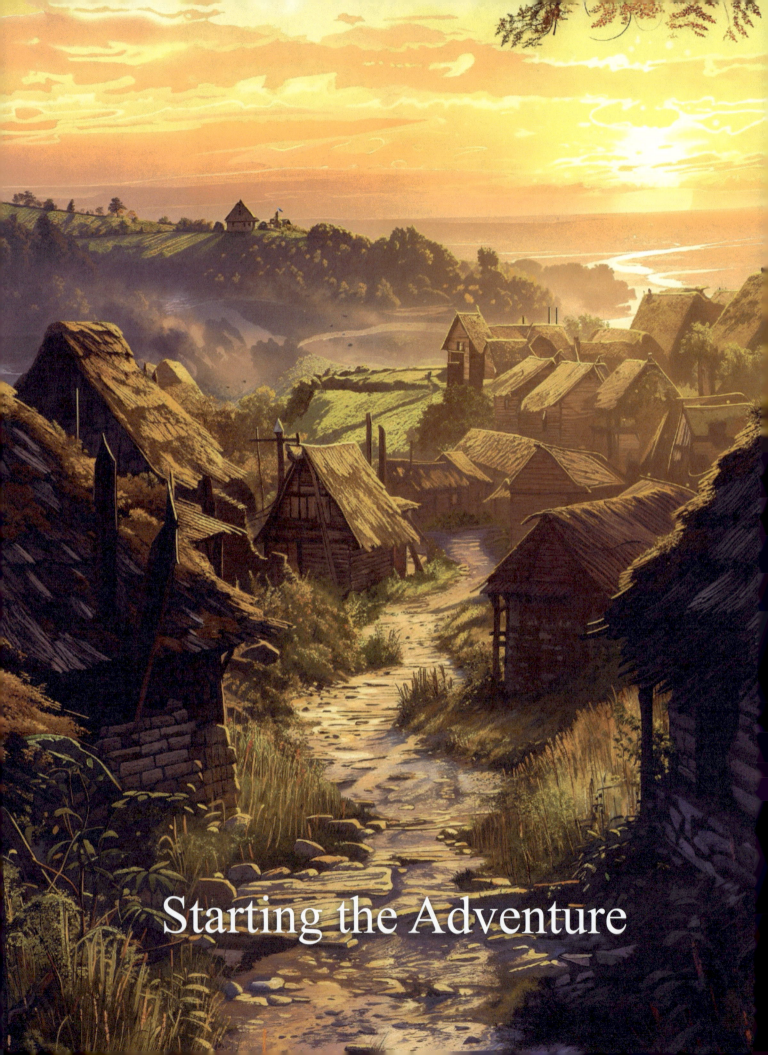
Starting the Adventure

Starting the Adventure

The objective of the adventure is to reunite the three parts of the mystical Triskelion, an ancient artifact of immense power, and use it to vanquish Fionnlagh, the Dark Sorcerer. Each part of the Triskelion is controlled by one of Fionnlagh's apprentices, hidden in different locations across the islands. The adventurers must collect all three parts, restore the Triskelion's power, and confront Fionnlagh to end his reign of terror.

Leveraging Gaelic Irish Myths

This adventure is deeply rooted in the rich tapestry of Gaelic Irish mythology. Players will encounter references to the Tuatha Dé Danann, the legendary race of gods and heroes, and the island's connection to these divine beings. Emphasize the mystical and ancient aspects of the setting, drawing on themes of nature, magic, and the eternal struggle between good and evil.

The Importance of the Fey

The fey play a crucial role in Gaelic stories, often acting as intermediaries between the mortal world and the divine. In this adventure, the fey serve as key NPCs who offer guidance, assistance, and sometimes, challenges to the players. They embody the enchantment and unpredictability of the natural world, providing both allies and adversaries who can significantly impact the course of the adventure.

Landscape and Settings

The landscape of this adventure is a reflection of the mythical Irish countryside, filled with lush forests, rural villages, ancient towers, and dramatic shorelines. Each location should evoke the timeless beauty and mystery of Gaelic folklore. Use descriptive language to paint vivid pictures of the environments, from the verdant hills of Inis Solais to the haunting cliffs of Oileán na nAmhrán. The settings are not just backdrops but integral parts of the narrative, offering opportunities for exploration, discovery, and encounters with the mystical and the unknown.

Key Locations and Descriptions

Inis Solais (Island of Light): The sacred island where the adventure begins, known for its ancient druidic sites and mystical properties. This island serves as a bastion of hope against the encroaching darkness.

- **Aerilon (Village)**: A sanctuary for scholars, warriors, and artisans, now overshadowed by fear and decay. The village is protected by ancient enchantments but currently struggles under Fionnlagh's dark influence.
- **Gleann na Marbh (Valley of the Dead)**: A somber, mist-shrouded battlefield where the spirits of ancient warriors rest uneasily, guarding the secrets of their final conflict.
- **Aillte na Mara (Cliffs of the Sea)**: The cliffs are home to numerous seabirds and are often wrapped in an eerie, supernatural mist.

Oileán na nAmhrán (Island of Songs): Renowned for its haunting beauty and musical heritage. Located to the west of Inis Solais, it can be reached by a treacherous sea journey or via the Bridge of the Rock.

- **Caisleán na Taibhse (Castle of the Ghost)**: A spectral castle inhabited by the spirit of a bard.
- **Uaimh Chráite (Ghost Cave)**: A cave system considered to be a portal to the Otherworld.
- **Aillte na nDeor (Cliffs of Tears)**: Cliffs named for a tragic love story, with stones said to be transformed tears.
- **Túr na nScáth (Tower of Shadows)**: The dark tower of Fionnlagh, shrouded in perpetual shadow.

Inis na nGaoth (Island of Winds): A small, rocky island with fierce winds and avian inhabitants, located southeast of Oileán na nAmhrán. It is a sanctuary for birds and a place where the wind carries the songs and messages of the gods. While not a primary location in the adventure, it offers:

- Potential refuge or a hidden location for important items or NPCs.
- Challenging terrain for skill-based encounters or tests of the party's resolve.
- A possible source of rare, wind-based magical components or artifacts.

The constant, howling winds make conventional sailing nearly impossible, often requiring magical means of transportation.

Act 1 - The Village of Aerilon

The village of Aerilon, nestled in the heart of Inis Solais, was founded centuries ago by a group of druids guided by the light of a celestial star. These druids sought a place where they could practice their sacred arts in peace, away from the conflicts and strife of the outside world. Upon discovering the radiant island of Inis Solais, they decided to settle and establish a sanctuary that would be a beacon of hope and knowledge. They cast powerful enchantments to protect the village and ensured that it would remain a haven for scholars, warriors, and artisans drawn to its promise of safety and enlightenment. Over the years, Aerilon grew into a vibrant community, flourishing under the watchful eyes of its druidic founders.

Village Summary

Aerilon is a sanctuary for scholars, warriors, and artisans, now overshadowed by fear and decay due to the sinister influence of Fionnlagh, the Dark Sorcerer. The village is protected by ancient enchantments cast by Eilidh the Druid. Key locations within the village include:

The Village Green: The heart of the village, used for gatherings and outdoor events. You can find Caoimhe, the village elder, here.

Blacksmith's Forge: The forge of Cionnaola Ó Dhonnaile, where weapons, armor, and tools are crafted and repaired.

The Celtic Knot: A cozy inn run by Fiona Ní Fágáin, offering food, drink, lodging, and local stories.

Homes: Residences for the remaining community of Aerilon, consisting of thatched cottages and bungalows.

You find yourselves in the serene village of Aerilon, nestled on the sacred island of Inis Solais. The air is thick with a sense of unease, and dark clouds loom over the once vibrant community. As you take a look around the village, you notice a cluster of charming cottages and bungalows, their thatched roofs and stone walls a testament to ancient craftsmanship. However, the once-vibrant atmosphere is now tainted by an eerie stillness. The crops are withered, and many homes stand abandoned. You notice the despair etched on the faces of the remaining villagers. The air, once filled with the scent of blooming flowers and freshly baked bread, now carries a subtle hint of decay, mingling with the distant sound of hushed whispers and nervous murmurs.

In the center of the village lies a large open space, the Village Green, where people likely once gathered for festivals and community activities. Now, while it still hosts more activity than any other part of the village, it seems a far cry from the lively bustle a village this size should have at this time of day. Nearby, the rhythmic clang of hammer on metal draws your attention to a sturdy building, no doubt where the village's blacksmith works with a grim determination. Further along, a faint light spills from the windows of a once-cozy inn, its warmth diminished by the pervasive sense of dread.

The Village Green

Players can find Caoimhe, the village elder, on the Village Green. She informs them of the magic wards protecting the village and guides them to Eilidh the Druid, who can be found two hours south of the village.

As you step into the heart of the village, you find yourselves in an open space surrounded by charming cottages and a small amount of activity. Unlike the emptiness observed through much of the village, here children play, villagers chat, and the air is filled with the scent of blooming flowers and fresh grass. Every now and again, a wary villager casts an anxious glance at the darkening sky. In the center of this relatively serene space stands an elderly woman with silver hair neatly braided, her eyes a striking shade of green that holds the wisdom of countless generations.

She smiles warmly as you approach, radiating an aura of calm and strength. "Welcome, travelers," she says, her voice soothing yet firm. "I am Caoimhe, the village elder. Are you here to help us?"

Meet with Caoimhe

The PCs arrive at the village of Aerilon, which has been sending out distress signals through various means to seek aid. This could include magical messages sent by village druids, word of mouth carried by traders, or even a message in a bottle found by the PCs along the shoreline. The village is in a state of anxiety and anticipation, hoping for heroes to answer their call.

As the PCs approach the Village Green, they are greeted by Caoimhe, the village elder, whose presence exudes calm and wisdom. With a gentle yet urgent voice, she beckons them closer.

"Brave adventurers, please aid our cause if you are able. The dark sorcerer Fionnlagh has brought ruin upon our village, his power growing each day as he corrupts the balance of nature. The ancient Triskelion, a symbol of harmony and power, has been shattered and its pieces scattered. Fionnlagh's apprentices guard these fragments, using their power for nefarious purposes. We need your help to retrieve the pieces of the Triskelion, restore its power to restore balance to the island, and put an end to Fionnlagh's corrupting influences over our lands and people once and for all. Our village's fate, and that of the entire island, rests in your hands."

PCs must succeed on a DC 12 Charisma (Persuasion) check to gain Caoimhe's trust and convince her to share detailed information about the wards and Eilidh, the druid who reinforced the ancient wards. Characters who succeed on a DC 14 Wisdom (Insight) check can discern Caoimhe's genuine concern and determine that she is withholding no information.

The Triskelion's Prophecy

Caoimhe will share with the PCs the following prophecy that has been handed down for generations. She fears that the time for the prophecy is now.

In the age when shadows rise and light falters, the island of Aerilon shall tremble under the weight of dark ambition. Three fragments, once whole, hold the balance of creation, destruction, and transformation.

First Fragment: Creation (Life Fragment)

Second Fragment: Destruction (Death Fragment)

Third Fragment: Transformation (Rebirth Fragment)

The prophecy speaks thus:

When the moon's pale light is shrouded in darkness,

And the land quakes with the fury of the storm,

Three shall seek the power to reshape fate,

But only one shall hold the key to the Triskelion's form.

Beware the path of corruption, for it leads to ruin.

Seek the heart of the forest, where ancient spirits dwell.

Unite the fragments under the sacred ritual,

In the heart of Coill Draíochta, where the secrets swell.

A hero born of shadow and light,

Must traverse the trials and face the dark night.

With courage, wisdom, and strength combined,

The Triskelion's power shall be realigned.

In the final hour, when hope seems lost,

And the dark sorcerer claims the throne at great cost,

The hero's resolve shall turn the tide,

For the prophecy's truth lies deep inside.

Only with purity of heart and clarity of mind,

Can the fragments' true power be intertwined.

To restore the balance and banish the blight,

The Triskelion must be made whole in the light.

The island shall bloom, its wounds shall heal,

When the hero fulfills the Triskelion's seal.

From the ashes of conflict, peace shall arise,

And the dawn of a new era will greet Aerilon's skies.

Additional Information Provided by Caoimhe

About the Triskelion

What is it? "The Triskelion is an ancient artifact imbued with the essence of nature and the balance of power. It is a sacred symbol representing harmony among the elements and the interconnectedness of all things."

Why is it important? "The Triskelion's power maintains the natural balance on the island. Without it, chaos and destruction threaten to overtake the land. It also acts as a barrier against dark forces, keeping malevolent entities at bay."

About Fionnlagh

His activities across the island: "Fionnlagh has been spreading his influence by corrupting natural sites, enslaving creatures, and spreading fear among the populace. His apprentices are positioned across the island, each guarding a fragment of the Triskelion."

Why is he doing this? "Fionnlagh seeks to harness the full power of the Triskelion for his own purposes. His ultimate goal is to dominate the island and bend its natural forces to his will, creating a realm of darkness under his control."

About Eilidh and the Wards

Eilidh's Role: "Eilidh is a powerful druid who has been reinforcing the ancient wards protecting Aerilon. These wards are crucial in delaying Fionnlagh's advances and buying time for the village to find a solution."

The Wards: "The wards are ancient protective spells woven into the very fabric of the land around Aerilon. They are designed to repel dark magic and protect the villagers from harm. However, their power is waning as Fionnlagh's corruption spreads."

Nature of the Wards

The village of Aerilon is protected by ancient magical wards that have recently been reinforced by Eilidh the Druid. These wards are designed to shield the village from dark magic and malevolent forces. The wards are woven into the very fabric of the village, anchored at key points around the Village Green, the Blacksmith's Forge, and the Celtic Knot Inn. Each ward is connected to the others through a network of ley lines that crisscross beneath the village, channeling the natural magic of the land to create a powerful barrier.

The wards have the following properties:

- **Protection from Evil and Good:** The wards provide a constant effect of the *Protection from Evil and Good* spell, shielding the village from fiends, undead, and other malevolent entities. Spellcasters have disadvantage at casting magic while in the village.
- **Alarm:** The wards are imbued with an *Alarm* spell, alerting the villagers to the presence of intruders or dark magic within the village boundaries. PCs with evil intentions will not be allowed into the village.
- **Healing Aura:** The wards generate a healing aura that grants villagers advantage on saving throws against diseases and poisons, and they recover from injuries at an accelerated rate (equivalent to a constant effect of the *Lesser Restoration* spell).

Fionnlagh, the Dark Sorcerer has been systematically weakening the wards through his dark magic and manipulation. His apprentices have infiltrated the village, subtly corrupting the ley lines and sowing discord among the villagers. The once-strong wards are now fragile, their power diminished by Fionnlagh's insidious influence.

The ways in which Fionnlagh has weakened the wards include:

Corruption of Ley Lines: Fionnlagh's apprentices have tainted the ley lines that power the wards, introducing dark energy that disrupts their function. This corruption manifests as black, thorny vines that emerge from the ground near the ward anchors. Touching the vines will immediately result in a cut causing 1d4 damage.

Dark Rituals: Fionnlagh has conducted dark rituals near the village, channeling negative energy into the wards to erode their strength. These rituals involve sacrifices and the summoning of dark spirits that feed on the wards' magic. The wards will be broken if the PCs take more than three days to stop Fionnlagh and his apprentices.

Psychological Warfare: Fionnlagh has spread fear and despair among the villagers, weakening their collective belief in the wards' power. The wards are partially sustained by the villagers' faith and hope, and as these dwindle, so does the strength of the wards.

Gather Information about Eilidh the Druid

PCs can ask Caoimhe about Eilidh the Druid and obtain directions to her location, which lies two hours' walk to the south of the village.

Intelligence Check using Cartographer's Tools (DC 13): Characters must succeed on a DC 13 Intelligence check (aided by proficiency with cartographer's tools) to understand Caoimhe's description and map out a clear path to Eilidh's location.

Survival Check (DC 15): Characters who succeed on a DC 15 Wisdom (Survival) check can prepare adequately for the journey, ensuring they avoid potential hazards along the way.

Lair Actions

Mystic Aura: Once per round, Caoimhe can create an aura of calm within a 30-foot radius. All hostile creatures must make a DC 15 Wisdom saving throw or be charmed until the end of their next turn.

Healing Light: Caoimhe can use her action to heal all allies within a 20-foot radius for 10 hit points.

Guiding Presence: Once per round, Caoimhe can grant advantage on the next attack roll, saving throw, or ability check made by one ally within 30 feet.

Blacksmith's Forge

Players can purchase weapons, armor, and tools from Cionnaola Ó Dhonnaile, the blacksmith. He is a key figure in maintaining the village's defenses.

You hear the rhythmic clang of hammer on metal as you approach a sturdy building with a plume of smoke rising from its chimney. Inside, the forge is alive with heat and activity. The walls are lined with racks of finely crafted weapons and tools, each piece bearing the mark of a master craftsman.

Behind the anvil stands a burly man with a thick beard and strong, calloused hands. He pauses his work to greet you with a nod.

Activities

Purchase weapons, armor, and tools.

Learn about the village's defenses and recent attacks.

Cionnaola Ó Dhonnaile, the Blacksmith

Cionnaola Ó Dhonnaile, known as "Cion" by the villagers, is Aerilon's blacksmith and a key figure in maintaining the village's defenses. His lineage traces back to the legendary smiths of the Tuatha Dé Danann, famous for their magical weapons and armor.

From a young age, Cionnaola showed exceptional skill in metalwork. Under his father Fiachra's tutelage, he mastered blacksmithing techniques and learned to respect the materials and traditions of their craft. Tragedy struck when raiders attacked Aerilon, killing Fiachra and many others. Driven by grief, Cionnaola vowed to become the best blacksmith, ensuring the village would never be unprepared again.

Years later, Cionnaola is now a pillar of strength in Aerilon, crafting functional and artistic weapons, armor, and tools. His creations are known for their durability and subtle enchantments. Despite the dark cloud cast by Fionnlagh, the Dark Sorcerer, Cionnaola remains steadfast, ensuring the village's defenders are well-equipped. His determination to honor his father's legacy and protect his village has earned him widespread respect and admiration.

Weapons, Armor and Tools

Below is a table of Gaelic-themed weapons that the PCs can buy in the village of Aerilon, with some weapons enhanced with minor magic properties.

Name	Damage	Properties	Cost	Weight
Claiomh Solais (+1 Sword of Light)	1d8 slashing	Versatile (1d10), Magic (+1 to attack and damage rolls)	200 gp	4 lb
Faobhar Fola (Blood Edge, a shortsword)	1d6 piercing	Finesse, Light, Magic (Deals an extra 1d4 necrotic damage)	150 gp	2 lb
Sleá Draíochta (Enchanted Spear)	1d6 piercing	Thrown (range 20/60), Versatile (1d8), Magic (Returns when thrown)	125 gp	3 lb
Tua Bais (+1 Axe of Death)	1d12 slashing	Heavy, Two-handed, Magic (+1 to attack and damage rolls)	250 gp	7 lb
Bogha Sí (Fey Bow)	1d8 piercing	Ammunition (range 150/600), Heavy, Two-handed, Magic (+1 to attack rolls)	150 gp	2 lb
Sciath Dubh (Black Shield)	N/A	Shield (+2 to AC), Magic (Advantage on saving throws against fear)	100 gp	6 lb
Claíomh Cogaidh (War Sword, a greatsword)	2d6 slashing	Heavy, Two-handed	50 gp	6 lb
Ga Cú Chulainn (Cú Chulainn's Spear)	1d8 piercing	Thrown (range 20/60), Versatile (1d10)	5 gp	4 lb
Truaill Trí (Triple Flail)	1d8 bludgeoning	Magic (Once per day, can cast *Thunderwave* as a 1st-level spell)	150 gp	5 lb
Scian Fola (Blood Knife)	1d4 piercing	Finesse, Light, Magic (Heals wielder for 1d4 HP on a critical hit)	50 gp	1 lb

Check for Cion's Trust

If the PCs are successful on a DC 15 Charisma (Persuasion) check, Cion will trust them and share detailed information. If they fail, he will only sell them items from his forge and will not provide any additional information.

Information Cion Shares if the PCs Gain His Trust

Wards and Enchantments: Eilidh the Druid has placed powerful wards around the village to protect against dark magic and physical attacks. These wards are fueled by ancient druidic magic and can repel lesser fiends and spirits.

Village Watch: A rotating guard of able-bodied villagers, trained by Cionnaola, patrols the village day and night. They are equipped with weapons and armor crafted by Cion, including enhanced items with minor magical properties.

Reinforced Buildings: Key buildings such as the blacksmith's forge, the Celtic Knot, and the village residences have been reinforced to serve as safe houses in case of an attack.

Recent Attacks

Shadow Beasts: Fionnlagh's apprentices have been sending shadow beasts to harass the village. These creatures are formed from dark magic and have been attacking livestock, spreading fear among the villagers.

Night Raids: On several occasions, groups of raiders, likely under Fionnlagh's command, have attempted to breach the village at night. The wards and the village watch have repelled these attacks, but not without casualties.

Disruption of Trade: Caravans and traders coming to Aerilon have been ambushed on the roads. Supplies are running low, and the villagers are becoming desperate as their connections to the outside world are being severed.

Lair Actions

Fiery Burst: Once per round, Cionnaola can cause a burst of flame to erupt from the forge, dealing 2d6 fire damage to all enemies within 10 feet (DC 13 Dexterity saving throw for half damage).

Hammer Strike: Cionnaola can use his action to make a powerful hammer strike, dealing an additional 1d6 bludgeoning damage on his next melee attack.

Iron Will: Once per round, Cionnaola can grant himself or an ally within 10 feet advantage on a Constitution saving throw.

The Celtic Knot

PCs can gather information about Oileán na nAmhrán and Fionnlagh from Fiona Ní Fágáin at her inn. This is also a place to hear local stories and legends.

Warm light spills from the windows of a cozy inn as you step inside, the smell of hearty stew and freshly baked bread welcoming you. The inn's common room is filled with the sound of cheerful conversation and the clinking of mugs. The walls are adorned with tapestries depicting scenes of local legends and folklore.

Behind the bar stands a woman with fiery red hair and a friendly smile. "Welcome to The Celtic Knot," she says, her voice warm and inviting. "I'm Fiona Ní Fágáin, and this is my establishment. Take a seat and make yourselves comfortable."

Activities

Learn about Oileán na nAmhrán (the Island of Songs) and Fionnlagh, the Dark Sorcerer.

Hear stories and legends from Fiona and the patrons.

Fiona Ní Fágáin

Fiona Ní Fágáin, the spirited owner of the Celtic Knot, is a beloved figure in the village of Aerilon. She inherited the inn from her parents, who were known for their hospitality and the rich tradition of storytelling that made the Celtic Knot a gathering place for travelers and villagers alike. Fiona grew up listening to the tales of ancient heroes, the fey, and the magic that shaped the land's history. This upbringing instilled in her a deep appreciation for her heritage and a fierce dedication to her community.

When Fionnlagh's dark influence began to spread over Aerilon, Fiona stood as a pillar of strength for the villagers. Despite the growing fear, she kept the Celtic Knot's doors open, providing a safe haven for those in need. Her resilience and unwavering spirit have earned her the respect and admiration of everyone who knows her. Fiona's knowledge of local legends and her connections with various travelers make her a valuable source of information about the fey and Fionnlagh's sinister plans.

People in the Celtic Knot

Name	Backstory	Information Known
Eamon O'Connell	A traveling bard who has been performing at the Celtic Knot for the past month. Eamon's songs and stories are filled with ancient lore and wisdom.	Eamon knows several songs about the fey and their ancient pacts. He has also heard rumors about Fionnlagh's apprentices and their activities on Oileán na nAmhrán, the Island of Songs.
Siobhan Ní Shuilleabhain	A local healer who frequents the Celtic Knot to share news and gather supplies. Siobhan is known for her herbal remedies and knowledge of mystical plants.	Siobhan has insights into the healing magic of the fey and the corrupting spells of Fionnlagh. She knows that Eilidh's druidic wards are weakening.
Brendan Ó Flannagáin	A retired soldier who now leads the village watch. Brendan often visits the inn to reminisce about his past adventures and share his military expertise.	Brendan has encountered fey creatures in his travels and has fought against dark magic similar to Fionnlagh's. He can provide tactical advice on dealing with shadow beasts and raiders.
Moira Ní Bhraonáin	A merchant who trades in rare goods and magical artifacts. Moira has a wide network of contacts and often brings news from other villages and towns.	Moira is a gossip and much of what she says is greatly exaggerated or outright lies. With that said, she does know about hidden fey artifacts that might aid the party.
Conor MacCarthaigh	A farmer whose lands have been ravaged by Fionnlagh's dark magic. Conor seeks solace at the Celtic Knot, hoping for a solution to his plight.	Conor has witnessed the effects of Fionnlagh's magic firsthand and can describe the shadow beasts and cursed plague in detail. He also knows which areas of the village are most vulnerable.

Items for Sale

Name	Description	Price
Aerilon Amber Ale	A smooth, golden ale brewed locally with a hint of honey.	3 cp
Stout of the Hills	A dark, rich stout with notes of coffee and chocolate.	4 cp
Highland Mead	A sweet, floral mead made from wildflowers and local honey.	5 cp
Fiery Spirit	A potent hard liquor with a spicy kick, distilled from barley.	8 cp
Druid's Blessing	A strong herbal liquor said to have restorative properties.	10 cp
Morning Porridge	A hearty bowl of oatmeal with dried fruits and honey.	2 cp
Farmer's Breakfast	Eggs, sausage, and fried potatoes, served with a slice of bread.	5 cp
Traveler's Stew	A thick stew of beef, vegetables, and barley, served with bread.	6 cp
Hunter's Pie	A savory pie filled with venison, root vegetables, and gravy.	7 cp
Fisherman's Lunch	Grilled fish with a side of roasted vegetables and lemon butter.	6 cp
Shepherd's Delight	A lamb and vegetable stew, seasoned with herbs and served with ale.	7 cp
Highland Feast	A large platter of roasted meat, potatoes, and seasonal vegetables.	10 cp
Sweetberry Tart	A slice of tart filled with sweet wild berries and cream.	3 cp
Lodging Room	A cozy room with a comfortable bed, suitable for a good night's rest.	1 sp per night

Residents

The residential homes provide background on the villagers' lives and their struggles. Players can interact with villagers to gain insights and additional quests.

Scattered around the village are charming thatched cottages and sturdy bungalows, each with its own unique character. Smoke rises from chimneys, and the smell of home-cooked meals wafts through the air. The homes are well-kept but show signs of the hardships faced by the villagers.

As you walk through the residential area, you see families going about their daily routines, their faces marked by worry and resilience. Children play quietly, and elders sit on porches, keeping watchful eyes on the horizon. The sense of community is strong here, despite the fear that hangs in the air.

Activities

- Speak with villagers to gain insights into their lives and concerns.
- Gather additional quests and information about recent events.

Speak with the Villagers

Below is a table of people in the village of Aerilon that the players could interact with as they are investigating the town:

Irish Gaelic Name	Phonetic Pronunciation	Backstory	Information
Bran Ó Ceallaigh	Bran oh KEL-lee	Bran is a skilled hunter and tracker who has lived in Aerilon all his life. He stays to protect his family and the village from the dark creatures that now lurk in the shadows. Despite the increased terror, his sense of duty keeps him from leaving.	Bran has seen Eoghan na Luí's scouts near the village, indicating they might be planning an ambush.
Sorcha Ní Bhraonáin	SOR-ka nee VREE-nawn	Sorcha is an herbalist and healer. She remained in Aerilon because she feels a deep connection to the land and believes her skills are crucial for helping the villagers survive. Her knowledge of herbs and potions is unparalleled.	Sorcha knows about Niamh an tSolais and her unique ability to heal both light and dark forces in the Sunset Forest.
Eilis Ní Chathasaigh	AY-lish nee HA-ha-see	Eilis is a storyteller and keeper of local legends. She hasn't left because she believes that preserving and sharing the village's history is essential, especially in dark times.	Eilis can share the legend of Claidheamh Solais (Sword of Light) and its connection to the Triskelion (see Magic Items section of the Appendix).
Liam Ó Domhnaill	LEE-am oh DO-nal	Liam is a blacksmith's apprentice, learning the trade from Cionnaola Ó Dhonnaile. He stayed because he believes his skills are crucial for defending the village.	Liam knows about the traps and defenses in Fionnlagh's tower, having helped Cionnaola forge some of the components.
Aoife Ní Riain	EE-fa nee REE-an	Aoife is a weaver known for her intricate tapestries that depict the village's history and myths. She stayed in Aerilon because she feels her work is a way to inspire hope and resilience among the villagers.	Aoife has heard rumors about Rivac possessing the Cruach Draíochta (Cauldron of Magic), a powerful and ancient magical artifact.
Conor Ó Braonáin	CON-or oh VREE-nawn	Conor is a fisherman who has a deep understanding of the island's waterways. He stayed because he believes his knowledge of the sea could be crucial for the village's survival and trade.	Conor has seen strange movements in the waters near Fionnlagh's stronghold and suspects that Maolmhuire, one of Fionnlagh's apprentices, is involved.
Deirdre Ní Fhearchair	DEER-dra nee FAR-har	Deirdre is a former warrior who now trains the village's defenders. She remained because she feels a responsibility to protect the people and pass on her combat skills.	Deirdre has insights into Eilidh, the Druid, and knows that Eilidh has crucial information about Maolmhuire, one of Fionnlagh's apprentices.
Rónán Mac Carthaigh	ROH-nawn mac CAR-hi	Rónán is a carpenter and builder, responsible for maintaining the village's structures. He stayed to ensure the village remains a safe and secure place.	Rónán has been working with Eilidh to reinforce the wards around the village and knows about the magical defenses she has put in place.
Máire Ní Dhuibhne	MAW-ra nee GWIV-na	Máire is a farmer who grows rare and magical plants. She stayed in Aerilon because she believes her crops are vital for the village's survival.	Máire knows about a hidden grove where Rivac often gathers rare ingredients for his magic, including those needed for the Cruach Draíochta (Cauldron of Magic).

Side Quests

The following side quests can be suggested by anyone in the village:

The Healing Grove

Description: Sorcha Ní Bhraonáin, the herbalist in Aerilon, needs rare herbs from a mystical grove deep in Coill Draíochta, the Enchanted Forest. The PCs must find the grove, collect the herbs, and return them to Sorcha to help heal the villagers.

Reward: Potions of Healing (3), Herbalist's Blessing (for one PC or the party as a whole: advantage on one Medicine check or healing-related skill check per day for a week).

Success Criteria: Collecting the required herbs from the grove and delivering them safely to Sorcha in Aerilon.

The Blacksmith's Apprentice

Description: Cionnaola Ó Dhonnaile, the blacksmith in Aerilon, has lost his prized hammer, taken by a mischievous fey creature. The PCs must venture into the Enchanted Forest, confront the creature, and retrieve the hammer.

Reward: A masterwork weapon of choice, forged by Cionnaola (grants a +1 bonus to attack and damage rolls).

Success Criteria: Recovering Cionnaola's hammer from the fey creature and returning it to him.

The Weaver's Request

Description: Aine Ní Dhálaigh, the weaver, needs special spider silk from a dangerous part of Coill Draíochta to create enchanted garments. The PCs must brave the spider-infested area, collect the silk, and return it to Aine.

Reward: Enchanted Garment (grants advantage on Dexterity (Stealth) checks).

Success Criteria: Successfully gathering the spider silk and delivering it to Aine.

The Old Hermit's Secret

Description: An old hermit in the Enchanted Forest claims to have knowledge about Fionnlagh's weaknesses. The PCs must find the hermit, gain his trust, and learn what he knows.

Reward: A detailed plan of Fionnlagh's defenses, providing advantage on Stealth and infiltration checks in Fionnlagh's territory.

Success Criteria: Earning the hermit's trust.

Lair Actions

Community Support: Once per round, a villager can assist the PCs, providing a +2 bonus to their next skill check.

Alert Neighbor: A watchful villager can warn the PCs of approaching danger, granting them advantage on their next Perception check.

Healing Touch: Once per round, a kind-hearted villager can use their action to heal a PC for 1d8 hit points.

Scaling the Village of Aerilon Encounter

Beginning Players (PC levels 1-5)

- Reduce the DC of skill checks by 2 (e.g., DC 15 becomes DC 13).
- Halve the HP of any NPCs if combat occurs.
- Reduce damage dealt by NPCs and lair actions by 1 die (e.g., 2d6 becomes 1d6).
- Make magical items less powerful (e.g., +1 weapons become masterwork weapons or have no bonus).
- Simplify side quests, focusing on gathering information and simple fetch quests.
- Emphasize roleplay and exploration over combat.

Intermediate Players (PC levels 6-10)

- Use NPC stat blocks as written.
- Offer magical items as written.
- Add complexity to side quests, incorporating combat and puzzle-solving elements.

Advanced Players (PC levels 11+)

- Increase the DC of skill checks by 2 (e.g., DC 15 becomes DC 17).
- Double the HP of any NPCs if combat occurs.
- Increase damage dealt by NPCs and lair actions by 1 die (e.g., 2d6 becomes 3d6).
- Enhance magical items (e.g., +1 weapons become +2 weapons).
- Make side quests more challenging, with high-stakes outcomes affecting the main storyline.
- Introduce powerful minions of Fionnlagh as potential combat encounters.
- Add complex political elements or moral dilemmas to the village's situation.
- Increase the urgency and scale of the threat to Aerilon.

Eilidh's Grove

This encounter introduces players to Eilidh the Druid, a key ally who provides crucial information about the Triskelion and the threats facing the land. The grove serves as a place of revelation and preparation for the challenges ahead.

As you trek through the dense forest, the air grows thick with an otherworldly mist. The trees seem to part before you, revealing a hidden clearing bathed in soft, ethereal light. The ground beneath your feet is carpeted with lush moss and dotted with vibrant wildflowers that seem to glow with an inner radiance.

In the center of this mystical glade stands an ancient oak tree, its massive trunk twisted into the semblance of a shelter. Tendrils of ivy with shimmering leaves cascade from its branches, creating a living curtain around the tree's base. The air here feels charged with magical energy, and you can hear the faint whispers of secrets carried on the breeze.

Activities

Speak with Eilidh to gain information about the Triskelion and Fionnlagh.

Receive a blessing or magical aid from Eilidh.

Search the grove for magical herbs or items.

Speak with Eilidh

When the players approach Eilidh, use the following guidelines:

Initial Interaction: PCs must first gain Eilidh's trust with a DC 13 Charisma (Persuasion) check. On a success, she speaks freely; on a failure, she's more guarded.

Information Gathering: Allow characters to ask questions. For each question, the PC must make a Charisma (Persuasion) check:

DC 10: Basic information

DC 15: Detailed information

DC 20: Secret or obscure information

Sample Questions and Answers (with associated Persuasion check DCs):

Q: "What is the Triskelion?"
Basic: "The Triskelion is an ancient artifact of immense power. Long ago, it was split into three parts."

Detailed: "Each piece of the Triskelion is now in the possession of one of Fionnlagh's apprentices. These pieces grants them extraordinary magical abilities, far beyond their natural talents."

Secret: "Now, this isn't common knowledge, but the true power of the Triskelion can only be awakened by performing a sacred ritual in the heart of Coill Draiochta, the Enchanted Forest. It's a closely guarded secret."

Additional Info:

What kind of immense power? What does it actually do? "The Triskelion holds power over nature and the elements. When whole, it can control weather, enhance crop yields, and even communicate with the spirits of the land."

Why was the Triskelion shattered? "It was shattered by the ancient druids to prevent it from being misused. They feared that its immense power, while inherently good and natural, could be corrupted and manipulated for evil purposes if it fell into the wrong hands."

How would reuniting the Triskelion's pieces into the single artifact affect the land and the island? "Reuniting the Triskelion would restore balance to the land, bringing prosperity, harmony, and peace back to the island."

Q: "Tell us about Fionnlagh."
Basic: "Fionnlagh is a dark sorcerer of considerable power. He's been threatening our lands with his corrupt magic for some time now."

Detailed: "He has three main apprentices, each controlling a fragment of the Triskelion. They've been causing havoc in different regions, each in their own way."

Secret: "There's something not many know about Fionnlagh. His power is tied to a corrupted ley line beneath his tower. If that connection could be severed, it might significantly weaken him."

Additional Info:

The Triskelion Prophecy

Why doesn't Fionnlagh bring the pieces together and use the Triskelion himself? "Fionnlagh, despite possessing the fragments, cannot unite them because the Triskelion's true power is inherently tied to the purity of its user. The artifact stands against dark magic and corrupt intentions, which makes it impossible for Fionnlagh to perform the sacred ritual required to harness its full power."

Why is he doing all of this, and what does he hope to gain? "Fionnlagh seeks to dominate the island and bend its natural forces to his will. He believes that by controlling the Triskelion, he can achieve ultimate power and immortality."

Why doesn't he bring the pieces together and use the Triskelion himself? "The Triskelion's power is based on harmony and balance, which is antithetical to Fionnlagh's corrupt nature. He cannot wield its full power, as it stands against his dark magic."

Who are Fionnlagh's apprentices? "Fionnlagh's apprentices are Conall, Róisín, and Maolmhuire. Conall is a necromancer with a dark past, Róisín is a master of elemental magic, and Maolmhuire is a shadow sorcerer whose touch corrupts. Each of them holds a fragment of the Triskelion and uses its power to further Fionnlagh's aims."

Where can I find information about them? "You should speak to those who have had direct encounters with the apprentices. Fiachra at the Battlefield can tell you about Conall, Rivac at the Hermit's Hut knows much about Róisín, and for information on Maolmhuire, I am the one with most knowledge."

Q: "How can we defeat Fionnlagh and his apprentices?"
Basic: "To have any hope against Fionnlagh, you'll need to retrieve each piece of the Triskelion from the apprentice who wields it and reunite the three parts. It's a formidable task, but essential."

Detailed: "Each of Fionnlagh's apprentices has a weakness. If you can identify and exploit these weaknesses, you might be able to defeat them and reclaim the pieces."

Secret: "There's an ancient druidic ritual, passed down through generations. It can purify the Triskelion once it's reassembled. With the purified Triskelion, you'd have a weapon powerful enough to challenge Fionnlagh himself."

Q: "Are there others who can help us?"
Basic: "Yes, the Fáinne na Sí, a group of the fey folk, reside in Coill Draiochta, the Enchanted Forest. They could be powerful allies."

Detailed: "You'll find them about half a day's walk to the Southeast. They're not easy to locate, mind you, but if you can find them, they can offer magical assistance and guidance unlike any other."

Q: "What can you tell us about Coill Draiochta/the Enchanted Forest?"
Basic: "Coill Draiochta is an ancient forest, teeming with magic and mystery. It's home to various fey creatures, both benevolent and mischievous."

Detailed: "Be cautious in there. The forest has a way of shifting and changing, as if it has a mind of its own. It's easy to lose your way if you're not careful."

Secret: "At the very heart of Coill Draiochta, there's a convergence of ley lines, a source of magical power beyond imagination. If you could find it and harness its energy, it might be key to defeating Fionnlagh."

Q: "Tell us about Maolmhuire."
The Shattered Soul: "In days long past, Maolmhuire was a soul not yet blackened. His heart sought light, but the shadows whispered secrets too alluring to resist."

The Apprentice of Darkness: "Fionnlagh, the master of shadows, found a kindred spirit in Maolmhuire. Beware, for their bond is forged in the fires of dark ambition and twisted dreams."

The Corrupting Touch: "His touch is that of decay. Those who feel his grasp wither as the autumn leaves, their strength sapped by the creeping tendrils of his power."

Keeper of the Life Fragment: "Within the heart of the Castle of the Ghost, which stands on Oileán na nAmhrán (the Island of Songs), a fragment of creation lies twisted in his grasp. Its purity now serves to spread corruption and fear, a cruel irony of fate."

The Broken Spirit: "Once, he was a guardian of the land, a friend to the forests and fields. But desperation drove him to the darkness, and the land weeps for his loss."

The Ritual of Shadows: "In the highest tower, under storm-wracked skies, he performs rituals most foul. His magic seeks to bind and corrupt, turning life into a mockery of itself."

The Phantom Snare: "Beware the traps he lays. The shadows themselves conspire with him, snaring the unwary in pits of despair and death."

A Glimpse of Redemption: "Though the shadows claim him, a sliver of light remains. Should you find it, there may yet be a way to turn him from his dark path."

The Key to Victory: "The Life Fragment is the source of his power. To strip it from him is to weaken his grasp on the land. But take heed, for it is bound tightly to his dark heart."

The Lucht Siúil: "Spirits wander the halls of his domain, the Lucht Siúil. Some seek knowledge, others hunger eternally. Their whispers hold secrets, if you have the courage to listen."

Receive a Blessing or Magical Aid from Eilidh

After the players have conversed with Eilidh and gained her trust, she may offer her assistance in the form of a blessing or magical aid. This process involves the following steps:

Eilidh's Offer: Eilidh will say, "You've a difficult journey ahead, and I'd like to offer you some aid. Each of you may approach me for a blessing or a bit of druidic magic to help you on your way."

Individual Approach: Each character must approach Eilidh individually. As they do, she'll ask them to share their greatest concern about the upcoming quest.

Wisdom Check: The PC must make a DC 14 Wisdom check. This represents their ability to articulate their concerns and connect with the natural energies Eilidh channels.

Blessing or Aid Determination: Based on the Wisdom check and the concern shared, Eilidh will provide one of the following (DM's choice based on what's most appropriate):

a) On a failed check:

- A minor blessing: Advantage on one saving throw of the DM's choice within the next 24 hours.

- A *Goodberry* spell cast for the PC (creates 10 berries that each restore 1 hit point and provide nourishment for one day).

b) On a successful check:

- A major blessing: Resistance to one damage type for 24 hours.

- A single-use ability to cast *Lesser Restoration* without using a spell slot.

- A charm that allows the PC to reroll one failed ability check or saving throw within the next 48 hours.

c) On a natural 20:

- Eilidh casts *Enhance Ability* on the character, which lasts for 8 hours without requiring concentration.

- A magical seed that, when planted, instantly grows into a tree that can be used once for the *Tree Stride* spell.

Druidic Mark: Regardless of the outcome, Eilidh places a small, temporary druidic mark on the character (a swirling pattern of leaves or vines). This mark lasts for 7 days and may help the character gain the trust of other druids or nature-aligned creatures they encounter.

Eilidh's Advice: As she bestows the blessing or aid, Eilidh will offer a piece of cryptic advice related to the character's stated concern. This advice should be roleplay-focused and potentially foreshadow upcoming challenges.

Group Harmony: After all PCs have received their individual blessings, Eilidh will perform a short ritual that grants the entire party the effects of a short rest, restoring hit points and expended resources as appropriate.

Search the Grove for Magical Herbs or Items

Players can search Eilidh's Grove for magical herbs or items. Each PC can make a DC 15 Wisdom (Perception) or Intelligence (Nature) check (aided by proficiency with the herbalism kit) to search the grove.

On a success, the character finds 1d4 herbs from the table below. On a critical success (natural 20), they find 1d4+1 herbs and have a chance to find a magical item (DM's discretion).

On a failure, they find nothing. On a critical failure (natural 1), they may have a minor negative encounter (e.g., disturbing a pixie's home, accidentally touching a poisonous plant).

The DM can decide how many search attempts are allowed based on time constraints and narrative pacing.

Below is a table of magical herbs that can be found in Eilidh's Grove:

Herb Name	Description	Herb Properties
Moonbloom	Silvery flowers that glow faintly in darkness	When consumed, grants the effects of a *Darkvision* spell for 1 hour.
Sunburst Leaf	Golden leaves that radiate warmth	Can be used as a component for *Light* or *Daylight* spells. If consumed, grants resistance to cold damage for 1 hour.
Whisperwind Grass	Tall, swaying grass that seems to murmur in the breeze	When a grass blade is held, grants advantage on Wisdom (Perception) checks relying on hearing for 10 minutes.
Dreamdew Petal	Iridescent petals covered in enchanted dew	If placed on the eyes before a long rest, grants the benefits of a Trance (as per the Elf racial trait) for that rest.
Thornheart Berry	Small, heart-shaped berries with tiny thorns	When consumed, grants 2d4 temporary hit points and advantage on Constitution saving throws for 1 hour.
Mistwalker Moss	Pale, ethereal moss that seems to shift and move	Can be used by casters to cast *Misty Step* once without using a spell slot. The moss disappears after use.
Truthroot	Gnarled root with a faint blue glow	When chewed, grants advantage on Wisdom (Insight) checks for 10 minutes, but disadvantage on Charisma (Deception) checks for the same duration.
Feylight Fungus	Bioluminescent mushrooms in various pastel colors	Can be used by casters to cast *Faerie Fire* once without using a spell slot. The fungus disappears after use.
Stormleaf	Leaves that crackle with tiny sparks when touched	Can be crushed to cast *Shocking Grasp* as a cantrip. Each leaf can be used once in this way by casters.
Heartwood Sap	Thick, amber sap from the grove's oldest tree	When applied to a weapon, grants a +1 bonus to damage rolls for 1 hour.

Note: These herbs are considered rare and magical. Their effects do not stack with similar magical effects, and a creature can only benefit from one type of herb at a time. The DM may adjust the properties or availability of these herbs as needed for game balance.

Terrain

The grove is considered difficult terrain due to the thick undergrowth and magical nature of the place. PCs must make a DC 12 Dexterity (Acrobatics) check to move at full speed; failure means they can only move at half speed. The magical atmosphere of the grove provides advantage on Wisdom (Perception) checks related to nature or magic while within its boundaries.

Lair Actions

Nature's Embrace: Eilidh can cause vines and roots to grapple up to three creatures of her choice within the grove. The targets must succeed on a DC 15 Strength saving throw or be restrained until the start of Eilidh's next turn.

Whispers of the Wind: Eilidh can create a gust of wind that carries whispered secrets. All creatures in the grove must make a DC 15 Wisdom saving throw. On a failure, they are disoriented and have disadvantage on their next attack roll or ability check. On a success, they gain insight and have advantage on their next Wisdom check.

Healing Bloom: Eilidh can cause healing flowers to bloom instantly. She and up to three allies of her choice within the grove regain 2d6 hit points.

NPC

Eilidh the Druid

Scaling Eilidh's Grove Encounter

Beginning Players (PC levels 1-5)

Reduce skill check DCs by 2 (e.g., DC 15 becomes DC 13).

Limit herb search to 1d4 herbs total for the party.

Simplify Eilidh's blessings:

- **Failed check**: Advantage on one saving throw within 24 hours.
- **Successful check**: Resistance to one damage type for 1 hour.

Reduce lair action save DCs to 13.

Limit magical aid to cantrips and 1st-level spells.

Focus on roleplay and information gathering over challenges.

Intermediate Players (PC levels 6-10)

Keep skill check DCs as written.

Allow each PC one herb search attempt.

Use Eilidh's blessings as written.

Keep lair action save DCs at 15.

Offer magical aid up to 3rd-level spells.

Add time pressure to gathering information.

Introduce minor combat encounters with fey creatures.

Advanced Players (PC levels 11+)

Increase skill check DCs by 2 (e.g., DC 15 becomes DC 17).

Allow multiple herb search attempts, with diminishing returns.

Enhance Eilidh's blessings:

- **Failed check**: Options from the intermediate tier.
- **Successful check**: Temporary HP equal to PC level, or advantage on all saves for 1 hour.

Increase lair action save DCs to 17.

Offer powerful magical aid, including custom boons.

Add complex moral choices or diplomatic challenges.

Introduce high-level threats, such as corrupted fey or minions of Fionnlagh.

The Battlefield - Gleann na Marbh (Valley of the Dead)

This encounter introduces players to Fiachra the Gravedigger, who provides crucial information about Conall's tactics and the Ghost Cave. The area is haunted by restless spirits.

As you approach the northern edge of the village of Aerilon, the landscape transforms dramatically. Before you stretches a vast, mist-shrouded valley, its ground pockmarked with countless grave markers and ancient monuments. The air grows heavy with an oppressive silence, broken only by the occasional whisper of wind through weathered stone.

In the center of this somber expanse, you spot a solitary figure moving methodically among the graves, shovel in hand. The mist seems to part around him, revealing more of the valley's grim features – shattered weapons half-buried in the earth, tattered banners fluttering weakly in the breeze, and here and there, the ghostly flicker of unearthly lights hovering above the ground.

Activities

Speak with Fiachra to gain information about Conall and the Ghost Cave.

Search for valuable artifacts or clues among the graves.

Perform a ritual to calm restless spirits.

Speak with Fiachra

When PCs approach Fiachra, he will be cautious at first. To gain his trust and information, follow these steps:

Initial Interaction: PCs must succeed on a DC 13 Charisma (Persuasion) check to gain Fiachra's trust. On a success, he speaks freely. On a failure, he is guarded and requires further convincing.

Information Gathering: Players can ask Fiachra questions about the apprentices. Due to his occupation and regular presence at gravesites, Fiachra possesses knowledge about one apprentice in particular, Conall, and his lair, the Ghost Cave. For each question, the PC must make a Charisma (Persuasion) check:

DC 10: Basic information

DC 15: Detailed information

DC 20: Secret or obscure information

Sample Questions and Answers

Q: "Tell us about Conall."
Basic: "Conall is one of Fionnlagh's apprentices. He controls the undead. He has recently been at the Battlefield to recruit the undead. These warriors died in honor, and Conall's demand to serve him appalls them."

Detailed: "Conall wields the Death Fragment of the Triskelion, granting him power over destruction and the dead. He's been raising fallen warriors as his servants."

Secret: "Conall's power is tied to a dark shrine hidden in the Ghost Cave on Oileán na nAmhrán. Destroying it could weaken him significantly."

Q: "Where is the Ghost Cave located?"
Basic: "The Ghost Cave is on Oileán na nAmhrán, the Island of Songs, west of this battlefield."

Detailed: "Conall has recently fled there. It's a treacherous journey across the water, and the cave itself is well-hidden along the island's western coast."

Secret: "There's a hidden path that can lead you safely to the cave. Look for a series of standing stones marked with spiral carvings near the western shore of Oileán na nAmhrán."

Q: "What dangers might we face in the Ghost Cave?"
Basic: "The cave is heavily guarded by Conall's undead minions."

Detailed: "Beware of various undead monsters protecting the cave entrance and its inner chambers. Conall has also set magical wards to alert him of intruders."

Secret: "At the heart of the cave lies a dark shrine, the source of Conall's power. It's likely protected by his strongest minions and deadly traps."

Fiachra's Demeanor: Fiachra speaks in a low, somber tone. His words are measured, and he often pauses to glance around, as if checking for eavesdroppers. He might say: "Tread carefully, for the path to Oileán na nAmhrán is perilous, and the Ghost Cave even more so. Conall's influence has turned that once-peaceful island into a haven for the restless dead. The very air around the cave seems to whisper with malevolent intent."

Additional Aid: If the players build a strong rapport with Fiachra (two or more successful Charisma checks), he offers additional help by way of a crude map showing the location of the Ghost Cave on Oileán na nAmhrán.

Wisdom Check: PCs can make a DC 14 Wisdom (Insight) check to determine if Fiachra is withholding any information.

Remember to roleplay Fiachra's somber and cautious nature, emphasizing his deep knowledge of Conall's activities and the dangers of Oileán na nAmhrán. His information should highlight the critical importance of finding and destroying the shrine in the Ghost Cave to weaken Conall's power over death and destruction.

Search for Valuable Artifacts or Clues Among the Graves

Players can search the Battlefield for magical items and clues. To do so, each PC can make a DC 15 Wisdom (Perception) or Intelligence (Investigation) check to search an area of the Battlefield. PCs proficient in History or Arcana have advantage on this check.

On a success, roll on the Artifact Location Table found below to determine what they find. On a critical success (natural 20), they find two items from the table.

On a failure, they find nothing of value. On a critical failure (natural 1), they may trigger a minor negative effect (e.g., disturbing a restless spirit, activating a latent curse).

The DM can limit the number of search attempts based on time constraints and narrative pacing.

Artifact Location Table

d8	Location	Item	Difficulty to Find
1	Warrior's Cairn	Claíomh Solais	DC 16 Strength check to move heavy stones
2	Overgrown Hero's Memorial	Sleá na Géine	DC 14 Nature check to safely part thick, thorny vines
3	Sunken Burial Mound	Sciath na Muintire	DC 15 Athletics check to dig through muddy earth
4	Ancient Tree Hollow	Fleasc Draíochta	DC 13 Perception check to spot the hidden compartment
5	Crumbling Stone Circle	Fáinne an Dúlra	DC 17 Arcana check to safely remove from its magical seal
6	Mist-Shrouded Obelisk	Clócá na Taibhsí	DC 16 Investigation check to decipher worn inscriptions
7	Forgotten Chieftain's Tomb	Corn na Féile	DC 18 Dexterity check using thieves' tools to unlock an ancient mechanism
8	Spectral Warrior's Rest	Lámh an Laoch	DC 15 Charisma check to respectfully request the item from the spirit

Magical Items Table

Item Name	Rarity	Description	Properties	Attunement	Lore
Claíomh Solais (Sword of Light)	Rare	A gleaming silver longsword that emits a soft, warm light	+1 to attack and damage rolls. Can cast *Light* spell at will.	Yes	Said to be wielded by Lugh, the god of light, in his battle against the Fomorians. Its light is said to reveal hidden truths and banish darkness.
Sleá na Géine (Spear of Precision)	Uncommon	A finely crafted spear with intricate knotwork designs	+1 to attack rolls. Once per short rest, can gain advantage on one attack roll.	No	This spear is believed to be a replica of Gae Assail, the magical spear of Lugh that never missed its target and always returned to the thrower's hand.
Sciath na Muintire (Shield of Kinship)	Rare	A round shield emblazoned with symbols of unity and protection	+1 to AC. Once per long rest, can cast *Shield of Faith* on self or an ally.	Yes	Inspired by the legendary shield of Sreng, a Fir Bolg warrior. It's said to strengthen the bonds between comrades in battle.
Fleasc Draíochta (Wand of Druidry)	Uncommon	A gnarled oak wand infused with nature magic	Can cast *Speak with Animals* and *Goodberry* once per day each.	Yes	Crafted by the druids of Tara, this wand is imbued with the essence of the sacred oak trees, connecting its wielder to the natural world.
Fáinne an Dúlra (Ring of Nature's Embrace)	Rare	A silver ring with an ever-changing gemstone that reflects the seasons	Grants advantage on Survival checks in natural environments. Can cast *Pass Without Trace* once per day.	Yes	Said to have belonged to Airmed, the goddess of healing and herbalism, allowing its wearer to move in harmony with nature.
Clócá na Taibhsí (Cloak of Spectral Form)	Rare	A shimmering grey cloak that seems to fade in and out of visibility	Grants advantage on Stealth checks. Can cast *Invisibility* on self once per day.	Yes	Woven from the mists of Tech Duinn, the otherworldly house of Donn, god of the dead. It allows the wearer to walk between the world of the living and the dead.
Corn na Féile (Horn of Festivity)	Uncommon	An intricately carved drinking horn	When drunk from, restores 2d4+2 hit points and grants advantage on Charisma checks for 1 hour.	No	This horn is said to be blessed by Dagda, the good god of fertility and abundance, ensuring that it never runs dry during times of celebration.
Lámh an Laoch (Gauntlet of the Hero)	Rare	A bronze gauntlet with swirling designs of courage and strength	Grants +1 to Strength and advantage on saves against fear.	Yes	Forged in honor of Cú Chulainn, Ireland's legendary hero. It's said to imbue its wearer with a portion of his legendary courage and strength.

Perform a Ritual to Calm Restless Spirits

Fiachra informs the PCs: "Conall's dark magic has disturbed the rest of the fallen warriors. Their spirits roam restlessly, causing havoc and potentially aiding our foes. If you can perform the ancient ritual of peace, you might calm these spirits and gain their favor."

Ritual Requirements

Gathering Materials:

- A handful of soil from a warrior's grave (DC 12 Intelligence (Investigation) check)
- A drop of water from a pure source (can be created by a *Create Water* spell or found in the area with a DC 14 Wisdom (Survival) check)
- A personal item from one of the PCs (freely given)
- Three candles (can be provided by Fiachra if the PCs don't have them)

Preparing the Ritual Site:

- Find a central location in the Battlefield (DC 13 Wisdom check to choose an appropriate spot).
- Arrange the candles in a triangle.
- Mix the soil and water in the center of the triangle.

Performing the Ritual:

- One PC must lead the ritual, making a DC 15 Intelligence (Religion) check.
- Two other PCs must assist, each making a DC 13 Charisma (Performance) check.
- The ritual takes 10 minutes to complete.

Ritual Process:

The lead PC must recite the following incantation (in Common or Gaelic): "Spirits of the fallen, hear our call. Your battles are over, your rest is earned. We honor your sacrifice and offer you peace. Return to your slumber, knowing your legacy endures."

As this is spoken, the assisting PCs should light the candles and sprinkle the soil-water mixture around the triangle.

Success Conditions:

If the lead PC succeeds on their check and at least one assisting PC succeeds, the ritual is successful.

If the lead PC rolls a natural 20, the ritual is automatically successful regardless of the assistants' rolls.

Rewards for Success:

- The restless spirits are calmed, making the Battlefield safer to navigate. The PCs gain advantage on saves against fear effects in this area.
- The grateful spirits bestow a boon: each PC gains 1d4 temporary hit points that last until their next long rest.
- Fiachra rewards the party with a Whisper Stone - a small, smooth river rock that, when held, allows the user to cast *Speak with Dead* once per day without expending a spell slot.

Consequences of Failure:

If the lead PC fails their check or both assisting PCs fail, the ritual is unsuccessful. The disturbed spirits become agitated, causing the following effects:

- Each PC must make a DC 14 Wisdom saving throw. On a failure, they are frightened for 1 hour.
- The Battlefield becomes more dangerous. Random spectral attacks occur every hour (50% chance each hour), dealing 2d6 necrotic damage to a random PC unless they succeed on a DC 13 Dexterity saving throw.
- Fiachra becomes disheartened and is less willing to help. Future Charisma checks to gain information from him have disadvantage.

Partial Success:

If the lead PC succeeds but only one assistant succeeds, the ritual is partially successful.

- The spirits are calmed in a 60-foot radius around the ritual site.
- PCs gain advantage on saves against fear effects only within this area.
- No temporary hit points or Whisper Stone are granted, but Fiachra provides the party with three Potions of Healing in thanks for their efforts.

Terrain

The valley is difficult terrain due to the uneven ground, scattered graves, and thick mist. PCs must make a DC 13 Dexterity (Acrobatics) check to move at full speed; failure means they can only move at half speed. Additionally, the mist obscures vision, limiting clear sight to 30 feet. Beyond this range, creatures and objects are lightly obscured, imposing disadvantage on Wisdom (Perception) checks that rely on sight.

Lair Actions

Ghostly Whispers: Spectral voices fill the air, forcing all creatures in the valley to make a DC 14 Wisdom saving throw or be frightened until the end of their next turn.

Mist Surge: The mist thickens dramatically in a 30-foot radius around a point of Fiachra's choosing. This area becomes heavily obscured until the start of Fiachra's next turn.

Grave Eruption: The ground trembles, and 1d4 skeletons burst from the earth in random locations within the valley. These skeletons are under Fiachra's control and act on his initiative.

Scaling the Battlefield - Gleann na Marbh Encounter

Beginning Players (PC levels 1-5)

Reduce all skill check DCs by 2 (e.g., DC 15 becomes DC 13).

Limit artifact searches to 1d4 total for the party.

Simplify the calming ritual:

- Reduce components to just soil and a personal item.
- Only require one PC to perform the ritual (DC 13 Performance check).

Weaken magical items:

- Remove attunement requirements.
- Limit uses to once per long rest.

Adjust lair actions:

- Reduce save DCs to 12.
- **Ghostly Whispers**: Disadvantage on next attack roll instead of frightened condition.
- **Grave Eruption**: Summon only 1 skeleton.

Intermediate Players (PC levels 6-10)

Keep skill check DCs as written.

Allow each PC one artifact search attempt.

Use the calming ritual as written.

Keep magical items as described.

Maintain lair actions as written.

Advanced Players (PC levels 11+)

Increase all skill check DCs by 2 (e.g., DC 15 becomes DC 17).

Allow multiple artifact search attempts with diminishing returns.

Enhance the calming ritual:

- Add component: a drop of PC's blood (safely drawn).
- Increase main Performance check DC to 17.
- On critical success, permanently calm a 100-foot area.

Upgrade magical items:

- Add an additional minor property to each item.
- Allow some items to regain charges on short rests.

Enhance lair actions:

- Increase save DCs to 16.
- **Ghostly Whispers**: Also deal 2d6 psychic damage.
- **Mist Surge**: Also heals undead creatures for 2d8 HP
- **Grave Eruption**: Additional skeletons bearing weapons and shields rise from the dead.

The Hermit's Hut

This encounter introduces players to Rivac Amretvo, the Storm Herald, who provides crucial information about Róisín and her weather manipulation abilities. The location offers a respite from the harsh weather and an opportunity to gain insights on defeating Róisín, who possesses the Rebirth Fragment of the Triskelion.

As you approach the edge of the towering cliffs of the sea, Aillte na Mara, you spot a small, weather-beaten hut perched precariously near the precipice. The structure seems to defy the elements, standing firm against the howling winds and lashing rain. Wisps of smoke curl from a crooked chimney, suggesting warmth and shelter within.

Drawing closer, you notice the hut is constructed from a patchwork of materials - driftwood, salvaged planks, and even pieces of shipwreck. The walls are adorned with various weather-worn objects: seashells, bleached bones, and curious symbols etched into the wood. A small garden of hardy, wind-resistant plants surrounds the hut, their leaves dancing in the ever-present breeze.

Activities

Speak with Rivac to gain information about Róisín and her weather manipulation abilities.

Examine the Cruach Draíochta and learn its properties.

Descend Aillte na Mara (the Cliffs of the Sea), find the boat and sail across the stormy waters.

Speak with Rivac

When the players approach Rivac to discuss Róisín and her abilities, use the following guidelines:

Initial Interaction: PCs must make a DC 13 Charisma (Persuasion) check to gain Rivac's trust. On a success, he speaks freely. On a failure, he is more guarded and requires further convincing.

Information Gathering: Allow characters to ask questions. For each question, the PC must make a Charisma (Persuasion) check:

DC 10: Basic information

DC 15: Detailed information

DC 20: Secret or obscure information

Sample Questions and Answers

Q: "What can you tell us about Róisín's powers?"
Basic: "Róisín controls the weather using the Rebirth Fragment of the Triskelion, which amplifies her power over the elements. This fragment makes her storms more potent and her magic more destructive. She can create devastating storms at will."

Detailed: "Her power extends for miles. She can summon lightning, create gale-force winds, and even alter the climate of entire regions."

Secret: "The Rebirth Fragment allows her to not only control weather but also to transform and adapt to different environments. This makes her incredibly resilient."

Q: "Where exactly can we find Róisín?"
Basic: "Róisín resides in the Storm Sanctum, a fortress built atop Aillte na nDeor, the Cliffs of Tears, directly west of here. You can see the storms ravaging the shoreline from here."

Detailed: "She's created a fortress of storm clouds at the highest point of the cliffs. The area is constantly battered by fierce storms, making it difficult to approach without proper preparation. It's nearly impossible to approach without her knowledge due to the constant tempests."

Secret: "There's a sea cave at the base of Aillte na nDeor that might provide a less guarded entrance. Look for a waterfall that seems to defy gravity, flowing upwards along the cliff face."

Q: "How can we reach Aillte na nDeor?"
Basic: "There are two ways: by sea or by land."

Detailed: "At the base of this cliff, you'll find a small boat. You can sail it across the waters to Aillte na nDeor, but beware of the treacherous storms."

Secret: "If you prefer land, trek two hours north to Droichead na Carraige, the Bridge of the Rock. It's a natural stone bridge connecting Inis Solais to Oileán na nAmhrán. It's safer, but it takes longer and Róisín might spot you crossing."

Q: "How can we counter Róisín's weather manipulation?"

Basic: "You will need to find a way to counteract her elemental magic. Seek out magical artifacts or spells that can shield you from her attacks. Protection from lightning and thunder damage is crucial. Magical shelter can also help."

Detailed: "Róisín's power wanes when she's far from natural weather patterns. If you can lure her into the sea cave, her powers might be diminished."

Secret: "The Rebirth Fragment is tied to the natural cycle of seasons. Disrupting this cycle - perhaps by using druidic magic to rapidly change seasons in an area - could temporarily nullify her powers."

Additional Info:

Is there any way to redeem Róisín? "Róisín's connection to nature was once pure and strong. If you can remind her of her former purpose and the good she used to do, there might be a chance to bring her back from the brink. However, be cautious, as her loyalty to Fionnlagh may be deeply ingrained."

Weather Reading: Rivac can perform a weather reading to gain insight into Róisín's current activities. This requires a DC 15 Wisdom (Nature) check from Rivac. Player characters can assist, granting advantage on the roll if they succeed on a DC 12 Nature check (using either Intelligence or Wisdom).

Storm Navigation: Rivac can teach the PCs how to navigate through Róisín's storms safely. This grants the party advantage on Survival or Vehicle (Water) checks to traverse the stormy seas or treacherous cliffs for the next 24 hours.

Wisdom Check: PCs can make a DC 14 Wisdom (Insight) check to determine if Rivac is withholding any information.

Examine the Cruach Draíochta

When the PCs express interest in the Cruach Draíochta (Cauldron of Magic), Rivac will bring it out from a hidden alcove in his hut. Use the following guidelines for this activity:

Initial Observation:

Allow PCs to make a DC 13 Intelligence (Investigation) check to examine the cauldron's exterior.

Success reveals intricate runes and Celtic symbols etched into the blackened iron surface.

Identifying the Cauldron:

PCs can make a DC 15 Intelligence (Arcana) check to recognize the cauldron as a powerful magical artifact.

Success provides basic knowledge of its magical nature and hints at its potential uses.

Unlocking the Cauldron's Secrets:

PCs can attempt to unlock the cauldron's abilities through various methods:

A. **Arcane Study** (Intelligence-based):
   - DC 17 Intelligence (Arcana) check to decipher the runes and symbols.
   - Success reveals one of the cauldron's abilities (DM's choice).
   - A natural 20 reveals all abilities.

B. **Intuitive Understanding** (Wisdom-based):
   - DC 16 Wisdom (Insight) check to intuitively grasp the cauldron's purpose.
   - Success provides a general sense of what the cauldron can do.
   - A natural 20 grants a vision of the cauldron being used by ancient druids.

C. **Magical Resonance** (Charisma-based):
   - Spellcasters can attempt a DC 15 Charisma (Arcana) check to attune themselves to the cauldron's magic.
   - Success allows them to sense one of the cauldron's abilities.
   - A natural 20 temporarily attunes them to the cauldron, granting advantage on checks to use it for 24 hours.

Rivac's Knowledge

If the players are struggling, Rivac can offer insights upon a successful DC 14 Charisma (Persuasion) check.

He can demonstrate one of the cauldron's abilities, chosen by the DM.

Practical Experimentation

PCs can attempt to use the cauldron to brew a simple potion.

This requires a DC 15 Intelligence (Arcana) or Wisdom (Nature) check (or any combination of these), depending on their approach.

Success allows the PC to brew a Potion of Healing and demonstrates the cauldron's accelerated brewing ability.

Attunement Attempt

A PC can attempt to attune to the Cruach Draíochta during a short rest.

This requires a DC 16 Charisma saving throw.

Success attunes them to the cauldron, granting full knowledge of its abilities and the power to use them.

Cauldron Abilities (revealed through successful checks or attunement):

- **Potion Brewing**: Potions can be brewed twice as fast and with fewer ingredients.
- **Spell Catalyst**: Spells cast through the cauldron gain increased potency (additional damage/healing die).
- **Rejuvenating Brew**: Once per day, brew a potion that restores 2d8 hit points and cures one condition.

Lore and History

A successful DC 16 Intelligence (History) check reveals legends about the cauldron's origins and its use by ancient druids (see Magic Items section of the Appendix).

This information could provide context for its powers and hint at potential uses against Róisín.

Descend Aillte na Mara (Cliffs of the Sea)

Climbing Down

PCs must make a DC 15 Strength (Athletics) check to climb down safely.

Characters using climbing gear may add their proficiency bonus to their roll.

Failure by 5 or less means the character slips and takes 2d6 bludgeoning damage but manages to catch themselves.

Failure by more than 5 results in a fall, dealing 4d6 bludgeoning damage.

Characters can choose to aid each other, granting advantage to one climber but imposing disadvantage on their own check.

Alternative Methods

Spells like *Feather Fall* or *Levitate* can bypass the climbing check.

Creative use of rope and pitons can lower the DC to 12.

Find the Boat

Locating the Hidden Cove

PCs must succeed on a DC 13 Wisdom (Perception) check to find the hidden cove where the boat is moored.

Characters proficient in Nature or Survival have advantage on this check.

Failure means an additional 30 minutes of searching, with each attempt increasing the DC by 1 due to mounting frustration.

The Boat

It's a sturdy, weathered fishing boat, large enough for the party but small enough for a few people to manage.

The boat contains basic supplies: oars, a small sail, and some rope.

Sail Across the Stormy Waters

Initial Navigation

The party must designate a navigator who will make the primary checks.

The navigator must make a DC 15 Intelligence (Nature) or Wisdom (Survival) check to plot the safest course.

Success grants advantage on the subsequent sailing checks.

Sailing Checks

The journey takes 1 hour, requiring three successful checks (one every 20 minutes).

The navigator must make a DC 16 Wisdom (Survival) or Intelligence (Vehicle: Water) check for each segment.

Other PCs can assist, using the Help action to grant advantage on one check.

Consequences of Failure

First Failure: The boat is blown off course, adding 20 minutes to the journey.

Second Failure: A large wave crashes over the boat. Each character must make a DC 14 Strength saving throw or be swept overboard, requiring a DC 15 Strength (Athletics) check to climb back in.

Third Failure: The boat capsizes. Characters must make DC 15 Constitution saving throws every 5 minutes to avoid gaining one level of exhaustion while swimming to shore.

Critical Failure (Natural 1): The boat takes damage, springing a leak. Characters must use an action each turn to bail water or the boat will sink in 1d4 rounds.

Critical Success (Natural 20): The navigator finds a calm path through the storm, reducing the journey time by 20 minutes and granting inspiration to all aboard.

Additional Challenges

Halfway through the journey, Róisín may notice the intrusion. The DC for the final sailing check increases to 18 as she intensifies the storm.

Lightning strikes may occur. Each character must make a DC 14 Dexterity saving throw or take 3d10 lightning damage (half on success) at a dramatic moment.

Remember to describe the harrowing journey vividly, emphasizing the towering waves, howling winds, and the small boat's struggle against the elements. This should be a tense and exciting part of the adventure, showcasing the power of Róisín's weather manipulation and the bravery of the characters.

Terrain

The area around the hut is difficult terrain due to the strong winds and slippery, rain-soaked ground. PCs must make a DC 13 Dexterity (Acrobatics) check to move at full speed; failure means they can only move at half speed. Additionally, any ranged attacks made outdoors suffer disadvantage due to the wind unless the attacker succeeds on a DC 15 Wisdom (Survival) check to account for the conditions.

Lair Actions

Wind Shield: Rivac summons a protective barrier of swirling winds around the hut. All creatures within 30 feet gain half cover against ranged attacks for 1 round.

Storm Surge: A sudden gust of wind sweeps through the area. All creatures within 60 feet of the hut must succeed on a DC 15 Strength saving throw or be pushed 10 feet away from the hut.

Calming Eye: Rivac creates a 20-foot radius zone of calm around the hut. Within this area, the effects of difficult terrain are negated, and creatures have advantage on Constitution saving throws against weather-based effects for 1 round.

NPC

Rivac Amretvo, the Storm Herald

Scaling the Hermit's Hut Encounter

Beginning Players (PC levels 1-5)

Reduce all skill check DCs by 2 (e.g., DC 15 becomes DC 13).

Simplify Cruach Draíochta examination:

- Reduce checks to a single DC 12 Arcana check.
- Limit to two basic abilities.

Cliff descent:

- Reduce climbing DC to 12.
- **Fall damage**: 1d6 per 10 feet, max 3d6.

Sailing:

- Reduce navigation DC to 13.

Lair actions:

- Reduce save DCs to 12.
- **Wind Shield**: Only grants disadvantage on ranged attacks against targets.
- **Storm Surge**: Reduce push distance to 5 feet.

Intermediate Players (PC levels 6-10)

No changes to content.

Advanced Players (PC levels 11+)

Increase all skill check DCs by 2 (e.g., DC 15 becomes DC 17).

Enhance Cruach Draíochta examination:

- Add a fourth, more powerful ability.
- Successful attunement grants a minor boon (e.g., resistance to thunder damage).

Cliff descent:

- Increase climbing DC to 17/
- Add magical winds requiring a DC 15 Strength save to avoid being pushed off.

Sailing:

- Increase navigation DC to 18.
- Require four successful checks for the journey.
- Add magical storms requiring DC 16 Constitution saves to avoid exhaustion.
- **Lightning damage**: increase to 4d10.

Enhance lair actions:

- Increase save DCs to 17.
- **Wind Shield**: Also deflects spells of 3rd level or lower.
- **Storm Surge**: Also deals 2d8 bludgeoning damage.
- **Calming Eye**: Also removes one level of exhaustion from allies.

Add a legendary action for Rivac:

- **Storm Burst**: Rivac calls down a bolt of lightning on a target within 60 feet, dealing 4d10 lightning damage (DC 16 Dex save for half).

Act 2 – The Fey

In the mystical world of *The Triskelion Prophecy*, the realm of the fey holds a prominent place, steeped in ancient magic and timeless enchantment. As the players embark on their journey through the fey realms, they will encounter Coill Draíochta, the Enchanted Forest, and Coill an Luí na Gréine, the Sunset Forest. These fey domains, each with their unique character and challenges, are integral to the quest for the Triskelion and the battle against the malevolent forces threatening the land.

Coill Draíochta, a living testament to the ancient powers of the Tuatha Dé Danann, is a forest of ever-changing paths and magical mysteries. Under the watchful eye of Ríona na Sí, the players must navigate this enchanted landscape, confronting fey creatures, solving riddles, and proving their worth. The forest's rich history, infused with the legacy of ancient gods, offers both wonder and danger at every turn. Similarly, the Sunset Forest, home to the enigmatic Twilight Kin, is a realm of perpetual twilight where the balance between light and dark is meticulously maintained. Here, the players will delve into the intricate politics and magical lore of the Twilight Kin, negotiating alliances, uncovering secrets, and confronting the fading magic that threatens this delicate equilibrium. As the players traverse these fey realms, they will forge crucial alliances, gain powerful allies, and face formidable challenges, all in the pursuit of restoring the Triskelion and defeating the dark sorcerer Fionnlagh.

Coill Draíochta, the Enchanted Forest

Coill Draíochta is a mystical, ever-changing forest that serves as a key location in the adventure. The players must navigate its magical paths, potentially encountering various fey creatures and supernatural events as they seek to reach the heart of the forest where Ríona na Sí resides.

As you step into the forest, you're immediately enveloped by an otherworldly atmosphere. The trees here are ancient and massive, their trunks wider than houses and their canopies so high they seem to touch the clouds. Shafts of golden sunlight filter through the leaves, creating a dappled pattern on the forest floor that seems to shift and move even when there's no breeze.

The air is thick with magic, shimmering motes of light dancing on the periphery of your vision. The forest sounds are unlike any you've heard before - bird calls that sound almost like music, the rustling of leaves that seems to whisper secrets, and the distant sound of trickling water that somehow sounds like laughter. Every path you see seems to twist and turn, leading into mist-shrouded depths that promise both wonder and danger.

History

Coill Draíochta has existed since time immemorial, said to be one of the first places the Tuatha Dé Danann, the ancient gods of Ireland, set foot when they arrived in the mortal world. When the Tuatha Dé Danann retreated from the world of men, they imbued this forest with their magic, creating a sanctuary for fey creatures and a bridge between the mortal realm and the Otherworld.

Over millennia, Coill Draíochta has been shaped by the magic of countless fey inhabitants, each leaving their mark on the land. The forest has seen the rise and fall of human kingdoms, remaining a constant source of mystery and wonder. It has been a place of refuge for magical creatures fleeing persecution, a source of inspiration for bards and poets, and a testing ground for heroes seeking to prove their worth.

In recent centuries, as the influence of the fey has waned in the wider world, Coill Draíochta has become one of the last bastions of true, wild magic. Under the stewardship of Ríona na Sí, the forest has maintained its enchanted nature, defying the encroachment of the mundane world and serving as a reminder of the ancient powers that once shaped the land.

Wandering the Forest

If players are wandering without a guide or map, use these rules:

- At the start of each hour of travel, the party leader must make a DC 15 Wisdom (Survival) check.
- Failure means the party becomes lost and moves in a random direction for that hour.

Random Encounters (1d10)

1. **Fairy Ring**: Player characters stumble upon a ring of mushrooms. If they step inside, they must make a DC 14 Charisma saving throw or be transported to a fey pocket dimension for 1d4 hours.
2. **Whispering Trees**: The trees begin to whisper secrets. Each PC can make a DC 12 Wisdom (Perception) check to gain a hint about the forest's layout or a nearby danger.
3. **Pixie Prank**: A group of 1d4+1 pixies appear and attempt to play tricks on the party. Use the pixie stat block from the *Monster Manual*.
4. **Enchanted Stream**: The party finds a stream of glowing water. Drinking from it grants the effects of a *Greater Restoration* spell, but doing so also requires a DC 15 Constitution saving throw. Upon a failure, the drinker is polymorphed into a small forest animal for 1 hour.
5. **Lost Traveler**: The party encounters another lost traveler (use the commoner stat block) who might join them or lead them astray (50% chance of either).
6. **Treant Guardian**: A treant (use standard treant stat block) awakens and questions the party's presence. It can be persuaded to help with a DC 15 Charisma (Persuasion) check.

7. **Fey Blessing**: The party receives a blessing from an unseen fey entity. Each member gains inspiration.
8. **Wild Magic Surge**: The area is saturated with wild magic. Any spell cast in the next hour triggers a wild magic surge (roll on the Wild Magic Surge table in the *Player's Handbook*).
9. **Moonlight Glade**: The party finds a glade bathed in eternal moonlight. Resting here grants the benefits of a long rest in only 4 hours.
10. **Shapeshifting Plants**: Plants around the party come to life (use awakened shrub stat block) and attempt to entangle them. DC 13 Strength check to break free.

Terrain

The forest floor is covered in soft moss and fallen leaves, interspersed with gnarled roots and sudden clearings. Treat the entire forest as difficult terrain unless on a clear path. Additionally:

Climbing trees requires a DC 12 Strength (Athletics) check.

There's a 25% chance each hour of encountering a small stream or brook that requires a DC 10 Dexterity (Acrobatics) check to cross without getting wet.

Dense fog appears randomly, limiting visibility to 30 feet and imposing disadvantage on Wisdom (Perception) checks relying on sight.

Lair Actions

Forest's Embrace: Vines and branches reach out to grapple intruders. Each creature must succeed on a DC 14 Dexterity saving throw or be restrained until the end of their next turn.

Fey Lights: Glowing wisps appear, leading travelers astray. Each creature must succeed on a DC 13 Wisdom saving throw or move up to half their speed in a random direction.

Nature's Renewal: A surge of healing energy flows through the forest. All plant creatures and fey regain 10 (3d6) hit points.

Edge of the Enchanted Forest

This encounter introduces players to Ciarán an Sióg, a playful fairy scout who tests the party's skills as they enter Coill Draíochta. The encounter also features the Saoi na Coille, an ancient and wise forest entity that may aid or challenge the players depending on their actions.

As you approach the Enchanted Forest, the air grows thick with an otherworldly mist, and the trees before you seem to shift and dance in impossible ways. The forest's edge is a mesmerizing blend of vibrant colors and ethereal light, with flowers that glow softly and vines that move of their own accord.

The path ahead splits and twists unpredictably, sometimes appearing to lead in multiple directions at once. Strange whispers echo through the branches, and you catch glimpses of small, darting creatures just at the edge of your vision. The very air tingles with ancient magic, hinting at the wonders and dangers that lie within this enchanted realm.

Ciarán's Reveal

As you take in the mystical surroundings, a soft, tinkling laughter fills the air. A small, radiant figure flits into view, hovering just above the ground. As the diminutive figure approaches, you see that it is a fairy scout bearing a mischievous glint in his eyes and wings that shimmer like sunlight on water.

"Welcome, travelers!" he exclaims, his voice like the chime of silver bells. "I am Ciarán an Sióg. You stand at the threshold of Coill Draíochta, the Enchanted Forest. To prove your worthiness to enter, you must first navigate a challenge I've prepared for you. Do you accept?"

If the PCs Reject the Challenge

Should the party choose to reject Ciarán's challenge, he flutters his wings in mock indignation. "Oh, but you must prove yourselves! The forest does not welcome those who shy away from a bit of fun."

If the PCs insist on bypassing the obstacle course:

Ciarán's Reaction: Ciarán attempts to bar their way with a playful but determined demeanor. "The forest has its rules, and I am its guardian. You must complete the challenge to enter."

Magical Barriers: Ciarán conjures a barrier of vines and shimmering light, making it impossible to proceed without accepting the challenge. PCs can attempt to dispel the barrier (DC 18 Intelligence (Arcana) or Wisdom (Nature) check) or find another way around.

Combat Option: If the PCs are aggressive or evil-aligned and choose to attack Ciarán, he will defend himself using illusions and evasive tactics. A successful attack will cause him to vanish in a puff of glittering dust, but the barrier remains, reinforced by the magic of the forest itself.

Consequences of Ignoring the Challenge

If the PCs bypass Ciarán's obstacle course without his permission, the forest itself will become hostile. They will face increased difficulty with navigation (all navigation checks are made with disadvantage), and the forest's creatures will be wary or aggressive towards them. This hostility will persist until they find a way to appease Ciarán or another forest guardian.

Navigate Ciarán's Magical Obstacle Course

Ciarán challenges the party to navigate through a magical obstacle course he's created to test their worthiness to enter the forest. This challenge consists of five stages, each requiring different skills and abilities.

Stage 1: Mischievous Mist Maze

Characters must navigate through a maze of magical mist.

Each PC makes a DC 14 Wisdom (Perception) check.

Success allows them to move through unhindered.

Failure results in becoming disoriented, imposing disadvantage on their next check in the course.

Stage 2: Tricky Tree Trunks

Characters must cross a series of fallen logs that shift and roll.

Each PC makes a DC 13 Dexterity (Acrobatics) check.

Failure results in falling prone and taking 1d6 bludgeoning damage.

Stage 3: Whispering Riddle Rings

Ethereal voices emanate from magical fairy rings pose riddles that must be solved to pass.

Players can attempt to solve a certain number of riddles in order to continue. Alternatively, PCs can roll Intelligence checks to decipher the riddles.

Failure to answer enough riddles correctly (as determined by the DM) results in temporary confusion, reducing the party's speed by half for the next stage.

Below is a table of fairy-themed riddles with varying complexities:

Type	Question	Answer	DC
Simple	I dance in the breeze, my colors so bright, I bring joy to fairies from morning to night. What am I?	A flower	10
Simple	Fairies use me to fly so high, I sparkle and shine in the night sky. What am I?	Pixie dust	10
Simple	I'm round and sprout from the ground, a fairy's favorite seat. In gardens I'm often where gnomes and elves meet. What am I?	A toadstool	10
Medium	Born in the forest, of neither flesh nor bone, I sing without voice, I dance without feet, I live without breath. What am I?	A leaf	13
Medium	Fairies guard me with all their might, I'm hidden by day but bloom at night. My petals are silver, my center pure gold, I grant wishes to those who are bold. What am I?	A moonflower	13
Medium	I'm a fairy's treasure, not silver or gold. I'm born from a tear, or so I'm told. Round and shiny, I catch the light, found in the morning after rainfall at night. What am I?	A dewdrop	13
Hard	I am the heart of the fairy realm, seen by few, yet known by all. I shift with the seasons, change with the moon, where time stands still, yet passes too soon. What am I?	A fairy ring	16
Hard	We are sisters, eternal and bright, one rules the day, one rules the night. We dance with the fairies in twilight's gleam, where reality blends into a dream. Who are we?	The sun and moon	16
Hard	I'm the bridge between your world and mine, visible to children, but adults seldom find. I appear when the veil is thin, a magical moment fleeting and rare. Cross me if you dare, but beware, for in fairy realms, time flows differently there. What am I?	A rainbow	16

Remember, these DC checks are for players who want to solve the riddle using an Intelligence check rather than trying to figure it out themselves. Adjust the DCs as needed to fit your campaign's difficulty level.

Stage 4: Enchanted Ecosystem

Players must identify and interact with magical plants and creatures.

Each PC makes a DC 14 Intelligence (Arcana or Nature) or a Wisdom (Animal Handling) check to identify and correctly interact with each plant or creature.

Failure causes a mild magical effect (use table below or DM's choice, e.g., temporary color change, speaking in rhymes for 1 minute).

Below is a table of magical plants and creatures for the Enchanted Ecosystem challenge:

Magical Plant/ Creature	Visual Description	Interaction	Success Effect	Failure Effect
Luminous Lily	A large, glowing flower with petals that shift colors	Gently stroke the petals in a circular motion	The PC gains darkvision until the next long rest.	The PC glows softly for 10 minutes, imposing disadvantage on Stealth checks
Whispering Willow	A small tree with leaves that rustle and murmur	Listen closely and repeat what you hear	The PC understands Sylvan for 1 hour	The PC can only speak in whispers for 10 minutes
Giggling Mushrooms	A cluster of colorful mushrooms that seem to laugh	Tell a joke to make them laugh louder	The PC gains advantage on their next Charisma check	The PC bursts into uncontrollable giggles for 1 minute
Butterfly Bloom	A flower with petals that flutter like butterfly wings	Offer a drop of water to the flower	The PC can hover 1 foot off the ground for 10 minutes	Butterflies follow the PC for 1 hour, imposing disadvantage on Stealth checks
Mirror Moss	A patch of moss that reflects like a perfect mirror	Look into the moss and state a truth about yourself	The PC gains advantage on Insight checks for 1 hour	The PC's reflection follows them for 1 hour, mimicking their actions
Melodic Mint	A fragrant herb that hums a soft tune	Hum along with the plant's melody	The PC gains inspiration	The PC can only speak in rhymes for 10 minutes
Tickling Tumbleweed	A rolling ball of twigs that seeks out creatures to tickle	Allow it to tickle you without laughing	The PC gains advantage on Dexterity saves for 1 hour	The PC is prone to fits of laughter for 10 minutes
Shimmering Sprite	A tiny, glowing humanoid creature that flits about	Offer a small, shiny object as a gift	The PC's steps leave glittering trails visible only to that PC until the next long rest, granting advantage on Survival checks to avoid getting lost	The PC's hair turns a random, glittering color for 24 hours
Prism Porcupine	A porcupine-like creature with crystal quills that refract light	Carefully pet its head without touching the quills	The PC's skin sparkles in sunlight for 24 hours, and they gain advantage on the next Persuasion check	Random objects around the PC change colors for 1 hour

These magical plants and creatures add whimsical and interactive elements to your Enchanted Ecosystem challenge. The effects are minor and fairy-themed, adding flavor to the encounter without significantly impacting gameplay balance. Adjust the durations or effects as needed to fit your campaign style.

Stage 5: Fey Flight Finale

This final stage of Ciarán's Magical Obstacle Course tests the party's agility, quick thinking, and ability to adapt to the whimsical nature of fey magic.

Setting: A wide chasm spans before the party, filled with swirling, colorful mists. Floating above the chasm are various platforms of different shapes, sizes, and materials (leaves, flowers, clouds, etc.). These platforms move, rotate, and sometimes vanish, reappearing elsewhere.

Challenge Components
Floating Platforms

Players must hop from platform to platform to cross the chasm.

Each leap requires a DC 15 Strength (Athletics) or Dexterity (Acrobatics) check, player's choice.

Failure results in falling, but Ciarán catches them with *Levitate*, returning them to the last stable platform.

Shifting Paths

The optimal path changes every round.

At the start of each PC's turn, they must make a DC 13 Wisdom (Perception) check to identify the best route.

Success grants advantage on their platform-jumping check.

Whimsical Wind

Unpredictable gusts of wind add an extra challenge.

When this happens, PCs must make a DC 12 Strength saving throw when jumping between platforms.

Failure doesn't cause a fall but pushes them to an adjacent platform, potentially off their planned route.

Illusion Interference

Some platforms are illusions that disappear when touched.

PCs can make a DC 14 Intelligence (Investigation) check to discern real platforms from illusions.

Stepping on an illusory platform counts as a failed jump.

Fairy Ring Finale

The final platform is a large, stable fairy ring.

To complete the challenge, PCs must perform a small "offering" (a dance, song, riddle, etc.).

This requires a DC 13 Charisma (Performance) check.

Failure doesn't reset progress but requires another attempt to "appease" the fairy ring.

Scoring

For each stage that is successfully passed, PCs earns 1 point.

Creativity and clever use of spells or abilities can earn bonus points at the DM's discretion for each stage.

Add the points for each completed stage plus the additional bonus points to determine how Ciarán will help you.

Total Scores:

0-1 points: Ciarán is disappointed but allows entry into the forest. However, he will not stay with the PCs and will not offer any guidance on how to navigate the forest.

2-3 points: Ciarán is impressed and offers a map of the forest providing direction to Ríona na Sí, leader of the fey in the Enchanted Forest.

4-5 points: Ciarán is delighted and will escort the PCs to Ríona na Sí, leader of the fey in the Enchanted Forest.

Aid from the Saoi na Coille

If the PCs successfully navigate the obstacle course, they will earn the favor of the Saoi na Coille. This ancient and wise forest entity may offer guidance, blessings, or even magical items to aid them on their quest. However, if they ignore or bypass the challenge, the Saoi na Coille will be less inclined to assist them, viewing them as disrespectful of the forest's customs.

Terrain

The forest floor is considered difficult terrain due to twisted roots, sudden sinkholes, and animated vegetation. Players must make a DC 13 Dexterity (Acrobatics) check to move at full speed; failure means they can only move at half speed. Additionally, the shifting nature of the forest requires a DC 14 Wisdom (Survival) check every hour to maintain the correct direction of travel.

Lair Actions

Whispering Winds: The forest creates confusing whispers. All creatures must succeed on a DC 14 Wisdom saving throw or be disoriented, having disadvantage on their next ability check or attack roll.

Entangling Roots: Roots burst from the ground in a 20-foot radius. Creatures in the area must succeed on a DC 15 Dexterity saving throw or be restrained until the end of their next turn.

Rejuvenating Mist: A healing mist fills a 30-foot radius. All creatures in the area regain 2d6 hit points.

The Enchanted Forest Clearing

This encounter introduces the players to the Saoi na Coille, an ancient and powerful forest guardian. The outcome of this interaction will significantly impact the party's journey through Coill Draíochta, potentially providing them with a valuable ally or a formidable adversary.

As you venture deeper into the forest, the trees seem to part before you, revealing a hidden clearing bathed in an ethereal, emerald light. The air here is thick with ancient magic, and you can feel the very pulse of the forest beating beneath your feet. Massive, gnarled roots intertwine to form natural archways and platforms, while delicate, luminescent flowers carpet the ground, their petals shifting colors with each gentle breeze.

In the center of this mystical glade stands an awe-inspiring sight: a colossal tree, its trunk wider than any you've ever seen, with bark that seems to ripple and move as if alive. As you watch, the tree begins to shift and change, its form twisting and reshaping until it takes on a vaguely humanoid appearance. Ancient, wise eyes open upon its face, regarding you with a gaze that seems to peer into your very souls.

Encounter Saoi na Coille

After completing Ciarán's Magical Obstacle Course, the PCs venture deeper into the forest. If Ciarán is not with them, then they will enter a clearing where they encounter the Saoi na Coille. If Ciarán is with the PCs, then he will know of Saoi na Coille and will act as diplomat to create a peaceful meeting.

Initial Encounter

The Saoi na Coille appears suddenly, emerging from the trees as if part of the forest itself.

It doesn't immediately attack, instead observing the party with a heavy, piercing gaze.

Interaction Options

Peaceful Approach: PCs can attempt to communicate peacefully with a DC 15 Charisma (Persuasion) check.

Success leads to a dialogue where the Saoi na Coille questions their intentions in the forest.

Failure may result in the Saoi na Coille viewing them as potential threats.

Show of Respect: PCs knowledgeable in druidic or fey customs can perform a respectful gesture (DC 14 Intelligence (Nature) check).

Success impresses the Saoi na Coille, granting advantage on further interactions.

Proof of Worth: The Saoi na Coille might challenge the party to prove their worth through a test of nature knowledge or respect for the forest.

This could involve a series of Nature or Survival checks (DC 15) or solving nature-themed riddles.

Potential Combat

If diplomacy fails or the PCs act aggressively:

Initiative: Roll for initiative if combat begins.

Battlefield: The clearing becomes a dynamic battleground with the Saoi na Coille controlling the terrain.

Lair Actions: Utilize the previously mentioned lair actions of the Coill Draíochta as well as the local lair actions below to make the environment challenging.

Combat Strategies: The Saoi na Coille prefers to entangle and restrain opponents rather than cause direct harm.

It summons forest allies (dryads or treants) to aid in combat.

It uses *Healing Touch* to sustain itself and its allies.

Resolving the Encounter

Peaceful Resolution: If the PCs successfully prove their good intentions, the Saoi na Coille becomes a valuable ally, offering guidance and possibly a boon (e.g., a magical seed, enhanced nature abilities).

Combat Resolution: If reduced to below half health, the Saoi na Coille retreats into the forest, leaving the PCs to face the consequences of battling a forest guardian.

Defeating the Saoi na Coille (reducing it to 0 HP) causes it to disperse into leaves and forest mist, reforming elsewhere in the forest.

Consequences: The outcome of this encounter should have lasting effects on the PCs' journey through the forest, either easing their path or making it more challenging.

Terrain

The clearing is considered magical terrain. Movement is difficult due to the constantly shifting roots and foliage. PCs must make a DC 13 Dexterity (Acrobatics) check to move at full speed; failure means they can only move at half speed. Additionally, the magical nature of the area interferes with certain spells. Any spell cast within the clearing requires a DC 12 Intelligence (Arcana) check to avoid wild magic surges.

Lair Actions

Forest's Embrace: The Saoi na Coille causes the trees and plants in a 30-foot radius to reach out and grasp at creatures. Each creature in the area must succeed on a DC 15 Strength saving throw or be restrained until the start of the Saoi na Coille's next turn.

Verdant Surge: A wave of healing energy pulses through the clearing. The Saoi na Coille and up to three creatures of its choice regain 10 (2d8 + 1) hit points.

Whispers of the Wild: The forest seems to come alive with whispers and murmurs. Each creature in the clearing must succeed on a DC 14 Wisdom saving throw or be charmed until the end of their next turn, finding themselves unable to take hostile actions against the forest or its denizens.

Monster

Saoi na Coille (Sage of the Forest)

Center of the Enchanted Forest

This encounter introduces the players to Ríona na Sí, the powerful leader of Coill Draíochta (The Enchanted Forest). The party must agree to rescue Tadhg an Airgid from the Twilight Kin to gain Ríona's assistance in their quest to restore the Triskelion.

As you push deeper into the heart of the forest, the air grows thick with ancient magic. The trees here are colossal, their trunks wider than houses, their canopies so high they seem to touch the sky. Shimmering motes of light dance through the air, and the very ground beneath your feet pulses with a subtle, magical energy.

You step into a vast clearing, where the trees form a perfect circle around a ring of towering standing stones. These monoliths, each easily twenty feet tall, are carved with intricate spirals and symbols that glow with a faint, otherworldly light. At the center of this stone circle stands a massive throne, hewn from a single piece of gleaming quartz crystal. The seat seems to capture and refract the light around it, creating a dazzling display of colors. A shimmering pool of crystal-clear water surrounds the throne, its surface as still as glass, reflecting the sky above. The entire area is bathed in an ethereal, silvery light that seems to emanate from the very air itself. As you take in this awe-inspiring sight, you sense a powerful presence watching you, evaluating your every move.

Activities

Meet and negotiate with Ríona na Sí, the fey leader of the Coill Draíochta.

Learn about and investigate Tadhg an Airgid's capture.

Receive information about the Sunset Forest and the Twilight Kin.

Meet and Negotiate with Ríona na Sí

Initial Approach: As the party enters, they must make a DC 14 Charisma (Persuasion) check to make a good first impression.

Formal Introduction: Ríona will ask each party member to state their name and purpose. This is an opportunity for roleplay.

State of Affairs: Ríona explains the current situation in Coill Draíochta and her concerns about the Triskelion.

Negotiation: Players can make offers or requests.

Each

significant point requires a DC 15 Charisma (Persuasion) check. Clever ideas or good roleplay can grant advantage.

Current Situation in Coill Draíochta

Ríona begins by explaining the dire situation in the Enchanted Forest:

"Coill Draíochta has long been a sanctuary of fey magic, a place where the natural and mystical worlds intertwine. However, our peace has been shattered. Tadhg an Airgid, our esteemed Keeper of Relics, has been captured by the Twilight Kin. His knowledge and the artifacts he protects are crucial to maintaining the balance of magic in our forest. Without him, we are vulnerable to corruption and chaos."

Who are the Twilight Kin?

"The Twilight Kin, or Clann na Coimhthrátha, reside in the Sunset Forest. They are a faction of fey who pride themselves on balance and diplomacy, often serving as mediators between various fey factions and mortal realms. However, in recent years, they have become more insular, focusing on accumulating knowledge and magical artifacts, leading to increased tensions with other fey groups, particularly us in Coill Draíochta."

Concerns about the Triskelion

"The Triskelion is an ancient artifact of immense power, symbolizing the harmony of the elements. Its fragments have been scattered and are now in the hands of Fionnlagh's apprentices. Reuniting the Triskelion is essential to restoring balance and preventing the spread of Fionnlagh's corrupt magic. Our fear is that without Tadhg's protection and the relics he guards, the Twilight Kin might misuse these powerful artifacts or even align with Fionnlagh, further tipping the scales towards chaos."

Investigate Tadhg's Capture

Ríona's Explanation: Ríona begins by explaining Tadhg's role: "Tadhg an Airgid is our Keeper of Relics, a position of great importance in Coill Draíochta. He safeguards artifacts of immense power and historical significance, many of which date back to the time of the Tuatha Dé Danann."

She elaborates on his duties:

- Maintaining a vast repository of magical items
- Studying and cataloging new artifacts
- Ensuring dangerous relics remain sealed and protected
- Advising the fey court on matters relating to ancient magic

Ríona stresses, "His knowledge is irreplaceable, and in the wrong hands, the relics he protects could upset the balance of power in our realm and beyond."

Circumstances of Capture: Players can ask questions about Tadhg's capture. Key information includes:

- **Time of capture**: Three nights ago, during the new moon
- **Location**: Near the Sunset Forest
- **Last known activity**: Tadhg was investigating reports of a newly uncovered ancient site

Sample Questions and Answers

Q: "Were there any witnesses?"

A: "A young dryad saw a group of shadowy figures surrounding Tadhg before he vanished."

Q: "Was anything left behind at the scene?"

A: "We found traces of unusual pollen, not native to our forest."

Q: "Has there been any ransom demand?"

A: "No direct communication, but there have been whispers of the Twilight Kin boasting about a 'valuable acquisition.'"

Investigation

On a successful DC 13 Intelligence (Investigation) check, PCs can uncover additional details:

- The pollen found at the scene is from a rare night-blooming flower that only grows in the Sunset Forest.
- Tadhg had recently expressed concern about increased Twilight Kin activity near ancient sites.
- A magical ward Tadhg always carried was found shattered at the scene, suggesting a powerful magical assault.

On a critical success (natural 20), the PCs might also learn that the attack coincided with a rare celestial alignment that temporarily weakens the barriers between fey domains.

Motive Discussion

Players can discuss potential motives with Ríona. She might suggest:

- The Twilight Kin could be after a specific artifact Tadhg protects.
- They might want to ransom Tadhg for political leverage.
- Tadhg's knowledge itself could be valuable to them.

On a successful DC 14 Wisdom (Insight) check, the PCs might deduce:

- The Twilight Kin's timing suggests they knew about Tadhg's movements, implying a possible spy in Coill Draíochta.

- The lack of ransom demand indicates they might be after something specific that they believe Tadhg can provide.
- The Twilight Kin might be planning a larger operation, with Tadhg's capture as just the first step.

On a critical success, the PCs might also realize that there could be a connection between Tadhg's capture and the fragmented Triskelion, possibly related to an artifact that could affect its power.

Rewards for Rescuing Tadhg

Ríona offers the following rewards for a successful rescue:

Ríona's Assistance: "Upon Tadhg's safe return, I pledge my full support to your quest. I will personally assist you in locating the three pieces of the Triskelion and aid you in your battle against Fionnlagh, the Dark Sorcerer and his apprentices."

Magical Gift: "As a token of our gratitude and to aid in your quest for the Triskelion, I will bestow upon you a powerful magical item from our sacred vault." (DM can choose an appropriate item based on the party's needs and level, such as a Cloak of Elvenkind, Boots of Speed, or a similar rare magical item.)

Knowledge: "Tadhg's vast knowledge of ancient relics and magic will be at your disposal. This could provide crucial insights into the Triskelion and strategies against Fionnlagh."

Fey Allies: "You will have earned the friendship of the Coill Draíochta. Our fey warriors and magicians will come to your aid in times of great need."

Consequences of Failure

Ríona also solemnly warns of the potential consequences should the mission fail:

Power Imbalance: "If the Twilight Kin retain Tadhg and gain access to our relics, the balance of power in the fey realms will shift dramatically. This could lead to conflicts that spread far beyond our forests."

Threatened Alliances: "We may be forced to capitulate to the Twilight Kin's demands, potentially compromising our ability to assist you in your quest against Fionnlagh."

Magical Catastrophe: "Some of the artifacts Tadhg protects are volatile. In inexperienced hands, they could cause magical disasters affecting both the fey and mortal realms."

Strengthened Adversaries: "There's a risk that the Twilight Kin might ally with Fionnlagh, armed with the knowledge and power from our relics. This would make your quest significantly more challenging."

Ríona's Assistance

Ríona details how she can aid the party:

Magical Tracking: "I possess the ability to sense the fragments of the Triskelion. While I cannot pinpoint their exact locations, I can guide you in the right direction."

Fey Network: "My connections throughout the fey realms will provide you with safe passage and vital information as you pursue each fragment."

Magical Support: "In crucial moments, I can channel the power of Coill Draíochta to you, granting temporary boons or assisting in battles from afar."

Strategic Insight: "My knowledge of Fionnlagh and his apprentices, gathered over centuries, can help you understand their weaknesses and predict their moves."

Ríona concludes, "Your success in this rescue mission is the first step in forming a powerful alliance. Together, we stand a chance against the darkness that threatens both our realms. Will you accept this quest, brave adventurers?"

Receive Information about the Sunset Forest and the Twilight Kin

Geographical Briefing: Ríona provides a map. PCs make a DC 12 Intelligence check to memorize key details.

Cultural Insights: Learn about the Twilight Kin customs. A DC 14 Intelligence (History) check reveals additional lore.

"The Twilight Kin, or Clann na Coimhthrátha, reside in the Sunset Forest. They pride themselves on balance and diplomacy, often serving as mediators between various fey factions and mortal realms. Their customs reflect their dual nature, emphasizing equilibrium between light and dark. This is manifested in their rituals, which often take place during twilight hours, symbolizing transition and balance. Unlike the more wild and whimsical fey, the Twilight Kin maintain structured societies with a focus on knowledge and preservation of ancient magic."

Key Figures: Discuss Eoghan na Luí and other important Twilight Kin. PCs can make a DC 13 Wisdom (Insight) check to understand political dynamics.

"Eoghan na Luí is the current leader of the Twilight Kin, known for his charisma and strategic mind. He is supported by a council of advisors, each representing different aspects of their society. Notable figures include:

- **Niamh an tSolais**: A powerful healer who oversees the Twilight Kin's medical and magical healing practices.
- **Caoimhín na Scáth**: The head of their scouts and intelligence, responsible for monitoring external threats and opportunities.

- **Sorcha na Réalta**: The chief diplomat, often engaging in negotiations with other fey courts and mortal representatives.

"The Twilight Kin's political dynamics are complex, with a delicate balance maintained between the desire for isolation to protect their knowledge and the necessity of interaction with other realms for trade and alliances."

Magical Aspects: Ríona explains unique magical properties of the Sunset Forest. An Intelligence (Arcana) check (DC 15) helps PCs grasp the implications.

"The Sunset Forest is a realm of perpetual twilight, where the boundaries between day and night, and often between worlds, are thin. This perpetual twilight enhances transformation and illusion magic, making it a powerful nexus for spells related to change, disguise, and subtlety. The forest's magic also affects time, creating pockets where time flows differently."

Successful Arcana checks made to understand the implications of the forest's magic reveal that these temporal effects can be harnessed to gain advantages in battle or to escape pursuit. However, they also pose risks, as miscalculations can lead to unintended time shifts or lost days.

For more detailed information on the Twilight Kin, their customs, and political dynamics, refer to the introduction of the Sunset Forest location in the next chapter and Eoghan's NPC entry in the Appendix.

Terrain

The clearing is considered sacred ground, suffused with powerful fey magic. Movement is normal, but any attempt to harm the environment or use destructive magic requires a DC 15 Wisdom saving throw to overcome the forest's protective aura. Failure results in the spell fizzling or the attack missing. Additionally, the magical nature of the area enhances nature-based magic; any druid or nature-based spells are cast as if one level higher.

Lair Actions

Forest's Whisper: Ríona causes the forest to whisper secrets. All creatures in the area must succeed on a DC 15 Wisdom saving throw or be compelled to speak only truth for the next minute.

Nature's Embrace: Roots and vines surge from the ground in a 30-foot radius, providing half cover to all creatures Ríona considers allies.

Fey Lights: Glowing motes of light swirl around the area. Ríona can grant one creature advantage on their next ability check, attack roll, or saving throw, or impose disadvantage on an enemy's next roll.

NPC

Ríona na Sí (friendly unless provoked)

Monster

Sídhe Sentinel (1d4, can be summoned to defend Ríona)

Scaling Coill Draíochta (Enchanted Forest) Encounters

Beginning Players (PC levels 1-5)

Reduce all skill check DCs by 2 (e.g., DC 15 becomes DC 13).

Random Encounters:

- Use only encounters 1-5.
- Reduce number of creatures in group encounters (e.g., 1d4-1 pixies).

Ciarán's Obstacle Course:

- Reduce stages to 3.
- Lower DCs for physical challenges to 11.

Saoi na Coille:

- Reduce HP by 25%.
- Lower spell save DC to 13.
- Remove legendary actions.

Ríona na Sí:

- Focus on roleplay, avoid combat.
- Offer simpler, level-appropriate quests.
- Provide uncommon magic items as rewards.

Intermediate Players (PC levels 6-10)

Keep skill check DCs as written.

Random Encounters: Use all encounters as written.

Ciarán's Obstacle Course: Use all 5 stages as described.

Saoi na Coille: Use stats as written.

Ríona na Sí: Offer full quest as described.

Advanced Players (PC levels 11+)

Increase all skill check DCs by 2 (e.g., DC 15 becomes DC 17).

Random Encounters:

- Add higher CR creatures to encounters (e.g., replace pixies with sprites).
- Introduce complex magical effects (e.g., wild magic surges)

Ciarán's Obstacle Course:

- Add a 6th stage involving complex illusions or magical puzzles.
- Increase DCs for physical challenges to 17.

Saoi na Coille:

- Increase HP by 50%.
- Raise spell save DC to 17.
- Add legendary actions:
  - Root Attack: Make one attack with its roots.
  - Healing Burst: Regain 10 (3d6) HP.

Ríona na Sí:

- Add combat encounter with 1d4+2 high-CR fey creatures as a "test".
- Offer more complex, multi-stage quests.
- Provide very rare magic items as rewards.

Lair Actions:

- Increase save DCs to 17.
- Enhance effects (e.g., Nature's Embrace provides 3/4 cover instead of half).

The Sunset Forest, Coill an Luí na Gréine

The Sunset Forest is a realm of perpetual twilight, home to the enigmatic Clann na Coimhthrátha (Twilight Kin). This encounter introduces players to a complex fey society balancing between light and dark, where they must navigate political intrigue and magical challenges to rescue Tadhg an Airgid.

As you step into the forest, you're immediately enveloped by an otherworldly twilight. The sky above is a perpetual canvas of deep purples, fiery oranges, and soft pinks, as if the sun is forever setting. The trees around you are tall and ancient, their leaves a vibrant tapestry of autumn colors - rich golds, deep reds, and burnished bronzes - that seem to glow in the eternal dusk.

The air is thick with magic, shimmering motes of light dancing between the trees like fireflies frozen in time. You can hear the soft whisper of leaves and the distant, ethereal sound of music carried on a breeze that doesn't seem to exist. The paths before you are clear but winding, disappearing into the twilight shadows between the trees. Everything here exists in a state of in-between, neither day nor night, a realm of transition and mystery.

History of the Sunset Forest

Coill an Luí na Gréine, the Sunset Forest, came into being during the great retreat of the Tuatha Dé Danann. As these ancient gods withdrew from the mortal world, one of their number, Crepuscule, the deity of twilight, chose to create a realm that would forever exist in the magical moment between day and night.

The forest is a place of eternal autumn, its trees forever clothed in the rich hues of the changing season. This perpetual state of transition makes it a powerful nexus of transformation magic. The very air shimmers with arcane energy, and the boundaries between the mortal world and the Otherworld are thin here.

While not as dense or wild as the Enchanted Forest (Coill Draíochta), the Sunset Forest is no less magical. It serves as a buffer zone between the mortal realm and the deeper, more volatile fey lands. Many fey creatures make their home here, particularly those associated with twilight, dreams, and transitions.

The relationship between the Sunset Forest and the Enchanted Forest is complex. While both are fey realms, the Sunset Forest is seen as more accessible to mortals, a place where the rules of reality are bent but not broken. It's often the first stop for those seeking to enter the deeper fey realms, and as such, its inhabitants are more accustomed to dealing with outsiders.

History of the Clann na Coimhthrátha, the Twilight Kin

The Clann na Coimhthrátha, or Twilight Kin, emerged as a distinct fey faction shortly after the creation of the Sunset Forest. They were originally a diverse group of fey creatures drawn to the unique twilight magic of the realm.

Over time, under the leadership of charismatic figures like Eoghan na Luí, they developed into a sophisticated society that prided itself on balance and diplomacy. The Twilight Kin see themselves as mediators between various fey factions, mortal realms, and even between the forces of light and darkness.

Their history is marked by both great achievements in magical research and diplomatic triumphs, as well as periods of internal strife when the balance between their light and dark aspects wavered. They've been instrumental in preventing several wars between fey courts and have often served as arbiters in disputes between mortals and fey.

In recent centuries, the Twilight Kin have become more insular, focusing on accumulating knowledge and magical artifacts. This shift has led to increased tensions with other fey groups, particularly those from the Enchanted Forest, who view their activities with suspicion.

Uncover the True Nature of the Sunset Forest's Fading Magic

As the party ventures deeper into the Sunset Forest, they begin to notice signs that something is amiss. The vibrant glow of the twilight magic seems to be dimming, and the forest feels less alive and more oppressive.

Investigation Checks

The following skill checks are necessary for the party to uncover the reasons behind the fading magic of the Sunset Forest:

Investigation: A DC 16 Intelligence (Investigation) check to spot clues in the environment. These clues include withering plants, unusual animal behavior, and areas where the twilight glow is weakest.

Arcana Knowledge: A DC 15 Intelligence (Arcana) check to recognize the symptoms of fading magic. The party can identify signs of magical depletion and corruption, such as residual dark energy traces and weakening magical auras.

Interviewing Fey: A DC 14 Charisma (Persuasion) check to gain trust and information from local fey creatures. These fey can provide insights into the forest's history and recent changes. Alternatively, the Twilight Kin themselves can offer more detailed information about the origins of the Sunset Forest and potential effects of various interactions between the forest and outside forces.

Perception Check: A DC 15 Wisdom (Perception) check to notice subtle magical disturbances. This includes sensing shifts in the magical currents and detecting faint pulses of dark energy.

Discovering the Causes

The party's investigations reveal that the fading magic is due to several interconnected factors:

Corruption from Outside Forces: Dark energies from Fionnlagh, the Dark Sorcerer's activities, are seeping into the edges of the forest. This corruption is slowly poisoning the twilight magic, causing it to wane.

Depletion of Magical Essence: The forest's magic is a finite resource that has been slowly consumed over millennia. Fionnlagh's apprentices have recently discovered that they too can absorb the magic of the Sunset Forest, leading to its accelerated depletion.

Ancient Pact Disruption: The Sunset Forest was created through an ancient pact between the Twilight Kin and the primordial forces of dusk and dawn. This pact has been slowly weakening due to the waning influence of old magic in the world and the increase of new magic from Fionnlagh.

By piecing together these clues, the party can understand the gravity of the situation and the need to restore the forest's magic to prevent further degradation.

Random Encounters (1d10)

1. **Twilight Wisps**: Glowing orbs lead PCs off the path. DC 13 Wisdom save or be charmed and follow for 1d4 hours.
2. **Shapeshifting Shadows**: Shadows come alive. Each PC must make a DC 14 Dexterity save or take 2d6 psychic damage.
3. **Time Pocket**: PCs enter an area where time flows differently. 1 hour here = 1 minute outside. Lasts for 1d4 hours of in-pocket time. PCs may not initially realize they are in a Time Pocket. Allow them to make a DC 15 Intelligence (Arcana) or Wisdom (Nature) check to notice subtle anomalies, such as the unusual stillness of the environment or the lack of typical forest sounds.
4. **Fey Revel**: Encounter a small fey party. DC 12 Charisma (Persuasion) to join and gain information.
5. **Whispering Winds**: Cryptic messages on the wind. DC 13 Intelligence (Investigation) for useful hints.
6. **Illusory Terrain**: Path suddenly ends. DC 15 Intelligence (Investigation) to see through illusion.

7. **Twilight Creature**: Encounter a Twilight Elk (use elk stats with resistance to psychic damage).
8. **Emotion Bloom**: Flowers release spores. DC 12 Wisdom save or be affected by the *Confusion* spell for 1 minute.
9. **Echo of the Past**: PCs witness a vision of past events. Wisdom (Insight) check (DC varies) to understand its significance.
10. **Fey Crossing**: Temporary portal to another part of the forest. DC 14 Intelligence (Arcana) check to determine or control its destination.

Terrain

The forest floor is covered in a carpet of fallen leaves in perpetual autumn colors. Treat areas off the main paths as difficult terrain. Additionally:

Climbing trees requires a DC 11 Strength (Athletics) check due to their smooth bark.

There's a 20% chance each hour of encountering a small stream that requires a DC 10 Dexterity (Acrobatics) check to cross.

The twilight conditions impose disadvantage on Perception checks relying on sight beyond 60 feet.

Lair Actions

Twilight Veil: The forest thickens and obscures the twilight. All creatures must make a DC 13 Wisdom save or be blinded until the end of their next turn.

Whispers of Fate: Disembodied voices offer cryptic advice. Each creature gains advantage on their next ability check if they can decipher the meaning (DC 12 Intelligence check).

Temporal Flux: Time briefly warps. Roll a d6: on odd, creatures age 1d4 years; on even, they regress 1d4 years. This is temporary and reverts after 1 hour.

The Center of the Sunset Forest

This encounter is the climax of the Sunset Forest arc, where PCs confront Eoghan na Luí and attempt to rescue Tadhg an Airgid. The situation is tense but potentially negotiable, with the fate of the Twilight Kin hanging in the balance.

As you push deeper into the heart of the forest, the twilight grows more intense, the shadows deeper and more alive. You emerge into a vast clearing dominated by an enormous, ancient oak tree. Its trunk, wider than a house, is gnarled and twisted, forming natural alcoves and chambers. The tree's canopy spreads out above, its leaves a mesmerizing swirl of deep purples and burnt oranges that seem to glow with an inner light.

The air here is thick with magic, shimmering motes of twilight energy dancing through the air like fireflies. The ground is carpeted with soft moss that seems to absorb sound, creating an eerie quiet broken only by the occasional whisper of wind through leaves. At the base of the tree, you see a group of figures, their forms partially obscured by the swirling, misty twilight that seems to emanate from the very ground.

Activities

- Negotiate with Eoghan na Luí for Tadhg's release.
- Repair the Brat Draíochta, the Cloak of Enchantment.
- Recover the captive Tadhg.
- Uncover the true nature of the Sunset Forest's fading magic.
- Form an alliance with the Twilight Kin.

Negotiate with Eoghan na Luí for Tadhg's Release

As your party approaches, you can make out more details of the figures standing beneath the ancient tree. In the center stands a tall and charismatic figure with dark, wavy hair and amber eyes, exuding an aura of authority and confidence. A small assembly of fey surrounds him, each one elegant and poised, their presence both commanding and unsettling.

Setting the Scene

These fey are a group of Twilight Kin, with their leader Eoghan na Luí commanding attention in the center, The assembly consists of Eoghan na Luí's closest advisors, including:

- Niamh an tSolais - powerful healer
- Caoimhín na Scáth - head of scouts and intelligence
- Sorcha na Réalta - chief diplomat

These individuals work to support Eoghan in major decisions and negotiations, ensuring the Twilight Kin's interests are protected.

Eavesdropping on the Twilight Kin

If the party successfully sneaks up on the fey assembly with a Group Stealth check (DC 16), they overhear Eoghan discussing the urgency of repairing the Brat Draíochta (the Cloak of Enchantment) and the potential political leverage Tadhg's knowledge provides. Eoghan expresses frustration at Tadhg's resistance and the importance of the cloak to their realm's stability.

Initial Approach

The party must make a DC 15 Charisma (Persuasion) check to gain Eoghan's attention without hostility.

Diplomatic Discussion: A series of three Charisma checks (player's choice of Persuasion, Deception, or Intimidation) follows. The DC starts at 15 and increases or decreases by 2 for each success or failure.

Possible Outcomes:

- **3 Successes:** Eoghan agrees to release Tadhg if the party helps repair an enchanted cloak—the Brat Draíochta, which has somehow been magically damaged.
- **1-2 Successes:** Eoghan demands additional favors or concessions.
- **0 Successes:** Negotiations fail, Eoghan becomes hostile.

Insight Check: A DC 16 Wisdom (Insight) check allows the party to discern that Eoghan's actions and decisions are driven by some sort of threat to the forest itself.

Eoghan's Initial Response: Eoghan is initially cautious but intrigued by the party's bold approach. He is not hostile but maintains a guarded demeanor, assessing the party's intentions with a mix of curiosity and suspicion.

Motivations of the Twilight Kin

Importance of the Cloak: The Brat Draíochta, or Cloak of Enchantment, is a powerful artifact that symbolizes the Twilight Kin's authority and connection to the Sunset Forest. It is currently damaged, and Eoghan believes that Tadhg's knowledge is crucial to its repair. The cloak's restoration would stabilize the magical balance in the Sunset Forest and enhance the Twilight Kin's power.

Reason for Capturing Tadhg: The Twilight Kin captured Tadhg because they believed he possessed critical knowledge about ancient artifacts and magical relics, including those necessary to repair the Brat Draíochta. Eoghan is willing to negotiate Tadhg's release if the party agrees to assist in the cloak's repair, as they have realized that Tadhg alone cannot solve their problem.

Waning Magic of the Forest: The Twilight Kin are well aware of the fading magic of the Sunset Forest, and cognizant of the connection between its health and the Cloak of Enchantment's current state of disrepair. If the PCs broach the subject of the forest's fading magic in conversation, Eoghan na Luí expresses concern over the magic's waning and urges the party to investigate the cause.

Brat Draíochta (Cloak of Enchantment)

Type: Wondrous item, legendary (requires attunement)

Description: This cloak appears to be woven from twilight itself, its fabric shimmering with deep purples, soft golds, and rich crimsons that shift and change as if caught in an eternal sunset. When worn, it seems to merge with the shadows around the wearer, its edges becoming indistinct.

Current State (Broken): The cloak's magic has become unstable. Its once-vibrant colors are now muted, and tears in the fabric reveal a dim, flickering light from within. The enchantments flicker unpredictably, sometimes failing altogether.

Properties (When Repaired):

- **Twilight Step**: As a bonus action, the wearer can teleport up to 60 feet to an unoccupied space they can see. This ability can be used 3 times per day.
- **Shadowmeld**: While in dim light or darkness, the wearer can use an action to become invisible until they move, take an action, or react.
- **Essence of Dusk**: The wearer gains advantage on Charisma (Persuasion) checks when interacting with fey.
- **Twilight Shield:** As a reaction when hit by an attack, the wearer can cause the attack to have disadvantage. This feature can be used 3 times per day.

Attunement: To attune to this item, the user must spend 1 hour meditating with the cloak during twilight, allowing its magic to merge with their own essence.

Lore: The Brat Draíochta was created by the first leaders of the Twilight Kin, imbued with the essence of the Sunset Forest itself. It was meant to serve as both a powerful magical artifact and a symbol of the Twilight Kin's authority. Legend says that as long as the cloak remains whole and powerful, the Sunset Forest will thrive.

The cloak's current broken state is deeply entwined with the fading magic of the Sunset Forest. Repairing it requires not just physical mending, but a complex ritual that involves reweaving the magical essence of twilight back into its fabric. This process demands extensive knowledge of both fey magic and artifact restoration, which is why Eoghan seeks Tadhg's expertise.

To repair the cloak, one must perform a ritual at the exact moment of twilight and use a combination of archaic fey spells and intricate magical weaving techniques. The process is delicate and potentially dangerous, as mishandling the cloak's unstable magic could have dire consequences for both the item and the surrounding area.

Repair the Brat Draíochta (Cloak of Enchantment)

To restore the Brat Draíochta, the PCs must perform a ritual requiring a successful DC 18 Arcana check. They need a rare component, a Dawn Blossom, which can be found in the heart of the Sunset Forest.

Recover the Captive Tadhg

Location and Restraint of Tadhg: Tadhg is held in a magically warded cell within Eoghan's camp, restrained by enchanted chains that suppress his magical abilities. If negotiations succeed, Eoghan will release Tadhg and remove the restraints. If the party opts for a rescue mission, they must bypass these wards and chains, which requires a successful DC 18 Intelligence (Arcana) check or a DC 20 Dexterity check using thieves' tools.

Tadhg's Cooperation: Tadhg has been mostly uncooperative, aware of the potential misuse of his knowledge. If the party rescues him by stealth or force, he can provide detailed insights into the Twilight Kin's plans and the relics' significance.

Attempting to Rescue Tadhg by Force or Stealth

Should negotiations fail, or the party decide to avoid diplomacy altogether, they can attempt to rescue the captive Tadhg by sneaking into the Twilight Kin's camp to locate him, or fighting their way through.

Stealth Approach

Group Dexterity (Stealth) check (DC 16) to approach undetected.

DC 15 Dexterity (Sleight of Hand) check to free Tadhg without alerting guards.

Force Approach

Initiative roll to determine order of combat.

Potential for surprise round if stealth was successful initially.

Tadhg's Escape

Once freed, Tadhg requires protection (AC 12, 30 HP).

DC 13 Wisdom (Survival) check to find a safe escape route.

Form an Alliance with the Twilight Kin

If Eoghan na Luí becomes aware that Fionnlagh and his apprentices are the central cause for the disruption of magic in the Sunset Forest, he will be inclined to align with the PCs to help defeat the Dark Sorcerer.

Negotiation

PCs can propose they form alliance with the Twilight Kin. A successful Charisma (Persuasion or Deception) check (DC 16) ensures the proposal is well received.

At the DM's discretion, this DC can vary based on what the party offers (15-18).

Proving Worth: Eoghan may ask the party to complete a small quest for the Twilight Kin (e.g., retrieving a magical artifact, DC set based on the task).

Sealing the Deal

The party may be asked to make a formal pact with the Twilight Kin. This requires a DC 15 Intelligence (Arcana) check to properly perform a fey pact ritual.

Spellcasters can use *Geas* or similar spells to magically bind the agreement.

Terrain

The clearing is considered sacred ground, suffused with volatile twilight magic. Movement is normal within the immediate area around the great tree, but the surrounding forest is difficult terrain due to twisting roots and shifting shadows. Additionally:

The magical twilight imposes disadvantage on Perception checks relying on sight beyond 60 feet.

Characters attempting to climb the central tree must make a DC 15 Strength (Athletics) check due to its smooth, magic-infused bark.

There's a 25% chance each round that a character using teleportation magic within the clearing arrives at a random location within it instead of their intended destination.

Lair Actions

Twilight Surge: Eoghan causes a wave of twilight energy to pulse through the area. All creatures must make a DC 15 Wisdom saving throw or be disoriented, having disadvantage on their next attack roll or ability check.

Shadow Veil: The shadows in the area deepen dramatically. Until the start of Eoghan's next turn, all creatures have three-quarters cover.

Temporal Shift: Time briefly warps around the tree. Eoghan can choose one creature to either age or regress by 1d4 years (their choice). This grants them either advantage or disadvantage on their next roll, depending on whether they aged or regressed.

NPCs

Eoghan na Luí

Tadhg an Airgid

The Magic Pond

In this encounter, PCs get to know Niamh an tSolais, a powerful healer who can become a valuable ally. The PCs must prove their worth through acts of kindness and healing, potentially gaining crucial support for their quest.

As you push through the perpetual twilight of the forest, you suddenly emerge into a clearing bathed in soft, golden light. Before you lies a tranquil pond, its surface mirror-smooth and reflecting the eternal sunset sky above. The water seems to glow from within, casting shimmering patterns on the surrounding trees and rocks.

Around the pond's edge, a vibrant array of flowers and herbs grow, their colors more vivid than any you've seen in this twilight realm. The air here is filled with a sweet, healing aroma that immediately makes you feel refreshed and invigorated. Near the water's edge, you spot a figure tending to the plants, their form radiating a gentle, warm light.

Activities

Approach and befriend Niamh.

Assist Niamh in healing wounded fey creatures.

Restore balance to a corrupted area of the forest.

Learn about and create healing potions with Niamh.

Approach and Befriend Niamh

Initial Approach: DC 13 Wisdom (Perception) check to notice any potential hazards or special features around Niamh.

First Impression: DC 14 Charisma (Persuasion) check to make a positive first impression.

Insight Check: DC 15 Wisdom (Insight) to gauge Niamh's intentions and current mood.

Cultural Understanding: DC 13 Intelligence (History) or Intelligence (Nature) check to recall appropriate fey etiquette.

Language Barrier (if applicable): DC 12 Intelligence check to communicate effectively if no common language is shared.

Assist Niamh in Heal Wounded Fey Creatures

For each of the creatures listed below, use the following formula to help cure them. Additional information is added with each creature.

Diagnosis: DC 14 Wisdom (Medicine) check to identify the fey creatures' ailments.

Herbalism: DC 15 Intelligence (Nature) check to identify and gather appropriate healing herbs.

Potion Brewing: DC 16 Intelligence check to assist Niamh in creating healing potions.

Magical Healing: Spellcasters can use healing spells. Each spell cast counts as a success.

Physical Aid: DC 13 Dexterity check to properly bandage or splint injuries.

Comforting Presence: DC 14 Charisma (Persuasion) check to calm distressed fey creatures.

Success Criteria: The party needs to accumulate 5 successes (adjusted for party size) across these checks to fully assist Niamh. Each failure adds 1 to the required number of successes.

Wounded Fey Creatures

Luminous Sprite

Description: A tiny, glowing humanoid with butterfly wings, its light dimmed by injury.

Diagnosis: Broken wing and energy depletion.

Herbalism: Gather moonblossoms and starlight ferns.

Potion Brewing: Infuse moonblossom petals in spring water under moonlight, add crushed starlight fern.

Physical Aid: Gently splint the wing with thin, flexible twigs and cobweb wrapping.

Comforting Presence: Speak in soft whispers and offer small, shiny objects as distractions.

Dryad Sapling

Description: A young tree nymph, bark cracked and leaves wilting.

Diagnosis: Dehydration and bark rot.

Herbalism: Collect sundew leaves and oakmoss.

Potion Brewing: Steep oakmoss in pure forest stream water, blend with sundew leaf extract.

Physical Aid: Apply a poultice of moist clay and herbs to the cracked bark.

Comforting Presence: Sing gentle melodies reminiscent of rustling leaves and flowing water.

Twilight Pixie

Description: A small, mischievous fey with gossamer wings, looking unusually lethargic.

Diagnosis: Magical exhaustion and minor cuts.

Herbalism: Gather twilight orchids and dewdrop crystals.

Potion Brewing: Dissolve dewdrop crystals in twilight orchid nectar, stir with a moonbeam.

Physical Aid: Clean and bandage cuts with soft spider silk.

Comforting Presence: Tell amusing stories of playful pranks and offer small sweets.

Faun Shepherd

Description: A half-human, half-goat creature with a twisted leg and a worried expression.

Diagnosis: Fractured leg bone and anxiety over separated herd.

Herbalism: Collect healing clover and mountain thistle.

Potion Brewing: Simmer healing clover in goat's milk, add ground mountain thistle.

Physical Aid: Set the leg with straight branches and bind with flexible vines.

Comforting Presence: Play soothing music on pipes or flutes, assure them of their herd's safety.

Will-o'-Wisp Essence

Description: A flickering ball of spectral light, pulsing weakly.

Diagnosis: Fading life force and ethereal disturbance.

Herbalism: Gather ghost orchids and firefly ferns.

Potion Brewing: Distill ghost orchid essence, mix with crushed firefly fern in a crystal vial.

Physical Aid: Create a protective sphere of interwoven moonbeams and shadows.

Comforting Presence: Mimic the pulsing light patterns of other will-o'-wisps, speak in gentle, echoing tones.

For each creature, a successful treatment would involve correctly diagnosing their condition (Medicine check), gathering the right herbs (Nature check), brewing the appropriate potion (Intelligence check), providing proper physical aid (Dexterity check), and offering suitable comfort (Charisma check).

Restore Balance to a Corrupted Area of the Forest

To help heal the corrupted areas of the forest, use the following formula:

Identify Corruption: DC 15 Intelligence (Arcana) or Wisdom (Nature) check to recognize the type and extent of corruption.

Cleansing Ritual: Perform the appropriate cleansing ritual using the following format:

Preparation: DC 14 Intelligence (Religion) check to set up the ritual correctly.

Performance: DC 16 Charisma (Performance) check to lead the ritual effectively.

Magical Support: Divine spellcasters can use purification spells (like *Protection from Evil and Good* or *Dispel Evil and Good*) to aid the process.

Combat Corruption: If corrupted creatures are present, initiative is rolled, and combat ensues.

Natural Remedy: DC 15 Wisdom (Survival) check to find and apply natural remedies to cleanse the area.

Harmonize with Nature: DC 14 Wisdom check to attune with the forest's natural energy and guide it towards balance.

Success Criteria: The party needs to succeed on at least 4 out of 6 of these checks (or equivalent combat success) to restore balance. Each significant failure (rolling 5 or lower) causes a minor setback, such as temporary corruption effects on a party member.

Corrupted Areas in the Forest

Withering Glade

Identify Corruption: Once-vibrant foliage now gray and wilting, ground covered in ash-like substance, air filled with sickly sweet scent.

Cleansing Ritual

Preparation: Create a circle of pure water around the glade's perimeter.

Performance: Chant in Sylvan while sprinkling purified forest dew in a spiral pattern.

Magic Support: Cast *Plant Growth* to reinvigorate the vegetation.

Combat Corruption: Defeat 1d4 Needle Blights that have sprouted from corrupted trees.

Natural Remedy: Brew a tincture of sunburst lichen and morning dew, spread it over the corrupted soil.

Shadowed Pool

Identify Corruption: Once-clear water now murky and dark, surrounded by twisted, blackened reeds. Faint whispers emanate from the depths.

Cleansing Ritual

Preparation: Place charged moonstones at cardinal points around the pool.

Performance: Perform a water blessing dance, moving clockwise around the pool.

Magic Support: Cast *Purify Food and Drink* on the water, moving around to affect the entire pool.

Combat Corruption: Confront and banish a shadow entity lurking in the water (use Shadow stats).

Natural Remedy: Introduce purifying algae and water lilies blessed by a druid or nature cleric.

Whispering Hollow

Identify Corruption: Trees with faces twisted in agony, leaves rustling with discordant whispers, ground covered in thorny vines.

Cleansing Ritual

Preparation: Hang wind chimes made of blessed silver throughout the hollow.

Performance: Play a harmonizing melody on a wooden flute, countering the discordant whispers.

Magic Support: Cast *Calm Emotions* to soothe the agitated spirits of the trees.

Combat Corruption: Overcome a series of hallucinations or illusions created by the corrupted whispers.

Natural Remedy: Plant seeds of harmony-restoring flowers (like "peaceful peonies") throughout the hollow.

Mist-Wreathed Stones

Identify Corruption: Ancient stone circle shrouded in sickly green mist, runes on stones glowing with an eerie light.

Cleansing Ritual

Preparation: Cleanse each stone with sacred oils in a specific order.

Performance: Recite the true names of ancient fey guardians at each stone.

Magic Support: Cast *Dispel Magic* on the corrupted runes.

Combat Corruption: Defeat animated stone guardians (use Earth Elemental stats) that have been twisted by the corruption.

Natural Remedy: Burn purifying herbs (sage, lavender, rosemary) in a brazier at the center of the circle.

Inverted Canopy

Identify Corruption: Trees growing upside-down, roots in the air and branches in the ground, causing disorientation.

Cleansing Ritual

Preparation: Create a complex mandala on the ground using colored sands.

Performance: Perform a gravity-defying acrobatic ritual among the inverted trees.

Combat Corruption: Navigate through the disorienting area while fending off corrupted bird-like creatures (use Kenku stats but with flying speed).

For each corrupted area, successful cleansing would involve correctly identifying the corruption (Arcana or Nature check), performing the ritual correctly (Religion and Performance checks), overcoming any combat challenges, and applying the natural remedy (Nature or Survival check).

Learn about and Create Healing Potions with Niamh

Below is a table of healing potions that Niamh can teach the PCs:

Name	Description	Properties	Weight	Niamh's Instructions
Twilight Elixir	A shimmering purple liquid that seems to contain swirling stars	Heals 2d4+2 HP and grants darkvision for 1 hour	1/2 lb	Brew twilight orchid petals in moonlit water, add a pinch of stardust. Stir with a silver spoon under the night sky for 10 minutes.
Sunburst Tonic	A bright golden liquid that radiates warmth	Heals 3d4+3 HP and grants advantage on the next saving throw against fear or charm effects	1/2 lb	Infuse sunflower petals and honey in spring water, add a drop of liquid sunlight. Heat gently over a flame for 1 hour, stirring clockwise.
Forest Heart Brew	A deep green potion with swirling patterns resembling leaves	Heals 2d6+4 HP and grants advantage on Constitution saving throws for 10 minutes	1/2 lb	Steep oak leaves, moss, and forest berries in pure stream water. Add a drop of dryad's tear. Let it sit in a grove for a full day and night.
Fey Mist Vapor	A misty, iridescent liquid that seems to shift colors	When the vial is opened, it creates a 5-foot radius of healing mist. Creatures in the mist at the start of their turn regain 1d4 HP	1/4 lb	Collect morning dew from fairy rings, mix with crushed rainbow flower petals. Distill the mixture in a crystal alembic under moonlight.
Vitality Salve	A thick, amber-colored paste with a sweet, earthy scent	Apply to wounds to heal 2d4+2 HP and end one disease affecting the target	1 lb	Grind healing herbs with honey and beeswax. Add powdered unicorn horn (or blessed oak bark as substitute). Heat and stir until it forms a thick paste.
Whisper of Life	A clear, effervescent liquid that makes a soft chiming sound when shaken	Instantly stabilizes a creature at 0 HP and restores 1 HP. Also cures paralysis	1/4 lb	Dissolve pixie dust in pure spring water, add a phoenix feather ash. Charge under a full moon for one night, then seal with a whispered prayer.

The potions' effects are balanced for low to mid-level play. Adjust the healing amounts and additional effects as needed for your campaign's level and difficulty.

For crafting these potions, PCs would typically need to make an Intelligence (Arcana) check or use an herbalism kit, with the DC varying based on the complexity of the potion (generally between DC 13-17). Some rare ingredients might require separate quests or skill checks to obtain.

Terrain

The area around the pond is considered sacred and magically enhanced. Movement is normal within 30 feet of the pond's edge. Beyond that, the Sunset Forest's difficult terrain rules apply. Additionally:

The pond's water has healing properties. Characters who drink from it gain the benefits of a short rest in just 10 minutes.

Plants within 30 feet of the pond are particularly potent. Proficiency with the herbalism kit not only allows the PC to add their proficiency bonus to any rolls made here using the kit, but also provides advantage to their potion crafting checks.

The magical nature of the area interferes with teleportation magic. Any attempt to teleport to or from this area requires a DC 15 Intelligence (Arcana) check to succeed.

Lair Actions

Restorative Mist: Niamh causes a healing mist to rise from the pond. All creatures within 30 feet regain 2d6 hit points.

Nature's Embrace: Vines and flowers rapidly grow, providing half cover to all creatures Niamh considers allies until the start of her next turn.

Purifying Light: A burst of radiant energy emanates from Niamh. All allies within 60 feet are cured of one disease or condition of Niamh's choice.

Scaling the Sunset Forest Encounters

Beginning Players (PC levels 1-5)

Reduce all skill check DCs by 2 (e.g., DC 15 becomes DC 13).

Random Encounters:

- Use only encounters 1-5.
- Reduce effects (e.g., 1d4 psychic damage instead of 2d6).

Negotiation with Eoghan:

- Reduce number of required successes to 2.
- Lower initial DC to 13.

Brat Draíochta Repair: Simplify to 3 checks total, DC 13 each.

Corrupted Areas:

- Reduce number of required successes to 3.
- Use easier monsters (e.g., Twig Blights instead of Needle Blights).

Healing Potions: Focus on basic healing potions (e.g., Twilight Elixir, Sunburst Tonic).

Niamh's Lair Actions:

- Reduce healing to 1d6.
- Limit purifying light to one condition.

Intermediate Players (PC levels 6-10)

Keep skill check DCs as written.

Niamh's Lair Actions: Use as written.

Advanced Players (PC levels 11+)

Increase all skill check DCs by 2 (e.g., DC 15 becomes DC 17).

Random Encounters:

- Enhance effects (e.g., 3d6 psychic damage).
- Add complex magical consequences to failures.

Negotiation with Eoghan:

- Increase number of required successes to 4.
- Add magical challenges (e.g., resist mind-reading, DC 17).

Brat Draíochta Repair:

- Add time pressure (e.g., complete within 45 minutes).
- Include magical backlash for failures (e.g., 2d10 force damage).

Corrupted Areas:

- Increase to 5 required successes.
- Use more challenging monsters (e.g., Glabrezu instead of Shadow).
- Add complex magical traps or environmental hazards.

Healing Potions:

- Introduce advanced potions with multiple effects.
- Allow experimentation to create unique potions.

Niamh's Lair Actions:

- Increase healing to 3d6.
- Add offensive options (e.g., radiant damage to enemies).
- Allow Niamh to grant temporary magical boons to allies.

Act 3

Act 3 – The Wicked Ones

Droichead na Carraige (Bridge of the Rock)

This encounter features a treacherous natural stone bridge connecting two islands over a dangerous tidal river. Players must navigate harsh weather conditions and potential magical defenses while avoiding detection by Róisín's forces.

Before you stretches a massive natural stone arch spanning a churning tidal river. The bridge, if it can be called that, is a precarious formation of weather-worn rock, its surface uneven and slick with sea spray. Jagged outcroppings and deep crevices mar its length, making the crossing appear as much a climb as a walk.

The howling wind carries salt and mist, obscuring your vision and threatening to throw you off balance. Far below, the river surges with frightening power, its waters periodically swelling with the tide.

Cross the Bridge of the Rock

The 200-foot journey across Droichead na Carraige is divided into four 50-foot segments, each presenting unique challenges.

Segment 1: The Approach

Slippery Incline: The first section slopes upward.

DC 13 Dexterity (Acrobatics) check to ascend without falling prone.

Segment 2: Narrow Pass

Tight Squeeze: The bridge narrows to 5 feet wide.

Medium creatures must move at half speed.

Large creatures must squeeze, moving at quarter speed and having disadvantage on Dexterity saves.

Gusty Winds: Strong crosswinds threaten to push characters off.

DC 14 Strength saving throw each turn to avoid being pushed 5 feet laterally.

Segment 3: The Gauntlet

Unstable Rocks: Sections of the bridge are crumbling.

DC 15 Wisdom (Perception) check to spot safe paths.

Failed check requires a DC 14 Dexterity save to avoid falling into a crevice (1d6 damage and must climb back up).

Magical Mist: A 20-foot section of heavy magical fog.

Heavily obscured area, creatures blinded while inside.

DC 13 Intelligence (Investigation) check to navigate through without getting turned around.

Segment 4: The Descent

Slick Decline: The final section slopes downward, made slippery by sea spray.

DC 14 Dexterity (Acrobatics) check to descend safely.

Failure results in sliding to the bottom, taking 1d6 bludgeoning damage.

Additional Challenges

Tidal Timing: The bridge is safest to cross during low tide.

PCs have 10 rounds before the tide rises, increasing all DCs by 2.

Stealthy Approach: PCs must periodically roll Dexterity (Stealth) checks (DC 14) to avoid detection by Róisín's forces. The number of Stealth checks required is at the DM's discretion, with a suggestion of three.

Party Tactics

Players can assist each other, granting advantage on checks.

Creative use of spells or abilities can mitigate challenges (e.g., *Levitate*, *Rope Trick*, *Pass without Trace*).

Characters with appropriate backgrounds (sailor, coastal dweller) may have advantage on certain checks.

Success Criteria

All party members reach the other side.

Crossing completed within 10 rounds (before high tide).

No more than two failed Stealth checks.

Lair Actions

Tidal Surge: The river below swells suddenly, sending a massive wave to crash over the bridge. All creatures on the bridge must succeed on a DC 15 Strength saving throw or be knocked prone and pushed 10 feet.

Howling Gale: A powerful gust of wind sweeps across the bridge. Each creature must succeed on a DC 14 Strength saving throw or be pushed 15 feet and have disadvantage on ranged weapon attacks until the start of its next turn.

Magical Mist: A thick, magical mist engulfs a 30-foot section of the bridge. This area becomes heavily obscured, and creatures within it have disadvantage on Wisdom (Perception) checks that rely on sight.

Scaling the Bridge of the Rock Encounter

Beginning Players (PC levels 1-5)

Reduce all skill check and saving throw DCs by 2 (e.g., DC 15 becomes DC 13).

Shorten the bridge to 150 feet (three 50-foot segments).

Increase time limit to 12 rounds before high tide.

Reduce damage from falls to 1d4.

Simplify lair actions:

- **Tidal Surge**: DC 13 save, pushed 5 feet.
- **Howling Gale**: DC 12 save, pushed 10 feet.
- **Magical Mist**: 20-foot section, disadvantage on Perception checks only.

Allow more frequent use of the Help action without penalties.

Intermediate Players (PC levels 6-10)

Keep all DCs and bridge length as written.

Maintain 10-round time limit.

Use damage values as written.

Implement lair actions as described.

Add optional challenges:

- Magical barriers requiring Arcana checks to bypass.
- Minor creatures (e.g., hostile birds) to combat while crossing.

Advanced Players (PC levels 11+)

Increase all DCs by 2 (e.g., DC 15 becomes DC 17).

Extend the bridge to 250 feet (five 50-foot segments).

Reduce time limit to 8 rounds before high tide.

Increase damage from falls to 2d6.

Enhance lair actions:

- **Tidal Surge**: DC 17 save, pushed 15 feet and 2d6 bludgeoning damage.
- **Howling Gale**: DC 16 save, pushed 20 feet and stunned until next turn on fail.
- **Magical Mist**: 40-foot section, creatures must succeed on a DC 15 Wisdom save or become lost for 1 round.

Add complex challenges:

- Sections of antimagic fields.
- Illusory duplicates of the bridge.
- Periodically phasing sections of the bridge.

Introduce patrol encounters:

- Róisín's aerial scouts (e.g., Wyvern Riders).
- Magical constructs guarding the bridge.

Caisleán na Taibhse (Castle of the Ghost)

This encounter features a haunted castle filled with corrupted beasts and dark magic, culminating in a battle against Maolmhuire for the Life Fragment of the Triskelion. Players must navigate traps and defenses while dealing with the enigmatic Lucht Siúil spirits.

As you approach the castle, its imposing stone towers loom before you, with twisted spires reaching into the darkening sky like gnarled fingers. Shadows seem to move of their own accord across the weathered facade, and a bone-chilling wail echoes from somewhere within. The air grows colder with each step, and you can't shake the feeling of unseen eyes watching your every move.

The massive wooden doors stand slightly ajar, as if inviting you into their haunted depths. An eerie mist swirls around the crumbling stone walls, and flickering, spectral lights are visible through some of the stained-glass windows. The very atmosphere seems charged with dark energy, promising danger and secrets within.

Locations in the Castle

Entrance Hall: Dimly lit, filled with shadowy corners and decaying tapestries.

Library: Dusty tomes and floating spectral lights; Lucht Siúil can be encountered here.

Dining Hall: Long table set for a ghostly feast, haunted by restless spirits of the Lucht Siúil.

Throne Room: Maolmhuire can be found here, surrounded by corrupted beasts.

Entrance Hall

As you push open the massive oak doors, they creak ominously, revealing a vast, dimly lit hall. The air is thick with dust and the musty scent of decay. Flickering torches cast long, dancing shadows across the walls, their meager light barely penetrating the gloom. Tattered tapestries, once vibrant with scenes of ancient battles and mythical beasts, now hang in moldering strips from the stone walls.

Notable Features

A grand chandelier, covered in cobwebs, hangs precariously from the vaulted ceiling.

Suits of armor line the walls, their metal corroded and twisted into grotesque shapes.

A faded, threadbare carpet runs the length of the hall, its pattern obscured by years of grime.

Large, cracked mirrors reflect distorted images of the room and its occupants.

Hidden Dangers

The chandelier is unstable and may fall if disturbed (DC 15 Dexterity save to avoid 3d6 bludgeoning damage).

Some floor tiles are loose, potentially triggering the Phantom Snare Trap (DC 14 Wisdom (Perception) to notice, DC 13 Dexterity save to avoid falling into a 10-foot pit).

Phantom Snare Trap

Description: This insidious trap combines mundane mechanisms with dark magic. When triggered, it not only causes physical harm but also attempts to drain the life force of its victims.

Trigger: Stepping on one of the loose floor tiles in the Entrance Hall.

Activation: The trap activates when more than 50 pounds of weight is placed on a loose tile.

Effect: The victim falls into a 10-foot pit lined with sharp spikes, taking 2d6 piercing damage. Additionally, spectral tendrils emerge from the pit walls, attempting to grasp the fallen character (escape DC 14). If grappled, the victim must make a DC 14 Constitution saving throw at the start of each of their turns or take 1d6 necrotic damage.

Detection: DC 14 Wisdom (Perception) check to notice the slightly uneven or discolored floor tiles. DC 16 Intelligence (Investigation) check to deduce the presence of the trap from subtle markings or wear patterns on the floor.

Disable: DC 15 Dexterity check using thieves' tools to jam the mechanism beneath the loose tile.

A successful casting of *Dispel Magic* (DC 14) on the pit will temporarily suppress the spectral tendrils for 1 hour.

Covering the loose tiles with a sturdy material (e.g., a thick plank) can allow safe passage over the trap.

Encounter

Shadows: 1d4 Shadows lurk in the corners, attacking unsuspecting intruders.

Loot

A tarnished silver candelabra (worth 25 gp) hidden behind one of the suits of armor.

A moldy spellbook containing two random 1st-level wizard spells, tucked away in a secret compartment (DC 16 Intelligence (Investigation) to find).

Library

When you push open the heavy wooden doors, the scent of old parchment and leather washes over you. Towering bookshelves line the walls, reaching up into the shadows of the vaulted ceiling. Dust motes dance in the air, illuminated by eerie, floating orbs of spectral light that drift lazily between the stacks. The floor creaks beneath your feet, and you notice that some of the books seem to shiver on their shelves as if alive.

Notable Features

A massive circular table dominates the center of the room, covered in open books and strange magical instruments.

An ornate lectern stands near one wall, a large tome chained to it.

Floating ladders that move of their own accord to reach high shelves.

Ghostly whispers can be heard emanating from certain sections of books.

A large, cracked mirror hangs on one wall, occasionally showing fleeting reflections of past readers.

Library Books

Below is a list of spellbooks found in the library, including the one chained to the lectern. These books offer a mix of benefits and potential dangers, adding depth and interactivity to the library encounter.

Chained Tome: *Whispers of the Veil*

Author: Moira the Shadowweaver

Description: A black leather-bound book with silver runes. It contains advanced necromancy spells and rituals for communicating with the dead.

Benefit: Grants advantage on Intelligence (Arcana) checks related to undead and spirits. Allows the reader to cast *Speak with Dead* once without using a spell slot.

Elemental Harmony: A Treatise on Planar Magic

Author: Archmage Zephyrian Stormcaller

Description: A blue and gold tome filled with intricate diagrams of elemental planes.

Benefit: Contains instructions for a ritual that grants resistance to one elemental damage type for 24 hours. Requires 1 hour and rare materials worth 50gp to perform. Only one creature can benefit from reading this book at a time, and each character can only benefit from it once.

Cryptic Codex of Ciphers

Author: Unknown (signed only with a mysterious symbol)

Description: A slim volume written entirely in magical ciphers.

Curse: Reading without deciphering causes *Confusion* (as the spell) for 1d4 hours.

Benefit: If deciphered (DC 18 Intelligence check), grants +2 to all Intelligence checks for 24 hours.

Remove Curse: Decode the entire book (three successful DC 18 Intelligence checks).

Flora Arcana: Secrets of Magical Botany

Author: Druid Elder Thorne Oakenheart

Description: A green, leaf-shaped book that smells of herbs and forest.

Benefit: Advantage on Nature checks related to magical plants. Allows the reader to cast *Goodberry* once without using a spell slot.

Chronomancer's Compendium

Author: Time Mage Aeon Flux

Description: An hourglass-shaped book that seems to shimmer and shift.

Curse: Randomly ages or de-ages the reader by 1d10 years for 24 hours upon reading.

Benefit: Grants the reader the ability to cast *Haste* once without using a spell slot.

Remove Curse: Spend 24 hours with the book, experiencing rapid aging and de-aging.

Illusions of the Mind's Eye

Author: Mirage, Master of Phantasms

Description: A book that appears different to each viewer, filled with moving illustrations.

Benefit: Grants advantage on saving throws against illusion spells for 24 hours after studying for 1 hour.

Graviturgist's Guide to Spatial Manipulation

Author: Sage Isotropa the Weightless

Description: A cube-shaped book that feels unusually light or heavy at random.

Benefit: Allows the reader to cast *Levitate* on themselves once without using a spell slot.

Runescript Grimoire

Author: Artificer Glyphtangle Sparkforge

Description: A metal-bound book with glowing runes on its cover.

Curse: Randomly triggers a wild magic surge (roll on Wild Magic Surge table in the *Player's Handbook*) when read.

Benefit: Allows the creation of a temporary magical rune once per day that can store one spell of 3rd level or lower for 24 hours.

Remove Curse: Successfully create and use 5 runes without triggering a wild magic surge.

Encounters

Lucht Siúil: 1d4 Lucht Siúil (Travelers) can be found here, initially neutral but potentially hostile if disturbed.

Animated Spellbook: An Animated Spellbook that attacks if certain forbidden tomes are touched.

Lucht Siúil Interaction

The Lucht Siúil here are more scholarly in nature. If approached respectfully, they might offer guidance or share knowledge:

DC 14 Charisma (Persuasion) check to gain their assistance in research.

Success grants advantage on Intelligence checks made to recall lore or gather information in the library.

Critical success might result in them revealing a secret about Maolmhuire or the castle's defenses.

Loot

Several rare spell scrolls (DM's choice, levels 1-3) hidden among the shelves.

Dining Hall

As you push open the massive double doors, they groan on rusted hinges, revealing a grand, yet eerie dining hall. A long, ornate table dominates the center of the room, stretching from one end to the other. It's set for a lavish feast, with tarnished silver plates, dusty crystal goblets, and moldering food that seems frozen in time. Tattered tapestries depicting scenes of grand banquets hang on the walls, their colors faded and images distorted. Ghostly whispers and the faint sound of phantom cutlery echo through the air.

Notable Features

A massive chandelier hangs precariously from the ceiling, swaying slightly despite the lack of breeze.

Several ornate chairs are overturned, as if their occupants left in a hurry.

A large fireplace at one end of the hall contains cold ashes and charred logs.

Serving carts are positioned around the room, bearing covered silver platters.

Mirrors line one wall, occasionally showing fleeting reflections of spectral diners.

Encounter

Lucht Siúil: 2d4 aggressive Lucht Siúil (Travelers) haunt this hall, their forms flickering in and out of visibility.

Lucht Siúil Interaction

The Lucht Siúil here are more hostile than their library counterparts. Their behavior is irritable and erratic, driven by an eternal, insatiable hunger, viewing living creatures as potential sustenance.

Initial reaction is hostile: DC 16 Charisma (Persuasion) check to avoid immediate aggression.

Failed checks result in the spirits attacking, attempting to drain life force from the characters.

Even if calmed, they remain unpredictable and may turn hostile again if provoked or if food is mentioned.

Unique Mechanic: Phantom Feast

The illusory food on the table seems to shimmer with spectral energy.

Characters who attempt to eat it must make a DC 15 Constitution saving throw.

Failure results in 2d6 necrotic damage and the Poisoned condition for 1 hour.

Success allows the character to regain 2d6 hit points and gain a random minor magical effect for 1 hour (DM's discretion).

Hidden Danger

The chandelier is unstable. Any loud noise or significant vibration causes it to fall.

DC 15 Dexterity saving throw to avoid 3d6 bludgeoning damage and being restrained under the wreckage.

Loot

A set of ornate silver cutlery (worth 75 gp) hidden in a serving cart.

A magical wine decanter that never runs empty (functions similarly to a Decanter of Endless Water, but produces wine).

Throne Room

As you approach the massive doors to the throne room, you feel an overwhelming sense of dread and malevolence. Pushing them open, you're greeted by a vast, dimly lit chamber. A long, tattered carpet leads to a raised dais at the far end, upon which sits a twisted, black throne. Shadows seem to writhe and dance along the walls, and the air is thick with dark energy. Corrupted beasts prowl the edges of the room, their forms warped and unnatural.

At the center of it all, seated upon the throne with an air of malicious authority, is a figure you recognize as Maolmhuire. His eyes gleam with dark power, and a cruel smile plays across his lips as he regards your entrance.

Notable Features

The black throne, seemingly carved from a single piece of obsidian, pulsates with dark energy.

Shattered stained glass windows depict scenes of conquest and corruption.

Twisted statues of former rulers line the walls, their faces contorted in agony.

A large, cracked mirror hangs behind the throne, occasionally showing glimpses of other realms.

Braziers filled with sickly green flames provide eerie illumination.

Unique Mechanic: Corrupting Aura

The room is suffused with corrupting energy.

At the start of each round, all creatures must make a DC 15 Constitution saving throw.

Failure results in 1d6 necrotic damage and disadvantage on their next attack roll or saving throw.

Maolmhuire and his Corrupted Beasts are immune to this effect.

Encounter

Maolmhuire, seated on the throne, ready to engage in combat.

Corrupted Beasts: 1d4+2 Corrupted Beasts prowl about the room, their forms warped and unnatural.

Maolmhuire's Tactics

He begins combat by using *Wall of Force* to divide the party.

Uses *Hold Person* to incapacitate strong melee fighters.

Casts *Blight* on grouped enemies.

Utilizes the Corrupted Beasts as a front line while he attacks from range.

Hidden Danger

The floor near the throne is unstable. Any creature that ends its turn within 10 feet of the throne must make a DC 14 Dexterity saving throw or fall into a 20-foot pit, taking 2d6 bludgeoning damage.

The Life Fragment

The Life Fragment of the Triskelion (embodying Creation) is embedded in the black throne. It can be removed with a DC 18 Strength check or by destroying the throne.

Terrain

The castle interior is dark and treacherous. Dim light conditions impose disadvantage on Perception checks relying on sight. Crumbling floors and unstable structures require DC 13 Dexterity (Acrobatics) checks when moving at full speed; failure results in falling prone. Areas of magical darkness require a DC 15 Intelligence (Arcana) check to navigate without disadvantage.

Lair Actions

Shadows Come Alive: Shadows in the room animate and attack, making one attack against each creature Maolmhuire chooses.

Spectral Wail: A horrifying scream echoes through the castle. All creatures must succeed on a DC 15 Wisdom saving throw or be frightened until the end of their next turn.

Corrupting Surge: Tendrils of dark energy erupt from the floor. Each creature of Maolmhuire's choice must make a DC 15 Constitution saving throw or take 3d6 necrotic damage.

NPC
Maolmhuire

Monsters
Lucht Siúil

Animated Spellbook

Corrupted Beast

Scaling the Castle of the Ghost Encounter

Beginning Players (PC levels 1-5)

Reduce all skill check and saving throw DCs by 2 (e.g., DC 15 becomes DC 13).

Entrance Hall:

- Reduce chandelier damage to 2d6.
- Simplify Phantom Snare Trap: remove magical effects, 1d6 damage.

Library:

- Reduce number of Lucht Siúil to 1d2.
- Remove Animated Spellbook encounter.

Dining Hall:

- Reduce number of Lucht Siúil to 1d4.
- Phantom Feast: DC 13 save, 1d6 damage or healing.

Throne Room:

- Maolmhuire uses lower-level spells (e.g., *Magic Missile* instead of *Blight*).
- Reduce number of Corrupted Beasts to 1d4.
- Corrupting Aura: DC 13 save, 1d4 damage.

Lair Actions:

- Reduce save DCs to 13.
- Corrupting Surge: 2d6 damage.

Intermediate Players (PC levels 6-10)

Keep all DCs as written.

Use all encounters and mechanics as described.

Throne Room: Use as written.

Lair Actions: Use as written.

Advanced Players (PC levels 11+)

Increase all DCs by 2 (e.g., DC 15 becomes DC 17).

Entrance Hall:

- Enhance Phantom Snare Trap: add paralysis effect (DC 17 Con save).
- Add 1d4 Wraiths to the Shadow encounter.

Library:

- Increase number of Lucht Siúil to 2d4.
- Add a spellcaster Lucht Siúil (use Mage stats).
- Use higher stats for Animated Spellbook (such as Young Red Dragon stats), but keep Small size.

Dining Hall:

- Increase number of Lucht Siúil to 3d4.
- **Phantom Feast**: DC 17 save, 3d6 damage or enhanced healing effect.

Throne Room:

- Maolmhuire uses 7th-9th level spells.
- Increase number of Corrupted Beasts to 2d4+2.
- Add 1d4 spellcaster Lucht Siúil (use Mage stats).
- Corrupting Aura: DC 17 save, 2d6 damage and additional negative effect.

Lair Actions:

- Increase save DCs to 17.
- Enhance effects (e.g., Spectral Wail also deals psychic damage).
- **Add a fourth Lair Action**: Reality Warp (alters terrain or gravity in the room).

Uaimh Chráite (Ghost Cave)

This encounter features a complex cave system where Conall, the necromancer, commands undead forces and guards the Death Fragment of the Triskelion. Players must navigate puzzles, defeat waves of undead, and face the enigmatic Scáthannaí to reach Conall and claim the fragment.

Once you approach the cave entrance, a chill runs down your spine. The air grows noticeably colder, and wisps of an unnatural mist curl around your feet. The cave mouth yawns before you, a dark void that seems to swallow all light. Faint, mournful whispers echo from deep within, carrying with them the unmistakable stench of decay.

Stepping inside, your eyes struggle to adjust to the gloom. The walls are slick with moisture, and pale, luminescent fungi cast an eerie glow throughout the cavern. Shadows seem to move of their own accord, dancing at the edge of your vision. The whispers grow louder, more insistent, as if the very cave itself is trying to speak to you.

Locations in the Cave System

Entrance Cave: Features ancient Celtic runes and a puzzle lock. 2d4 Scáthannaí guard this area.

Bone Chamber: A vast cavern filled with skeletal remains. 1d6 skeletons and 1 Scáthannaí patrol here.

Summoning Chamber: Where Conall performs his necromantic rituals. Conall is found here, along with 2 Scáthannaí.

Shadow Sanctum: A small, pitch-black chamber connected to the Summoning Chamber. The Death Fragment (Destruction) of the Triskelion is hidden here.

Entrance Cave

As you step deeper into the cave, the narrow entrance opens into a vast, circular chamber. The walls are smooth and curved, as if carved by unnatural forces. Pale, bioluminescent fungi cling to the rocky surfaces, casting an eerie, ghostly light throughout the space. The air is thick with mist, and you can hear the faint sound of dripping water echoing in the distance.

Your attention is immediately drawn to the far wall, where an enormous stone door stands. Its surface is covered in intricate Celtic knotwork and spirals, all seeming to radiate from a central, circular indentation. Ancient runes, glowing with a faint blue light, arc across the top of the door. The floor leading up to the door is inlaid with stone tiles, each bearing different Celtic symbols.

Notable Features

A massive stone door with Celtic designs and runes.

A circular indentation in the center of the door, about the size of a dinner plate.

Stone tiles on the floor, each with a different Celtic symbol.

Bioluminescent fungi providing dim, bluish light.

Small channels in the floor that seem to lead to the door.

Puzzle Lock

The door is sealed by an ancient magical lock based on Celtic symbolism and the cycle of life and death. To open it, PCs must:

Decipher the Runes: A DC 15 Intelligence (Arcana) check is required to decipher the runes above the door. The translated message reads: "From seed to tree, from life to beyond, follow the path of existence to open the way."

Nine Tiles: The floor contains 9 tiles in a 3x3 grid, each depicting a different Celtic symbol:

- Spirit (ghostly face), Tree (Celtic tree of life), Phoenix (bird in flames)
- Elder (wise man), Sprout (triskele), Gravestone (Celtic cross)
- Warrior (sword), Seed (spiral), Skull (stylized Celtic skull)

Correct Sequence: The correct sequence to step on is:

- Seed
- Sprout
- Tree
- Warrior
- Elder
- Skull
- Gravestone
- Spirit
- Phoenix

This sequence represents the cycle of life, death, and rebirth.

Activation: As each correct tile is stepped on, it glows with a soft blue light. Once the correct sequence is activated, channels in the floor fill with spectral blue energy, flowing to the door.

Unlocking the Door: A PC must then place their hand in the circular indentation on the door, which will magically draw a small amount of their life force (1d4 necrotic damage) to unlock the door and lead into the Bone Chamber.

Incorrect Sequence

If a PC steps on an incorrect tile, one of the following effects occurs (roll a d6):

1. **Darts:** The tile shoots poison darts. The character must make a DC 13 Dexterity saving throw. On a failure, they take 2d4 piercing damage and 2d4 poison damage.
2. **Falling Rocks:** Small rocks fall from the ceiling. The character must make a DC 13 Dexterity saving throw. On a failure, they take 2d6 bludgeoning damage.
3. **Spectral Hands:** Ghostly hands emerge from the tile, attempting to grapple the character. They must make a DC 13 Strength saving throw or be restrained until the end of their next turn.
4. **Necrotic Pulse:** The tile releases a pulse of necrotic energy. The character takes 3d6 necrotic damage (DC 13 Constitution save for half damage).
5. **Confusion:** The tile releases a burst of disorienting magic. The character must make a DC 13 Wisdom saving throw or be affected as if by the *Confusion* spell until the end of their next turn.
6. **Fire Burst:** The tile erupts in a burst of flames. The character takes 3d6 fire damage (DC 13 Dexterity save for half damage).

After any incorrect step, all glowing tiles fade, and the sequence must be restarted from the beginning.

Hint Mechanism: If the players are struggling, they might notice that touching the circular indentation on the door provides fleeting visions of the correct symbols in order, but at the cost of 1 point of necrotic damage per use.

Hidden Danger

Pressure plates near the entrance trigger a cave-in if stepped on. DC 14 Wisdom (Perception) check to notice, DC 13 Dexterity save to avoid 2d6 bludgeoning damage from falling rocks.

Encounter

Scáthannaí: 2d4 Scáthannaí (Shadow Walkers) guardians lurk in the shadows of the chamber. They initially remain hidden, only revealing themselves if:

- Players try to force the door open without solving the puzzle
- Players take too long to solve the puzzle (more than 10 minutes)
- Players trigger the cave-in trap

Tactical Considerations

The Scáthannaí use their Shadow Step ability to appear suddenly from dark corners.

They create shadow portals to confuse and separate the party.

The dim lighting gives them advantage on Stealth checks.

Loot

A Celtic torc hidden in a small crevice (DC 15 Perception to find) that grants advantage on saving throws against fear while worn (worth 50 gp).

Bone Chamber

As you enter this vast cavern, the air grows noticeably colder and a sense of dread washes over you. The chamber stretches out before you, its ceiling lost in the darkness above. The ground crunches beneath your feet - a carpet of bones extends as far as you can see, punctuated by larger mounds and grotesque sculptures crafted from skeletal remains.

Eerie, blue-green light emanates from patches of phosphorescent fungi clinging to the cavern walls, casting long, dancing shadows across the bone-strewn floor. The walls themselves seem to be weeping, a constant trickle of water adding a disconcerting backdrop of quiet dripping to the oppressive silence.

Notable Features

A massive central pillar, formed entirely of interlocked bones and skulls.

Several large bone pits scattered throughout the chamber.

Crude altars made of stacked skulls, some bearing faintly glowing runes.

A partially collapsed section of wall revealing a glimpse of a natural underground river.

A narrow, foreboding tunnel leading deeper into the cave system, towards the Summoning Chamber.

Massive Central Pillar

Description: A 30-foot tall, 10-foot diameter pillar made entirely of interlocked bones and skulls. Faint whispers can be heard emanating from it.

Interaction: PCs can attempt to climb the pillar (DC 15 Athletics check).

Benefit: From the top, PCs gain advantage on Perception checks within the chamber due to the elevated view.

Detriment: Failed climbing attempts alert nearby monsters. Each failed check has a 25% chance of causing 1d4 bones to fall, dealing 1d6 bludgeoning damage to creatures within 5 feet.

Special: A DC 18 Intelligence (Arcana) check reveals that the pillar is a conduit for necromantic energy. Damaging it (AC 15, 50 HP) weakens all undead in the chamber, imposing disadvantage on their attack rolls and saving throws for 1 hour.

Large Bone Pits

Description: 20-foot diameter, 10-foot deep pits filled with bones and a viscous, dark liquid.

Interaction: PCs can search the pits (DC 14 Intelligence (Investigation)) or attempt to cross them.

Benefit: Searching may yield valuable items (roll on the following Random Loot Table).

Detriment: Entering a pit requires a DC 15 Strength saving throw to avoid being pulled under. Escaping requires a DC 15 Strength (Athletics) check. Failures result in 1d6 necrotic damage per round and the restrained condition.

Special: The liquid has alchemical properties. A successful DC 16 Intelligence (Arcana) check allows a character to harvest 1d4 vials, each granting temporary resistance to necrotic damage for 1 hour when consumed.

Crude Skull Altars

Description: 5-foot tall altars made of stacked skulls, some bearing glowing runes.

Interaction: PCs can attempt to decipher the runes (DC 16 Intelligence (Arcana) check) or disturb the altars.

Benefit: Successfully deciphering grants insight into Conall's rituals, providing advantage on the next save against his spells.

Detriment: Failed checks or disturbing the altars triggers a Wraith to emerge (use standard Wraith stats), which attacks the party.

Special: When touching a rune-etched skull, a PC with a spell slot available can choose to sacrifice that slot to imbue their next spell cast with additional necrotic damage equal to the slot level.

Partially Collapsed Wall

Description: A 15-foot wide breach revealing a fast-flowing underground river.

Interaction: Players can attempt to navigate the river (DC 16 Strength (Athletics) check) or use it to cleanse cursed items.

Benefit: Successfully navigating the river provides a shortcut directly to the Shadow Sanctum.

Detriment: Failed checks result in being swept away, taking 2d6 bludgeoning damage and ending up a half day's walk south of the entrance to the cave.

Special: Immersing a cursed item in the river for 1 minute has a 50% chance of removing the curse without using the *Remove Curse* spell.

Narrow Tunnel to Summoning Chamber

Description: A 5-foot wide, winding tunnel with strange echoes and an acrid smell.

Interaction: Players must navigate the tunnel carefully (DC 13 Dexterity (Stealth) check to move quietly).

Benefit: Successful Stealth checks allow the party to surprise occupants in the Summoning Chamber.

Detriment: Failed checks alert Conall, allowing him to prepare defenses.

Special: Listening carefully (DC 15 Wisdom (Perception) check) allows PCs to overhear parts of Conall's ritual, granting advantage on saving throws against his first spell in the upcoming encounter.

Random Loot Table

d6	Item Name	Description	Value
1	Torc of the Tuatha	A twisted gold neck ring once worn by the Tuatha Dé Danann. It grants the wearer advantage on Charisma checks when interacting with fey creatures.	750 gp
2	Brigid's Eternal Flame	A small, never-extinguishing flame contained in a bronze lantern. It sheds bright light in a 20-foot radius and dim light for an additional 20 feet.	500 gp
3	Dagger of Lugh	A finely crafted silver dagger that glows in the presence of Fomorians. It deals an extra 1d6 radiant damage to giants.	650 gp
4	Manannán's Cloak Brooch	A silver brooch shaped like a ship. Once per day, the wearer can cast *Water Walk* without using a spell slot.	800 gp
5	Ogham Stone Fragment	A piece of an ancient stone bearing Ogham inscriptions. A character proficient in History can use it to cast *Comprehend Languages* once per day.	400 gp
6	Dagda's Harp String	A single string from the legendary harp of the Dagda. When tied around a musical instrument, it grants advantage on Performance checks made with that instrument.	550 gp

Encounters

Fey Skeletons: 1d6 Fey Skeletons patrol the chamber, their bones adorned with twisted vines and spectral wisps.

Scáthannaí: 1 Scáthannaí (Shadow Walker) lurks in the darker corners, overseeing the undead guardians.

Hidden Dangers

Quicksand-like Bone Pits: DC 14 Perception check to notice, DC 15 Strength save to avoid being pulled under.

Triggered Bone Avalanches: Certain areas can collapse if disturbed, requiring a DC 13 Dexterity save to avoid 2d6 bludgeoning damage.

Bone Formation Puzzle

The safe path across the chamber is marked by subtle patterns in the bone arrangements. The correct pattern follows the concept of the Celtic triskele, representing the three realms of earth, sea, and sky.

Correct Pattern

Earth: Bones arranged in spiral patterns on the ground.

Sea: Wave-like formations of smaller bones and ribs.

Sky: Arches made of longer bones like femurs and spines.

To navigate safely, PCs must step on or touch these formations in the correct order: Earth, Sea, Sky, repeating this pattern until they reach the exit.

Decoding the Pattern

PCs can attempt a DC 15 Intelligence (Investigation) check to discern the correct pattern.

A successful History check (DC 13) might provide a hint about the significance of the triskele in Celtic mythology.

Characters proficient in Religion get advantage on the Investigation check.

Traversing the Chamber

The chamber is divided into 6 sections, each requiring a correct step.

One character can make the Investigation check for the whole party.

If successful, the party can move safely across all 6 sections.

On a failure, each PC must make individual Dexterity (Acrobatics) checks (DC 14) for each section they cross.

Consequences of Incorrect Steps

Minor Mistake (failed by 1-3): The bones shift ominously. The character takes 1d4 piercing damage from sharp bone edges.

Moderate Error (failed by 4-6): A gout of necrotic energy erupts. The character takes 2d6 necrotic damage and must make a DC 13 Constitution save or be poisoned for 1 hour.

Major Blunder (failed by 7+): The bones collapse, creating a 10-foot diameter pit. The character falls in, taking 2d6 bludgeoning damage and becoming restrained. A DC 15 Strength (Athletics) check is required to escape.

Critical Failure (natural 1): The disturbance awakens 1d4 Fey Skeletons, which immediately attack.

Additional Interactions

Casting *Detect Magic* reveals faint necromantic auras along the correct path.

A druid or character proficient with the Nature skill might recognize the patterns as representing natural elements (advantage on the check).

Creative use of spells (like *Mage Hand* to test paths) could grant advantage on checks or provide safe passage for one section.

Loot

Ancient Celtic jewelry hidden among the bones (DC 16 Perception to find). Use the Random Loot Table for rewards for completing activities in the room.

Tactical Considerations

The bone piles provide half cover for small or medium creatures.

The Scáthannaí uses the shadows cast by the bone pillar to ambush intruders.

Fey Skeletons can burrow through the bone carpet, potentially surrounding the party.

Connecting Tunnel

The tunnel leading to the Summoning Chamber is narrow and winding. As PCs approach:

The air grows warmer and filled with an acrid, smoky scent.

Faint chanting can be heard echoing from ahead.

Spectral wisps of energy occasionally pulse along the walls.

Environmental Effect

The oppressive atmosphere of death in this chamber weighs heavily on the living. At the start of each turn, living creatures must make a DC 12 Wisdom saving throw or be frightened until the end of their next turn.

Summoning Chamber

As you enter this cavernous chamber, the air grows thick with the acrid smell of dark magic and decay. The rock walls are adorned with pulsing, eldritch runes that cast an eerie, sickly green light throughout the space. In the center of the room, a massive circular sigil is etched into the stone floor, its lines glowing with barely contained necromantic energy.

Surrounding the sigil are numerous black candles, their flames flickering an unnatural purple. At the far end, you see a raised dais upon which stands an obsidian altar, covered in mysterious arcane implements and what appear to be fresh bloodstains. The very atmosphere feels heavy, as if the boundary between the world of the living and the dead is paper-thin here.

Notable Features

The large necromantic sigil (20-foot diameter) on the floor in the center of the room.

The obsidian altar on the raised dais.

Four stone pillars inscribed with runes, one in each corner of the room.

Numerous arcane implements and components scattered around the chamber.

A small, ominous door made of blackened wood, located behind the altar, leading to the Shadow Sanctum.

A shimmering, spectral portal next to the door, pulsing with dark energy.

Encounter

Conall, performing a ritual at the altar.

Scáthannaí: 2 Scáthannaí, guarding the chamber and assisting in the ritual.

Conall's Tactics

Prioritizes keeping the party away from the door to the Shadow Sanctum.

Uses *Wall of Force* to create a barrier in front of the door.

Casts *Cloudkill* near the door to deter approach.

Uses *Create Undead* to summon minions that focus on guarding the door.

Employs *Counterspell* to prevent any attempts to magically open or bypass the door.

Scáthannaí Tactics

One Scáthannaí always remains near the door to the Shadow Sanctum.

They use *Shadow Step* to intercept any party member getting close to the door.

Create shadow portals to redirect characters away from the door.

Use their Shadow Tendrils ability to pull characters away from the door area.

Large Necromantic Sigil

Description: A complex pattern of intersecting lines and arcane symbols etched into the stone floor, 20 feet in diameter, glowing with a sickly green light.

Disruption: Players can attempt to disrupt the activated sigil (DC 18 Intelligence (Arcana) check).

- **Successful Disruption:** The sigil weakens all undead in the room, imposing disadvantage on their attacks and saving throws for 1d4 rounds.
- **Failure to Disrupt:** The sigil pulses with energy, dealing 2d8 necrotic damage to the character (DC 15 Constitution save for half damage).

Empowerment: Players can attempt to further empower the activated sigil (DC 18 Intelligence (Arcana) check).

- **Successful Empowerment:** The sigil releases a wave of necromantic energy, granting all necromancy spells cast within the sigil an additional +2 bonus to spell save DCs for 1d4 rounds. During this time, the sigil's glow intensifies and dark shadows swirl within it.
- **Failure to Empower:** The sigil backfires, releasing chaotic necromantic energy that deals 2d8 necrotic damage to all creatures within 10 feet (DC 15 Constitution save for half damage).

Special: A spellcaster standing within the sigil gains a +2 bonus to spell save DCs for necromancy spells, but must make a DC 13 Wisdom save at the end of each turn or take 1d6 psychic damage from the sigil's corrupting influence.

Obsidian Altar on the Raised Dais

Description: A 5-foot-long, 3-foot-wide altar made of polished obsidian, covered in strange symbols and fresh bloodstains.

Interaction: Players can investigate the altar (DC 15 Investigation check) or attempt to use it (DC 17 Arcana check), which involves a ritual sacrifice of a small animal or a vial of their own blood.

Benefit: Successfully using the altar allows a character to cast one necromancy spell of 3rd level or lower without expending a spell slot.

Detriment: Failed attempts to use the altar cause the altar to drain 1d6 hit points from the character, healing Conall for the same amount if he's within 30 feet.

Special: Any healing spell cast within 10 feet of the altar functions as if cast at one level higher.

Four Runic Stone Pillars

Description: 10-foot-tall stone pillars, each inscribed with a different set of glowing runes representing death, decay, rebirth, and spirit.

Interaction: PCs can attempt to decipher (DC 16 Arcana check) and manipulate (DC 15 Intelligence check) the rune on each pillar. Alternatively, PCs can instead choose to decipher and disrupt a pillar rune (requiring only a single DC 17 Arcana check).

Benefit: Successfully manipulating a pillar's rune grants a unique effect upon that PC for 1 minute:

- **Death Pillar**: Resistance to necrotic damage
- **Decay Pillar**: Advantage on Constitution saving throws
- **Rebirth Pillar**: Regain 1d6 hit points at the start of each turn
- **Spirit Pillar**: Ability to see and attack incorporeal creatures as if they were corporeal

On the other hand, successfully disrupting a pillar's rune weakens Conall's spells, imposing disadvantage on his spell attack rolls for 1d4 rounds.

Detriment: A failed attempt to interact with a pillar's rune causes that rune to flare, dealing 2d6 force damage to the character and alerting Conall to their location.

Special: If all four pillars are activated simultaneously, they create a zone of anti-undead energy, turning all undead creatures in the room for 1 minute (DC 15 Wisdom save to resist).

Arcane Implements and Components

Description: Various magical tools, reagents, and focus items scattered on tables and shelves around the room.

Interaction: Players can scan for useful items (DC 14 Perception) and attempt to use them in combat (DC 15 Arcana or Religion check to quickly identify and use a given item).

Benefit: Successfully finding and identifying an implement grants one of the following (d6 roll):

1. A scroll of *Animate Dead*
2. A potion of Necrotic Resistance
3. A wand with 1d4 charges of *Inflict Wounds* (3rd level)
4. A vial of ectoplasm that can be thrown to create difficult terrain in a 10-foot radius
5. A spirit focus that grants advantage on saving throws against possession for 1 hour
6. A bone whistle that can be used to cast *Command* on undead creatures (DC 15)

Detriment: Failed Intelligence (Arcana or Religion) checks while using these items in combat causes them to backfire, dealing 1d8 force damage to the user and granting Conall a free use of *Misty Step*.

Special: A character proficient in Arcana can choose to spend an action to identify the function of a specific implement without needing to roll.

Spectral Portal

The spectral portal next to the blackened wood door was created to serve as a conduit for summoning spirits from the Plane of Shadow to aid in Conall's dark rituals. This portal connects directly to the Shadowfell, allowing Conall to pull through powerful entities or communicate with malevolent spirits.

A PC can determine the portal's original purpose and destination with a successful DC 16 Intelligence (Arcana) check. Upon examining the runes around the portal and the magical energies emanating from it, the character will discern its design for dark summoning purposes. However, with the right magical knowledge and effort, this portal can be repurposed to create an escape route or to summon help (DC 18 Arcana check).

Shadow Sanctum Door

The door is locked with a complex magical lock (DC 20 Dexterity check using thieves' tools to pick).

Protected by a *Glyph of Warding* (DC 16 Investigation to detect, DC 16 Arcana to identify the glyph), which is triggered by opening (or attempting to open) the door. When triggered, the glyph inflicts 5d8 necrotic damage (DC 16 Dexterity save for half damage).

Conall wears the key to the sanctum, which ends in a small obsidian skull, on a chain around his neck.

Environmental Hazards

Necrotic Pulses: At initiative count 20, the floor sigil pulses with energy. All living creatures within 10 feet of the sigil must make a DC 15 Constitution save or take 2d6 necrotic damage.

Sanctum's Call: Every round, any character within 10 feet of the Shadow Sanctum door must make a DC 14 Wisdom save or be compelled to open the door, using their action to do so if possible.

Escape Routes

The spectral portal at the back of the Summoning Chamber can be repurposed (DC 18 Arcana check) to create an escape route, but it leads to a random location. Roll 1d6 on the Random Location Table to determine the location the portal will transport the PC:

1d6	Location
1	Battlefield (Valley of the Dead)
2	The Sunset Forest
3	Island of Winds (see Key Locations and Descriptions section in Starting the Adventure)
4	Tower of Shadows
5	The Enchanted Forest
6	Entrance to the Ghost Cave

If the PCs manage to open the door to the Shadow Sanctum during combat, they can potentially use it as an escape route, but they'll face whatever dangers lie within.

Shadow Sanctum

As you open the door, you're confronted by absolute darkness - a void so complete it seems to swallow even magical light. The air is unnaturally still and cold, carrying the faint scent of ozone and decay. As you step inside, you feel a weight pressing down on you, as if the very shadows were trying to crush you. The silence is deafening, broken only by the sound of your own heartbeat echoing in your ears.

Notable Features

Impenetrable darkness that resists normal and magical light.

A circular pedestal in the center of the room.

Whispering shadows that seem to move independently.

Floating orbs of negative energy.

A wall of shifting, incorporeal faces.

Magical Properties

The room negates all sources of light, magical or otherwise. Even darkvision is reduced to a 10-foot range.

Characters must make a DC 15 Wisdom saving throw upon entering. Failure results in the frightened condition while in the room.

The Death Fragment

The Death Fragment of the Triskelion (embodying Destruction) rests on the central pedestal, pulsing with dark energy. It appears as a twisted, black metal shard that seems to absorb light.

Interactions

Navigating the Room

Characters must make a DC 14 Dexterity (Acrobatics) check to move without stumbling in the dark. Failure results in falling prone.

Alternatively, a DC 16 Wisdom (Perception) check allows a character to navigate by sound and air currents.

Whispering Shadows

These insidious shadows attempt to mislead characters. PCs must make a DC 15 Wisdom saving throw to resist their influence. Failure causes the character to move in a random direction.

A successful DC 17 Intelligence (Arcana) check can interpret the enchanting whispers, granting that PC advantage on saves against the room's effects for 1 minute.

Negative Energy Orbs

Balls of negative energy that hover in various places throughout the room, dealing 2d6 necrotic damage on contact.

These floating hazards can be dispersed with radiant damage or healing magic.

Wall of Faces

The wall attempts to possess any character that touches it. DC 16 Charisma saving throw to resist.

If possessed, the character is under the effect of the *Confusion* spell until they leave the room.

Claiming the Death Fragment

Touching the Death Fragment on the pedestal requires a DC 18 Constitution saving throw. Failure results in 4d6 necrotic damage and the poisoned condition for 1 hour.

Removing the Death Fragment from the pedestal triggers a collapse of the sanctum's magic, causing 6d6 force damage to all creatures inside (DC 17 Dexterity save for half).

Puzzle Element

To safely remove the Death Fragment from the central pedestal, PCs must counteract the room's dark energy. This can be done by:

- Casting *Daylight* or a similarly powerful light spell (automatically dispels the magical darkness for 1 minute)
- Performing a ritual using radiant energy (requires three successful DC 15 Religion checks)
- Sacrificing hit points, for which each character can contribute (needs a total of 30 hit points sacrificed).

Escape the Sanctum

When done safely, once the Death Fragment is removed, the room's magic becomes unstable. Characters have 3 rounds to escape before the Shadow Sanctum collapses, potentially trapping them in a pocket dimension.

Terrain

The cave floor is uneven and slippery. Characters must succeed on a DC 12 Dexterity (Acrobatics) check when moving at full speed or fall prone. Failure also alerts nearby undead. The cave is in dim light due to the glowing fungi, except for the Shadow Sanctum which is in total darkness. The mist obscures vision beyond 30 feet, making the cave heavily obscured.

Lair Actions

Whispers of the Damned: Ghostly whispers fill the cave, forcing all living creatures to make a DC 15 Wisdom saving throw or be frightened until the end of their next turn.

Necrotic Surge: Waves of necrotic energy pulse through the cave. Each living creature takes 2d6 necrotic damage, while undead creatures heal for the same amount.

Shadow Veil: Shadows thicken in a 20-foot radius area, creating magical darkness that even darkvision can't penetrate.

NPC

Conall

Monsters

Scáthannaí

Fey Skeleton

Scaling the Ghost Cave Encounter

Beginning Players (PC levels 1-5)

Reduce all skill check and saving throw DCs by 2 (e.g., DC 15 becomes DC 13).

Entrance Cave:

- Simplify puzzle to 3 tiles instead of 9.
- Reduce number of Scáthannaí to 1d4.

Bone Chamber:

- Reduce number of Fey Skeletons to 1d4, remove Scáthannaí.
- Simplify bone formation puzzle to 3 sections instead of 6.

Summoning Chamber:

- Conall uses lower-level spells (e.g., *Burning Hands* instead of *Cloudkill*).
- Reduce number of Scáthannaí to 1.
- Necrotic Pulse deals 2d6 damage instead of 3d6.

Shadow Sanctum:

- Reduce damage from negative energy orbs to 1d6.
- Claiming the Death Fragment deals 2d6 necrotic damage instead of 4d6.

Lair Actions:

- Reduce save DCs to 13.
- Necrotic Surge deals 1d6 damage instead of 2d6.

Intermediate Players (PC levels 6-10)

Keep all DCs as written.

Use all encounters and mechanics as described.

Summoning Chamber: Add 1d4 Fey Skeletons to the encounter.

Shadow Sanctum: Add a minor guardian creature (e.g., Shadow).

Lair Actions: Use as written.

Advanced Players (PC levels 11+)

Increase all DCs by 2 (e.g., DC 15 becomes DC 17).

Entrance Cave:

- Add a complex magical trap (e.g., *Forcecage* or *Symbol*).
- Increase number of Scáthannaí to 3d4.

Bone Chamber:

- Increase number of Fey Skeletons to 2d6, add 2 Scáthannaí.
- Add a powerful undead creature (e.g., Bone Devil).

Summoning Chamber:

- Conall uses higher-level spells (e.g., *Circle of Death*).
- Add 2d4 Fey Skeletons and 1d4 Wraiths.
- Necrotic Pulses deal 3d6 damage.

Shadow Sanctum:

- Add a powerful shadow creature (e.g., Shadow Demon).
- Claiming the fragment deals 6d6 necrotic damage.
- Increase collapse damage to 8d6.

Lair Actions:

- Increase save DCs to 17.
- **Add a fourth Lair Action**: Time Warp (manipulates initiative order).

General:

- Add time pressure (e.g., cave collapse in 1 hour).
- Introduce more complex magical traps throughout the cave system.

Aillte na nDeor - Cliffs of Tears

This encounter features a treacherous, storm-ravaged cliffside where Róisín wields her weather-controlling powers. Players must navigate harsh environmental challenges and face elemental creatures before confronting Róisín to claim the Rebirth Fragment of the Triskelion.

As you approach, you're confronted by towering cliffs that seem to pierce the stormy sky above. The air is thick with salt spray and the deafening roar of waves crashing against the rocky shore below. Rain lashes down in sheets, driven by howling winds that threaten to sweep you off your feet.

The cliffside is a maze of jagged rocks and narrow ledges, punctuated by small caves and crevices. Halfway up, you spot a precarious path zigzagging its way to the summit. At the top, barely visible through the storm, you can make out the silhouette of what appears to be an ancient stone circle, where flashes of lightning seem to converge.

Locations in the Cliffs

Cliffside Path: Navigate the treacherous path from the pebble beach up the cliffside, battling strong winds and slippery terrain.

Druidic Stone Circle: Solve an ancient druidic puzzle at the stone circle to gain access to Róisín's inner sanctum.

Storm Sanctum: Confront Róisín and her elemental minions in a final battle atop the cliff.

Cliffside Path

Before you stretches a daunting path that winds its way up the face of the cliff. The narrow trail is little more than a ledge in places, slick with sea spray and treacherously uneven. Fierce winds howl around you, threatening to pluck you from the cliff face at any moment. Above, dark storm clouds roil ominously, occasionally illuminated by flashes of lightning.

Path Details

The path is approximately 500 feet long, rising about 200 feet in elevation.

It's divided into five 100-foot sections, each presenting unique challenges.

The path varies in width from 3 to 5 feet, with some sections narrowing to just 1 foot wide.

Navigating the Path

For each 100-foot section, PCs must make the following checks:

- DC 14 Strength (Athletics) or Dexterity (Acrobatics) check to maintain footing.
- DC 13 Constitution saving throw to resist the buffeting winds.

Failure on either check results in one of the following (d4 roll):

1. Slip and fall prone, risking sliding off the path.
2. Get pushed 5 feet by the wind, potentially off the path.
3. Become disoriented, losing half movement speed for the next turn.
4. Suffer 1d6 bludgeoning damage from being slammed against the cliff face.

Specific Hazards

Choose one hazard per 100-foot section of the Cliffside Path (which contains 5 total sections).

Crumbling Ledge: DC 15 Dexterity save to avoid falling rocks (2d6 bludgeoning damage on fail).

Wind Tunnel: DC 16 Strength save or be pushed 10 feet and knocked prone.

Slippery Algae Patch: DC 15 Dexterity (Acrobatics) to cross without falling.

Lightning Strike Zone: DC 14 Dexterity save to avoid 3d10 lightning damage (taking half damage on success).

Nesting Seabirds: Agitated birds force the PCs to make DC 13 Wisdom (Animal Handling) check in order to pass them without provoking attacks.

Small Caves

There are three small caves along the path which can be used for shelter:

- Located at 150 feet up
- Located at 300 feet up
- Located at 450 feet up

Each cave is about 10 feet deep and 15 feet wide, and provides full cover from the wind and rain.

PCs may take a much-needed short rest in any of these caves.

A DC 12 (Wisdom) Perception check might reveal useful items left by previous climbers (rope, pitons, etc.)

Storm Intensification

Every 10 minutes, roll a d20. On a 15 or higher, the storm intensifies for 1d4 rounds. During intensification:

- All DCs increase by 2.
- Lightning strikes become more frequent (25% chance each round for each exposed character).
- Wind speed doubles, potentially pushing characters off the path (DC 15 Strength save to resist).

Using Equipment

Climbing gear grants advantage on Strength (Athletics) checks.

Rope can be used to create a safety line, allowing a DC 15 Dexterity save to catch oneself if falling.

Pitons can be hammered into the cliff (takes an action) to create an anchor point.

Spells and Abilities

Levitate or *Fly* spells trivialize the climb but require Concentration checks (DC 10 + damage taken) each time the caster is hit by winds or debris.

Feather Fall can save a falling character but doesn't help with the ascent.

Characters with a climb speed still need to make saving throws against the wind and other hazards.

Druidic Stone Circle

As you reach the cliff's summit, you find yourself in a wide, flat area dominated by a circle of towering standing stones. Each monolith is easily 15 feet tall and covered in weathered carvings. At the center of the circle stands a large, flat altar stone. The air here crackles with magical energy, and despite the raging storm around you, the interior of the circle remains eerily calm.

Circle Details

The circle consists of 8 standing stones arranged in a perfect circle, 50 feet in diameter.

Each stone represents one of the Celtic seasonal festivals: Samhain, Imbolc, Beltane, Lughnasadh, and the solstices and equinoxes.

The altar stone in the center is 6 feet in diameter and covered in spiraling patterns.

Stone Circle Puzzle

To gain access to Róisín's inner sanctum, the PCs must align the energies of the Stone Circle correctly. This involves:

Identifying the Stones

DC 15 Intelligence (History or Nature) check to correctly identify which stone represents each festival.

Success grants advantage on subsequent checks related to the puzzle.

Deciphering the Altar

The altar stone contains a riddle written in Ogham script. PCs must make a DC 16 Intelligence (Investigation) check to decipher the script. The riddle, once translated, reads: "When fire and frost join hands, and harvest bows to rebirth, the way shall open. Speak the name of balance to enter."

Aligning the Energies

Characters must touch the correct sequence of stones to "join" the energies.

Correct Sequence: Beltane (fire) → Samhain (frost) → Lughnasadh (harvest) → Imbolc (rebirth)

Each correct touch causes the stone to glow with magical energy.

An incorrect sequence causes the stones to emit a burst of elemental energy (2d6 damage of an appropriate type) and summons a minor elemental (use Scout stats with appropriate elemental damage) that must be defeated or dispelled.

The Final Key

Once the correct sequence is activated, a character must stand on the altar stone and speak the word "Meán Earraigh" (Spring Equinox in Irish), representing balance.

This requires a DC 14 Intelligence check to deduce or remember from earlier clues.

Challenges and Interactions

Weather Interference

The raging storm occasionally breaches the circle's calm. PCs may need to make DC Constitution saving throws to maintain concentration on the puzzle during these moments.Time Pressure

The longer the players take to solve the puzzle, the more the storm intensifies outside the circle.

After 10 minutes, there's a cumulative 10% chance each minute that Róisín notices the intrusion.

Druidic Insight

Characters with proficiency in Nature or Religion can attempt a DC 15 check using that skill to gain a hint about the correct sequence or the final key word.

Magical Resonance

Spellcasters can attempt to attune to the circle's energy with a successful DC 15 Intelligence (Arcana) check.

Success grants advantage on one puzzle-related check.

Solving the Puzzle

When the puzzle is correctly solved:

- The altar stone splits open, revealing a staircase descending into Róisín's hidden sanctum.
- The stone circle creates a protective barrier against the storm, granting safe passage into the sanctum.
- PCs gain inspiration for successfully navigating the ancient druidic magic.

Failure Consequences

Multiple failures might alert Róisín, causing her to emerge and confront the party directly.

The storm could intensify to dangerous levels, forcing a retreat if the puzzle isn't solved in time.

Storm Sanctum

Upon descending the long, turning staircase, you emerge into a vast, open-air platform on an adjacent cliffside. The full fury of the storm rages around you, yet a shimmering dome of energy keeps the worst at bay. At the center stands Róisín, her wild hair crackling with electricity, a staff of twisted wood and storm-blue crystal clutched in her hand. Around her, elemental creatures of wind and lightning dance in chaotic patterns. Róisín's eyes lock onto you, a mix of anger and excitement flashing across her face. "So," she calls out over the howling wind, "you've come to challenge the mistress of storms? Let's see if you can weather what I have in store!"

Battlefield Layout

A circular platform, 80 feet in diameter.

Four lightning rods at the cardinal points.

A central altar where Róisín stands.

Patches of slippery, wet stone scattered about.

Swirling wind vortexes that appear and disappear randomly.

Circular Platform (80 feet in diameter)

Description: A massive stone platform with intricate weather-related symbols etched into its surface. The edge is surrounded by a low (3-foot) wall of swirling mist.

Interactions:

- **Movement**: Treated as difficult terrain due to high winds. PCs must succeed on a DC 13 Strength (Athletics) check to move at full speed or move at half speed on a failure.
- **Investigation check (DC 15)**: Reveals patterns in the symbols that hint at safe zones from lightning strikes.
- **Arcana check (DC 16)**: Allows a character to temporarily stabilize a 10-foot area, granting normal movement for 1 round.

Benefits:

Successful navigation allows strategic positioning.

Understanding the patterns grants advantage on Dexterity saves against lightning strikes.

Detriments:

Failure to navigate properly might position characters in hazardous areas.

The misty edge obscures the cliff's drop, requiring a DC 12 Wisdom (Perception) check to notice when within 5 feet of the edge.

Four Lightning Rods

Description: 15-foot tall metal spires stand, one at each of the four cardinal points, crackling with electrical energy. Each lightning rod is surrounded by a 5-foot radius of intensified wind.

Interactions:

- **Athletics check (DC 15)**: Climb the rod to gain an elevated position.
- **Arcana check (DC 17)**: Successfully redirect the rod's energy.
- **Attack**: AC 15, 30 HP. Destroying a rod releases a burst of lightning in a 20-foot radius, inflicting 4d10 lightning damage (Dexterity save for half damage).

Benefits:

Successfully redirecting a rod's energy grants resistance to lightning damage for 1 minute.

Destroying all four lightning rods weakens Róisín's control over the storm, imposing disadvantage on her lightning-based attacks.

Detriments:

Any failed interaction check causes 2d10 lightning damage to the PC.

Róisín's lightning spells deal an additional 4d6 lightning damage when she is near the metal spires as long as all four rods are intact.

For each destroyed lightning rod, Róisín's lightning spell damage decreases by 1d6. This damage reduction applies only within the area near the lightning rods.

Central Altar (where Róisín stands)

Description: A 15-foot diameter, 5-foot high circular stone altar, upon which stands Róisín. Swirling patterns of wind and lightning are carved into its sides, glowing with magical energy.

Interactions:

- **Athletics check (DC 14)**: Climb onto the altar.
- **Arcana check (DC 16)**: Successfully disrupt the altar's magic.
- **Religion check (DC 15)**: Recognize the altar as a focus for weather control rituals.

Benefits:

Standing on the altar grants a +2 bonus to spell save DCs for weather-related spells.

Disrupting the altar's magic weakens the storm, granting advantage on saves against weather effects for 1 minute.

Detriments:

The altar periodically releases bursts of wind. Characters on or within 10 feet of the altar must succeed on a DC 14 Strength saving throw or be pushed 15 feet and knocked prone.

Failed attempts to disrupt the magic cause 3d8 force damage to the character.

Róisín's Tactics

Starts upon the central altar, 15 feet above the main platform.

Uses her Weather Manipulation to create advantageous conditions.

Casts *Chain Lightning* to hit multiple opponents.

Uses *Thunderwave* to push characters towards the edge of the platform.

When heavily damaged, she uses *Gaseous Form* to retreat temporarily.

Elemental Minions

Peist Dhraíochta: 1d4+2 Peist Dhraíochta (Magic Serpents) hover nearby, unfazed by the fearsome weather around them, ready to defend Róisín and act on her command.

Environmental Hazards

Lightning Rods: Each round, there's a 25% chance a rod is struck. Characters within 10 feet must make a DC 15 Dexterity save or take 3d10 lightning damage.

Slippery Patches: DC 13 Dexterity (Acrobatics) check to move across without falling prone.

Wind Vortexes: Appear randomly. Characters starting their turn in one must make a DC 14 Strength save or be moved 15 feet in a random direction.

Platform Edge: Characters pushed off the edge must make a DC 15 Dexterity save to catch the edge or fall 100 feet.

The Rebirth Fragment

The Rebirth Fragment of the Triskelion (embodying Transformation) is embedded in Róisín's staff. The fragment glows brightly during the battle, occasionally releasing bursts of transformative energy.

Disarm: If Róisín is disarmed (DC 18 Strength check or specific disarming attack), the staff falls to the ground.

Special Abilities Granted by the Fragment

Transformative Blast: Róisín can use an action to fire a beam of energy that polymorphs a target into a small, harmless creature (as per *Polymorph* spell) for 1 minute (DC 17 Wisdom save negates).

Adaptive Form: As a bonus action, Róisín can adapt her body to resist the last type of damage she took. This grants her resistance to that damage type for 1 minute. This ability can resist any damage type, including physical damage (slashing, piercing, or bludgeoning).

Renewal: Once per battle, when reduced to 0 HP, Róisín can use her reaction to regain 50 HP and continue fighting.

Battle Phases

Initial Confrontation: Róisín stays near the altar, sending minions to attack while she casts spells.

Elemental Fury: At 2/3 HP, Róisín intensifies the storm, increasing the frequency of environmental hazards.

Desperate Measures: At 1/3 HP, Róisín uses her staff's full power, gaining the ability to teleport between lightning rods as a bonus action.

Claiming the Rebirth Fragment

If Róisín is defeated or her staff is taken, the Rebirth Fragment can be removed from it with a DC 16 Intelligence (Arcana) check.

Failing the check causes a surge of transformative energy. The character must make a DC 15 Constitution saving throw or be polymorphed into a random creature for 1 minute.

Victory Conditions

Condition 1: Defeat Róisín and claim the staff.

Condition 2: Convince Róisín to surrender (requires exceptional roleplay and likely multiple high-DC Charisma checks).

Condition 3: Destroy or disrupt all four lightning rods, weakening Róisín's connection to the storm.

Defeating Róisín (Condition 1) and **Convincing Róisín to Surrender** (Condition 2) are alternative paths to victory; only one of these needs to be completed to claim the staff.

Destroying or Disrupting the Lightning Rods (Condition 3) is optional but can be completed to weaken Róisín and make the combat encounter easier.

Terrain

The cliffside is extremely treacherous. Characters must make a DC 15 Strength (Athletics) or Dexterity (Acrobatics) check every 100 feet of vertical climb. Failure results in falling 1d6 x 5 feet or until caught by a rope or magic. The storm imposes disadvantage on these checks and on any ranged attacks. Visibility is limited to 30 feet due to the heavy rain and mist.

Lair Actions

Gale Force: Róisín summons a powerful gust of wind. All creatures must succeed on a DC 15 Strength saving throw or be pushed 15 feet and knocked prone.

Lightning Strike: A bolt of lightning strikes a point Róisín can see. Creatures within 10 feet must make a DC 15 Dexterity saving throw, taking 4d10 lightning damage on a failed save, or half as much on a successful one.

Misty Veil: Thick mist suddenly envelops a 30-foot radius area. This area is heavily obscured until the start of Róisín's next turn.

NPC

Róisín

Monster

Peist Dhraíochta

Scaling the Cliffs of Tears Encounter

Beginning Players (PC levels 1-5)

Reduce all skill check and saving throw DCs by 2 (e.g., DC 15 becomes DC 13).

Cliffside Path:

- Reduce length to 300 feet, 3 sections.
- Reduce hazard damage to 1d4.
- Use only 2 small caves.

Druidic Stone Circle:

- Simplify puzzle to 4 stones.
- Reduce Elemental Guardian CR (use Tribal Warrior stats).

Storm Sanctum:

- Reduce platform size to 60 feet diameter.
- Use only 2 lightning rods.
- Róisín uses lower-level spells (e.g., *Thunderwave* instead of *Chain Lightning*).
- Reduce number of Peist Dhraíochta to 1d4.

Lair Actions:

- Reduce save DCs to 13.
- Lightning Strike deals 3d10 damage.

Intermediate Players (PC levels 6-10)

Keep all DCs as written.

Use all encounters and mechanics as described.

The Storm Sanctum: Add 1d4 Air Elementals to the encounter.

Advanced Players (PC levels 11+)

Increase all DCs by 2 (e.g., DC 15 becomes DC 17).

Cliffside Path:

- Extend to 700 feet, 7 sections.
- Add complex magical hazards (e.g., gravity shifts, time distortions).

Druidic Stone Circle:

- Add a time limit to solve the puzzle.
- Use Elemental stats for Elemental Guardians.

Storm Sanctum:

- Increase platform size to 100 feet diameter.

- Add 2 more lightning rods (total 6).
- Róisín can cast 9th level spells.
- Increase number of Peist Dhraíochta to 2d4+2.
- Add 1d4 Young Rocs as flying threats.

Lair Actions:

- Increase save DCs to 17.
- **Add a fourth Lair Action**: Elemental Surge (summons temporary elemental).

General:

- Introduce more complex weather effects (e.g., localized tornadoes, hail).
- Add magical wards that must be dispelled during combat.

Túr na nScáth (Tower of Shadows)

This encounter is the final confrontation with Fionnlagh in his tower, where he attempts to unleash the Triskelion's full power. The players must navigate the tower's defenses and face Fionnlagh in an epic battle that tests all their acquired skills and knowledge.

Before you looms a towering structure that seems to defy the laws of nature. Its obsidian walls twist and spiral upwards, disappearing into the swirling dark clouds above. Shadows dance across its surface, giving the illusion that the very stone is alive and writhing.

As you approach the Tower of Shadows, you feel an oppressive weight bearing down on you, as if the tower itself is trying to crush your will. The air crackles with dark energy, and whispers of forgotten languages echo in your minds. This is unmistakably the seat of Fionnlagh's power, a bastion of corruption in the heart of the land.

Activities

Infiltrate the Tower of Shadows, navigating through the tower's defenses and traps.

Defeat Fionnlagh and claim the Triskelion.

Rooms in Túr na nScáth

Ground Floor: Entrance Hall - A grand, shadowy chamber with twisted statues and shifting floor patterns.

2nd Floor: Armory of Corrupted Relics - Weapons and armor infused with dark magic line the walls. Some items may try to possess those who touch them.

3rd Floor: Chamber of Corrupted Nature - A mockery of a natural environment, filled with twisted plants.

4th Floor: Ritual Chamber - Where Fionnlagh performs his dark magics, adorned with arcane circles and eldritch artifacts.

Ground Floor: Entrance Hall

Once you step through the ominous doorway, you find yourselves in a vast, circular chamber. The ceiling arches high above, lost in shadows that seem to move of their own accord. Pale, sickly light emanates from twisted iron sconces, casting long, dancing shadows across the walls and floor.

Lining the perimeter of the room are a dozen statues, each more disturbing than the last. They appear to be crafted from a black, oily stone that glistens wetly in the dim light. The statues depict various figures - some humanoid, others decidedly not - all contorted in poses of agony or ecstasy.

The floor beneath your feet is a dizzying mosaic of interlocking spirals and Celtic knots, crafted from stones of deep purple and midnight blue. As you watch, the patterns seem to shift and change, creating a nauseating sense of movement.

At the far end of the hall, a grand staircase of the same black stone as the statues spirals upwards, disappearing into the gloom above.

The Entrance Hall on the first floor sets the tone for the twisted nature of Fionnlagh's tower and presents immediate challenges for the party to overcome.

Shadow-Casting Sconces

The eerie light sources create exaggerated, moving shadows.

Characters must succeed on a DC 13 Wisdom saving throw when entering the room or be unable to distinguish between real threats and shadow movements, having disadvantage on Perception checks for 10 minutes.

Shifting Floor Mosaic

The floor patterns constantly change, requiring a DC 14 Dexterity (Acrobatics) check to move at full speed. Failure means the character moves at half speed and must make a DC 12 Constitution save or become disoriented, suffering disadvantage on their next attack roll or ability check.

A DC 16 Intelligence (Arcana) check reveals safe paths through the mosaic, granting advantage on the Acrobatics checks for 1 minute.

Twisted Statues

There are 12 statues around the room. Each depicts a different figure in various states of transformation or torment.

A DC 15 Wisdom (Perception) check reveals that the eyes of the statues seem to follow the party's movements.

If a character touches a statue, they must make a DC 14 Wisdom saving throw or be subjected to horrifying visions, becoming frightened for 1 minute.

Grand Staircase

The winding staircase that leads to the second floor seems to shift and move subtly, ending abruptly on the second floor. However, the second and third floors each contain a new, hidden staircase leading to the next floor of the tower. Every third round, the staircase turns into a slide at one random stair, requiring a DC 15 Dexterity save to avoid sliding back to the bottom. At the DM's discretion, every staircase in the tower bears this hazard.

Hidden Dangers

Shadow Tendrils: At initiative count 20 each round, 1d4 shadow tendrils emerge from the darkest corners of the room, attempting to grapple random characters (DC 14 Dexterity save to avoid, DC 14 Strength check to escape).

Whispering Voices: Every 5 minutes, characters must succeed on a DC 14 Wisdom saving throw or be compelled to approach and touch one of the statues.

Gravity Flux: Once during the encounter, Fionnlagh can use his magic to suddenly alter gravity in the room. Everyone must succeed on a DC 15 Dexterity saving throw or fall 20 feet in a random direction.

The Corruption Sequence Puzzle

The twelve statues around the room represent different stages of corruption, from pure to fully corrupted. The correct sequence mimics Fionnlagh's own descent into darkness.

Introducing the Puzzle: DMs can choose to apply various PC skill checks (active or passive) to provide direction or hints to the party as necessary. For example, a DM may utilize their PCs' passive Investigation scores to allow a PC with high enough skill to deduce the presence of the puzzle involving the statues.

It is recommended to provide players with a typed list of the statue descriptions (provided below) in **randomized** order, as the list below is already in correct sequence and serves as the answer key.

Statue Descriptions/Answer Key (in correct order):

1. "The Innocent": A child-like figure with a hopeful expression
2. "The Seeker": A scholar holding an open book
3. "The Tempter": A figure offering an apple with a sly smile
4. "The Bargainer": Two figures shaking hands, one slightly shadowed
5. "The Tainted": A figure with small tendrils creeping up their legs
6. "The Conflicted": A figure with half their face visibly corrupted
7. "The Fallen": A figure on their knees, head in hands
8. "The Embraced": A figure willingly accepting tendrils of darkness
9. "The Transformer": A figure mid-change into a monstrous form
10. "The Corruptor": A sinister figure extending a hand to others
11. "The Abomination": A horrifically twisted, barely humanoid shape
12. "The Void": A statue that seems to absorb all light around it

Puzzle Mechanics

PCs must identify the correct sequence of the statues, with the option to roll DC 16 Intelligence (History) or Wisdom (Insight) checks to recognize the method of progression or obtain hints.

Each statue must be touched in order, with the touching character risking the vision effect (DC 14 Wisdom save or be frightened for 1 minute).

A successful sequential touch causes the statue's eyes to glow faintly.

Correct Pattern: PCs must touch the statues in the order listed above, from "The Innocent" to "The Void".

Consequences of Incorrect Attempts

Minor Mistake (touching statues out of order):

The touched statue emits a pulse of necrotic energy. The touching character takes 2d6 necrotic damage.

All correctly activated statues reset, requiring the sequence to be started again.

Moderate Error (touching a statue more than 3 steps out of sequence):

The statue animates and attacks the touching character (use Stone Golem stats, but only for one round).

All characters must make a DC 15 Wisdom saving throw or be frightened for 1 minute.

The floor pattern shifts violently, requiring DC 15 Dexterity saves to avoid falling prone.

Major Mistake (touching "The Void" statue out of sequence):

A wave of corruption sweeps the room. All characters must make a DC 16 Constitution saving throw or gain one level of exhaustion.

The room is plunged into magical darkness for 1 minute.

1d4 Shadow Demons (found in the *Monster Manual*) are summoned and attack the party.

Critical Failure (failing the puzzle 3 times):

The tower's entrance seals shut.

The entire room begins to fill with a toxic shadowy substance. Characters take 1d10 necrotic damage per round until they solve the puzzle or find another way out.

Fionnlagh is alerted to their presence, and will be prepared for them on the upper floors.

Successful Completion

When the puzzle is correctly solved:

The staircase stabilizes, glowing with a soft blue light that counters the tower's disorienting effects.

A hidden compartment opens in the base of "The Innocent" statue, revealing a cache of useful items:

- Cloak of Protection
- 2d4 Potions of Greater Healing
- Scroll of *Protection from Evil and Good*
- +1 weapon (type determined by the DM based on party composition)

The oppressive atmosphere in the room lifts, granting the party a moment of respite and clarity before they ascend to face the challenges above.

2nd Floor: Armory of Corrupted Relics

As you ascend the staircase to the second floor, you enter a vast chamber that appears to be an armory, but one unlike any you've ever seen. The walls are lined with weapon racks and armor stands, each holding items that radiate an aura of malevolence. The air is thick with the scent of metal and ozone, and you can hear faint whispers emanating from the relics themselves.

Sickly green flames flicker in iron braziers, casting an eerie glow across the room. The floor is a polished black stone that seems to absorb light, creating the unsettling illusion that you're walking on a void. At the center of the room stands a large, circular dais with a pedestal, upon which rests a large, pulsing dark crystal.

Corrupted Weapon Racks

Dozens of weapons line the walls, each twisted and altered by dark magic.

A DC 15 Wisdom (Perception) check reveals that some weapons seem to move slightly of their own accord.

Any character approaching within 5 feet of a weapon rack must make a DC 14 Wisdom saving throw or feel an overwhelming urge to pick up and use one of the weapons.

Possessed Armor Stands

Suits of armor in various styles stand at attention around the room.

A DC 16 Intelligence (Arcana) check reveals that the armors are infused with trapped spirits.

There's a 25% chance each round that 1d4 suits of armor animate and attack the party (use Animated Armor stats from the *Monster Manual*).

Central Dais and Dark Crystal

A 15-foot-diameter raised platform with a pedestal at its center.

The black crystal, which rests upon the pedestal, pulses with dark energy, seeming to react to the presence of the party.

Characters who move within 10 feet of the dark crystal must make a DC 15 Constitution saving throw or suffer 2d6 necrotic damage and have disadvantage on their next attack roll or ability check, which lasts for 1 minute. Characters must make this saving throw each round they remain within range.

Whispering Relics

The whispers from the weapons and armor can be heard throughout the room.

Every 5 minutes, characters must succeed on a DC 13 Wisdom saving throw or be affected by the *Confusion* spell for 1 minute.

Corrupted Weapons Table

Below is a table of weapons found in the Armory of Corrupted Relics:

Name	Description	Damage	Properties	Weight	Corruption Level
Shadowfang	A curved dagger that seems to drink in light	1d4+2 piercing	Finesse, light; deals additional 1d4 necrotic damage	1 lb	High
Soulreaver	A greatsword with runes that glow a sickly green	2d6+2 slashing	Heavy, two-handed; on a critical hit, target must make DC 14 Wis save or be frightened for 1 minute	6 lbs	Very High
Whisperbolt	A longbow that emits a faint screaming sound when drawn	1d8+2 piercing	Ammunition (150/600), heavy, two-handed; ignore up to half cover	2 lbs	Medium
Frostgrave Axe	A battleaxe with a blade that radiates intense cold	1d8+2 slashing	Versatile (1d10); deals additional 1d6 cold damage	4 lbs	High
Mindshatter Mace	A mace with a head that appears to be a screaming face	1d6+2 bludgeoning	On hit, target must make DC 13 Int save or be stunned until end of next turn	4 lbs	Very High
Voidtouched Spear	A spear that seems to bend light around it	1d6+2 piercing	Thrown (20/60), versatile (1d8); +2 to hit against surprised creatures	3 lbs	Medium
Heartseeker	A shortbow that whispers the fears of its targets	1d6+2 piercing	Ammunition (80/320), two-handed; advantage on attacks against frightened creatures	2 lbs	High
Doomhammer	A warhammer that grows heavier with each kill	1d8+2 bludgeoning	Versatile (1d10); gains +1 to damage (max +3) for each creature killed, resets daily	2 lbs	Very High
Truthslicer	A shortsword that glows when lies are spoken nearby	1d6+2 piercing	Finesse, light; grants advantage on Insight checks while held	2 lbs	Low
Stormcaller Javelin	A javelin that crackles with barely contained lightning	1d6+2 piercing	Thrown (30/120); returns to thrower's hand, can cast *Call Lightning* 1/day	2 lbs	High
Bloodthirst Flail	A flail with spiked chains that writhe like tentacles	1d8+2 bludgeoning	Reach; when you hit, you can choose to take 1d4 damage to deal an extra 2d4 damage	2 lbs	Very High
Peacekeeper	A simple-looking quarterstaff with calming runes	1d6+2 bludgeoning	Versatile (1d8), can cast *Calm Emotions* (DC 15) 3/day	4 lbs	Low

Note: All weapons are considered magical +2 weapons for the purpose of overcoming resistance and immunity to nonmagical attacks and damage. The magical +2 to damage is already factored in on the damage dice.

The "Corruption Level" is on a scale of Low, Medium, High, and Very High. When a PC uses a corrupted weapon they will need to roll a 1d6 to see if the weapon will inflict the properties are reversed or inflicted on the PC. For a Low corruption level, the player must roll 2 or higher on a 1d6; for Medium they must roll 3 or higher; for High, they must roll 4 or higher; and for Very High they must roll 5 or higher each time they use the weapon.

Corrupted Armor Table

Below is a table of armor found in the Armory of Corrupted Relics:

Name	Description	Armor	AC	STR	Stealth	Lbs.	Corruption Level	Magic Properties
Shadow Weaved Cloak	A cloak that seems to be made of living shadows	Light	12 + Dex modifier	-	Advantage	4 lbs	High	Grants advantage on Stealth checks and the ability to cast *Invisibility* once per day.
Boneplate Mail	Armor forged from the bones of fallen warriors	Heavy	19	Str 15	Disadvantage	65 lbs	Very High	Grants resistance to necrotic damage and the ability to cast *Animate Dead* once per week.
Whispersilk Robes	Robes that constantly murmur dark secrets	Light	12 + Dex modifier	-	-	4 lbs	Medium	Grants advantage on saving throws against being frightened and the ability to cast *Detect Thoughts* once per day.
Voidforged Plate	Pitch-black plate armor that seems to absorb light	Heavy	19	Str 15	Disadvantage	65 lbs	Very High	Grants advantage on Stealth checks in dim light or darkness and the ability to cast *Darkness* once per day.
Skinwalker Leather	Leather armor that occasionally ripples as if alive	Light	12 + Dex modifier	-	-	10 lbs	High	Grants the ability to cast *Alter Self* once per day.
Spiritchain Mail	Chainmail that faintly glows with trapped souls	Heavy	17	Str 13	Disadvantage	55 lbs	High	Grants resistance to psychic damage and the ability to cast *Speak with Dead* once per week.
Mindshield Helm	A helm that whispers warnings of danger	-	+1 to AC	-	-	3 lbs	Low	Grants advantage on saving throws against being charmed and the ability to cast *Detect Magic* at will.
Doomplate Armor	Heavy armor adorned with screaming faces	Heavy	19	Str 15	Disadvantage	65 lbs	Very High	Grants resistance to fear effects and the ability to cast *Bane* once per day.
Featherfall Cloak	A cloak that softly billows, even without wind	Light	12 + Dex modifier	-	-	4 lbs	Low	Grants the ability to cast *Feather Fall* at will.
Souldrainer Gauntlets	Gauntlets that pulse with a hungry red glow	-	+2 to AC	-	-	2 lbs	Very High	Grants the ability to drain 1d6 hit points from a target on a successful melee attack, healing the wearer for the same amount.
Thornweave Shirt	A shirt made of intricately woven thorny vines	Light	13 + Dex modifier	-	-	8 lbs	Medium	Grants the ability to cast *Entangle* once per day.
Stormcaller Shield	A shield that crackles with contained lightning	Shield	+3 to AC	-	-	6 lbs	High	Grants resistance to lightning damage and the ability to cast *Call Lightning* once per day.

The "Corruption Level" is on a scale of Low, Medium, High, and Very High. When a PC uses a corrupted armor they will need to roll a 1d6 to see if the weapon will inflict the properties are reversed or inflicted on the PC. For a Low corruption level, the player must roll 2 or higher on a 1d6; for Medium they must roll 3 or higher; for High, they must roll 4 or higher; and for Very High they must roll 5 or higher if they wear the armor..

Interactable Elements

Corrupted Weapons: If a character touches or wields a corrupted weapon, they must make a DC 16 Charisma saving throwOn a failure, they are possessed by the weapon's spirit and attack the nearest ally for 1d4 rounds.

On a success, they can wield the weapon, which functions as a magical +2 weapon but requires a DC 13 Wisdom save at the start of each turn to avoid becoming possessed.

Possessed Armor: If a character attempts to wear a piece of armor, they must make a DC Constitution saving throw.

On a failure, they take 3d6 necrotic damage and are paralyzed for 1 round as the armor attempts to crush them.

On a success, they can wear the armor, which functions as magical +1 armor but imposes disadvantage on saving throws against magical effects.

Dark Crystal: Characters can attempt to destroy or remove the crystal (AC 18, 50 HP, immune to nonmagical damage).

If destroyed, it releases a shockwave of necrotic energy (60-foot radius, DC 16 Constitution save, 6d6 necrotic damage).

If removed intact, it can be used as a powerful focus for necromantic spells (+2 to spell attack rolls and save DCs for necromancy spells).

Hidden Dangers

Soul-Draining Floor: Every minute, characters touching the floor must make a DC 14 Constitution saving throw or lose 1d4 hit points as the floor drains their life force.

Miasma of Corruption: The air is toxic. Every 10 minutes, characters in the room must succeed on a DC 13 Constitution saving throw or gain one level of exhaustion.

Relic Surge: Once during the encounter, all relics in the room surge with dark energy. All characters must make a DC 15 Dexterity saving throw or take 4d6 force damage from flying weapons and armor pieces.

The Dark Crystal Purification Puzzle

The Dark Crystal

Appearance: A jagged, obsidian-like crystal about the size of a human head. It pulses with a sickly purple light and seems to absorb shadows around it.

Properties: The crystal is the source of corruption in the room. It has AC 18, 50 HP, and is immune to nonmagical damage.

Effect: Characters who move within 10 feet of the crystal must make a DC 15 Constitution saving throw each round they remain within range or take 2d6 necrotic damage and have disadvantage on their next attack roll or ability check, which lasts for 1 minute.

Puzzle Mechanics

Perceiving the Puzzle: The faint whispers of the relics can clue in the PCs to the presence of the puzzle and its challenge. These whispered messages should be somewhat cryptic, e.g., "Place the relics least vile to purify what is corrupt."

DMs can utilize the party's passive Perception scores or apply various other PC skill checks to provide further direction or hints as needed.

Identifying the Least Corrupted Items: Characters must make a DC 17 Wisdom (Insight) check to identify the least corrupted items, of which there are four total. Note that only three items fit on the triangle, so the PCs must carefully determine which items to use and their placement.

Success reveals the items' auras are slightly different, appearing less tainted.

Failure means they identify the wrong items, leading to negative consequences if used in the ritual.

Deciphering the Whispers: The whispers in the room contain clues about item placement.

DC 15 Intelligence (Investigation) check to decipher the whispers.

Clues are cryptic, e.g., "The cloak of feathers guards the rising sun," indicating the Featherfall Cloak should be placed on the eastern point of the dais.

Correct Placement: The dais has three marked points around the center pedestal holding the crystal, which form a triangle. A successful DC 14 Intelligence check determines that each corner of the triangle marks a cardinal point, which represent (respectively): North (Truth), East (Balance), and West (Purity).

Correct placement:

- **North**: Mindshield Helm
- **East**: Featherfall Cloak
- **West**: Peacekeeper

Performing the Cleansing Ritual: A character must succeed on a DC 16 Intelligence (Religion or Arcana) check.

The ritual involves channeling purifying energy through the placed items into the crystal.

Takes 1 minute to perform, during which the performer cannot move or take other actions.

Consequences of Incorrect Attempts

Wrong Item Identification: If a corrupted item is used, it releases a burst of dark energy.

All characters within 20 feet take 3d8 necrotic damage (DC 15 Dexterity save for half).

The wrongly placed item is destroyed.

Incorrect Placement: Misaligned energies cause the crystal to pulse violently.

All characters in the room must make a DC 14 Wisdom saving throw or be frightened for 1 minute.

The crystal gains 10 temporary hit points.

Failed Ritual Check: The ritual backfires, channeling corruption into the caster.

The caster takes 4d10 psychic damage and gains one level of exhaustion.

All correctly placed items are flung to random points in the room.

Critical Failure (rolling a natural 1 on the check): The crystal overloads, releasing a massive wave of corruption.

All characters take 6d10 necrotic damage (DC 18 Constitution save for half).

All items in the room become animated and attack the party for 1d4 rounds.

Time Pressure: Each failed attempt strengthens the crystal's influence.

After three failed attempts, the corruption starts to spread beyond the room, potentially alerting Fionnlagh.

Successful Completion

When the puzzle is correctly solved:

The crystal shatters with a blinding flash of purifying light.

All corrupted items in the room are cleansed, becoming standard magical items without negative effects.

A secret passage opens in the north wall, revealing a staircase that leads to the next floor.

A hidden hatch pops open in the floor, exposing a cache of beneficial items:

- Potion of Supreme Healing
- Scroll of *Greater Restoration*
- +1 Shield of Spell Turning
- Ring of Protection

The room's oppressive atmosphere lifts, granting the party a moment of respite and clarity.

3rd Floor: Chamber of Corrupted Nature

As you ascend to the third floor, you're met with a sight that defies expectation. The chamber before you is a vast, enclosed garden, but one warped beyond recognition. Sickly light filters through windows on the outer walls of cracked, dark glass, casting an eerie glow over the twisted vegetation below.

The air is thick with a cloying, sweet scent that makes your head swim. Gnarled trees with bark-like, charred flesh line winding paths of pale, ashen soil. Flowers of impossible colors and shapes bloom and wither in moments, their petals seeming to scream silently as they die. Vines with thorns that ooze a viscous, dark liquid writhe along the walls, and in the center of the room, a great tree stands, its branches reaching towards the ceiling like grasping fingers.

Notable Features

The Corrupted Great Tree

A massive, twisted oak dominates the center of the room. Its trunk appears to be breathing, expanding and contracting slowly. Faces occasionally form in the bark, moaning silently before disappearing. A successful DC 15 Intelligence (Nature) check reveals it's the source of corruption for the entire chamber.

Pools of Mutagenic Sludge

Several pools of bubbling, iridescent liquid are scattered throughout the room. Any plant or creature that touches the liquid begins to mutate rapidly. If touched, the character must succeed on a DC 16 Constitution save or suffer 3d6 acid damage and gain a random mutation (see table below).

Carnivorous Flora

Patches of beautiful but deadly plants are spread across the chamber, scattered among areas of harmless vegetation. A successful DC 14 Intelligence (Nature) check identifies dangerous areas. Failing to avoid these areas triggers an attack from the plants: +6 to hit, 2d8 piercing damage, and the PC is automatically grappled (DC 13 Strength check to escape).

Plant Table

Below is a table of plants found in the Chamber of Corrupted Nature:

Name	Description	Properties	Special Traits	Actions	Corrupted/ Uncorrupted
Shadowleaf Oak	A massive tree with black leaves that absorb light	Bark feels like cold flesh	Whispers dark thoughts to those nearby	Branch Attack: +6 to hit, 2d8 bludgeoning damage	Corrupted
Bloodthorn Rose	Roses with petals like razors, oozing a red substance	Thorns cause continuous bleeding	Regenerates rapidly when damaged	Thorn Spray: 15 ft cone, DC 13 Dex save, 3d6 slashing damage	Corrupted
Whisperweed	Tall grass that sways without wind, making hushing sounds	Muffles all sound within 10 ft	Reveals secrets to those who listen closely	Disorienting Whisper: DC 14 Wis save or be confused for 1 round	Corrupted
Voidfruit Tree	Tree bearing fruit that looks like small black holes	Fruit appears to absorb small objects	Eating fruit grants 5 temporary hit points, but risks corruption (DC 15 Wis save)	Void Touch: +5 to hit, 2d6 cold damage and grappled, pulls target 5 ft closer	Corrupted
Gloomshroom	Mushrooms that emit a sickly, dim light	Spores cause hallucinations	Thrives in complete darkness	Spore Cloud: 10-ft radius, DC 13 Con save or poisoned for 1 minute	Corrupted
Heartblossom	Small, heart-shaped flowers with a soft, pulsing glow	Petals have minor healing properties	Wilts in the presence of strong negative emotions	Soothing Pollen: Heals 1d4 HP to all creatures within 5 ft	Uncorrupted
Truthroot	A gnarled root system with crystal-clear sap	Sap acts as a truth serum	Cannot grow in soil tainted by lies	Root Entangle: DC 13 Dex save or restrained	Uncorrupted
Sunburst Fern	Fern with fronds that emit warm, golden light	Light counters magical darkness	Strengthens other uncorrupted plants nearby	Radiant Burst: 15 ft radius, 2d6 radiant damage to corrupted creatures	Uncorrupted

This table provides a mix of corrupted and uncorrupted plants, each with unique properties and potential uses or dangers. PCs can identify a given plant with a DC 14 Intelligence (Nature) check. The uncorrupted plants could be key to solving the puzzle to Purifying the Great Tree, while the corrupted ones present various challenges and hazards for the party to navigate.

Hazards and Interactions

Toxic Pollen Bursts

Certain flowers release clouds of toxic pollen when approached.

DC 15 Dexterity save to avoid, or suffer 2d8 poison damage and be blinded for 1 minute.

Living Vines

Vines attempt to ensnare and crush characters.

DC 14 Dexterity save to avoid being restrained.

Restrained characters take 2d6 bludgeoning damage at the start of their turn.

Corrupted Fruit

Trees bear fruit that looks incredibly tempting.

Eating the fruit heals 2d8+2 hit points but requires a DC 15 Wisdom save or be charmed by Fionnlagh for 1 hour.

Shifting Terrain

The floor occasionally shifts and bubbles like a living thing, creating difficult terrain. Any character attempting to move at full speed must make a DC 13 Dexterity (Acrobatics) check to do so. However, a failed check causes the character to be knocked prone and take 1d6 bludgeoning damage.

Mutation Table (d6)

The following table can be used to create random plant effects to the PCs:

1. **Bark Skin**: AC increases by 2, but vulnerable to fire damage.
2. **Venomous Touch**: Unarmed strikes deal an extra 1d4 poison damage.
3. **Photosynthesis**: No need to eat, but vulnerable to necrotic damage.
4. **Thorn Growth**: Deal 1d4 piercing damage to any creature that hits you with a melee attack.
5. **Root Legs**: Speed increases by 10 feet, but vulnerable to lightning damage.
6. **Spore Cloud**: As an action, release spores in a 10-ft radius, obscuring the area heavily for 1 minute.

Puzzle Element: Purifying the Great Tree

To progress and weaken Fionnlagh's power, the party must purify the Corrupted Great Tree:

- Identify three types of uncorrupted plants hidden in the chamber (DC 16 Nature check to find the right plants).
- Collect sap from these plants (DC 14 Survival check, failure deals 2d6 poison damage).
- Mix the saps together and apply the mixture to the tree's roots while reciting a purification spell (DC 16 Religion or Arcana check).

Consequences of Failure

Each failed step causes the tree to attack with its branches: +8 to hit, 3d8 bludgeoning damage.

Three total failures cause the tree to animate fully, becoming a corrupted treant that attacks the party.

A critical failure (rolling a 1 on the final check) causes all plants in the room to animate and attack for 1d4 rounds.

Successful Completion

The tree shudders and transforms, its corruption falling away.

During the tree's transformation, its shifting form reveals a hidden staircase to the next floor.

The entire chamber gradually becomes purified, making it safe to rest here if needed.

4th Floor: Ritual Chamber - Final Confrontation

As you burst into the vast circular chamber atop Túr na nScáth, you're immediately assaulted by a maelstrom of magical energies. The domed ceiling opens to a stormwracked sky, flashing with eldritch lightning. At the center of the room, standing before a massive obsidian altar, Fionnlagh, the Dark Sorcerer turns to face you, his eyes blazing with arcane power.

"Ah, the meddlesome heroes arrive at last," Fionnlagh's voice booms, resonating with otherworldly echoes. "You're just in time to witness the culmination of my life's work!"

The floor beneath your feet pulses with violet light, an intricate mosaic of magical circuits stretching from wall to wall. Surrounding the room, eldritch artifacts on pedestals hum with barely contained power, while towering bookshelves filled with forbidden tomes line the walls between warped, reality-bending mirrors.

Fionnlagh raises his arms, and the swirling vortex of dark energy above the altar expands, tendrils of chaos reaching out across the chamber. "The barriers between worlds grow thin," he cackles, "and true power shall be mine!"

Fionnlagh's Appearance and Actions

Fionnlagh stands tall and imposing, his form wrapped in robes that seem to be woven from shadows themselves. His long, silver hair whips about in an unfelt wind, and his eyes glow with an inner fire of ambition and madness.

In one hand, he clutches an ornate staff topped with a pulsating crystal, while his other hand manipulates strands of pure magical energy. As he moves, reality seems to warp around him, colors shifting and space bending in his wake.

Initial Battle Setup

Fionnlagh starts the battle on the central dais, near the obsidian altar.

He is in the process of completing a major ritual, which the party must disrupt to prevent catastrophic consequences.

Several of his most powerful creations (perhaps 2-3 of the unique monsters previously described) guard him, positioned around the room.

Fionnlagh's Battle Tactics

Ritual

The ritual has 5 stages, each requiring 3 successful actions to complete.

Each round, Fionnlagh can use his bonus action to progress the ritual.

He must succeed on a DC 15 Constitution check to maintain concentration while under attack.

Players can disrupt the ritual by:

- Dealing damage to Fionnlagh (forcing concentration checks)
- Destroying ritual components on the altar (AC 15, 30 HP each)
- Using *Counterspell* or similar effects (DC 18)

Each completed stage grants Fionnlagh a new ability:

- **Stage 1**: Gain resistance to nonmagical damage
- **Stage 2**: Can cast one additional spell per turn
- **Stage 3**: Gain legendary actions (3/round)
- **Stage 4**: Can summon one high-level demon as an action
- **Stage 5**: Ritual completion - catastrophic event (campaign-dependent)

Success Conditions

Fionnlagh successfully completes all 5 stages of the ritual.

This requires a total of 15 successful actions (3 per stage).

Failure Conditions

Fionnlagh is defeated (reduced to 0 HP) before completing all 5 stages.

All ritual components on the altar are destroyed before the ritual is complete.

The players manage to consistently disrupt the ritual, preventing its completion within a set number of rounds (e.g., 20 rounds).

Tracking System

Use a tracker with 15 slots, divided into 5 stages of 3 slots each.

Each time Fionnlagh successfully uses his bonus action to progress the ritual, mark off one slot. If he completes a stage, apply the corresponding ability.

If PCs successfully disrupt the ritual:

- Erase the last marked slot.
- If this removes a completed stage, also remove the corresponding ability.

Keep track of:

- Number of successful ritual actions
- Current stage of the ritual
- Rounds elapsed since the battle began

Fionnlagh succeeds if he fills all 15 slots. He fails if he's defeated, all components are destroyed, or a pre-set round limit is reached before he can complete the ritual.

Artifact Manipulation

There are 5 major artifacts around the room:

- **Chronos Hourglass**: Manipulates time (slowing enemies or granting extra actions)
- **Void Siphon**: Creates gravity wells or anti-gravity zones
- **Elemental Nexus**: Summons elemental creatures or creates damaging elemental fields
- **Mirror of Echoes**: Creates duplicate illusions of Fionnlagh or his minions
- **Soul Cage**: Drains life force from enemies to heal Fionnlagh or his minions

Activating an artifact requires an action and a DC 16 Intelligence (Arcana) check.

Each artifact can be used once per round.

Artifacts can be destroyed (AC 18, 50 HP) to prevent their use.

Spellcasting

Fionnlagh has access to 9th level spells. Some favorites include:

Time Stop: To make significant ritual progress or set up combos

Meteor Swarm: For massive damage across the battlefield

Maze: To temporarily remove troublesome heroes

Psychic Scream: To potentially incapacitate multiple foes

Wish: As a last resort, to try and force his will upon reality

He uses *Counterspell* liberally to protect his ritual.

Fionnlagh may have unique, homebrew spells at your discretion.

Environmental Control

Gravity Flux: Fionnlagh can change gravity as a bonus action, potentially causing enemies to fall or restricting their movement.

Temporal Pockets: He can step into areas of slowed time to avoid attacks or gain extra actions.

Planar Rifts: Fionnlagh can open or close minor rifts as reactions, potentially disrupting enemy actions or protecting himself.

Mirror Navigation: He can use the room's mirrors to teleport short distances as a bonus action.

Minion Coordination

Fionnlagh has 3-4 powerful minions (use previously created monster stats).

He issues commands as free actions on his turn.

Potential tactics include:

- Forming a protective ring around himself or ritual components
- Sending minions to activate artifacts or disrupt spellcasters
- Using larger minions as mobile cover
- Sacrificing minions to power up spells or artifacts

If a minion is destroyed, Fionnlagh can use his action to rapidly create a new one from the chaotic energies in the room (limited use).

Dynamic Battle Elements

Arcane Mosaic Activation

At the start of each round, roll a d6 to determine which effect activates:

1. **Flame Runes**: 15-foot radius areas of fire damage (2d6 fire damage, DC 15 Dex save).
2. **Frost Sigils**: Creates difficult terrain and deals 1d6 cold damage to creatures that end their turn on it.
3. **Lightning Glyphs**: Arcs of lightning between sigils (3d6 lightning damage, DC 15 Dex save).
4. **Gravity Wells**: Localized areas of intense gravity (creatures must use double movement to leave).
5. **Healing Springs**: Specific sigils heal 2d6 HP to any creature ending its turn there.
6. **Teleportation Circles**: Creatures stepping on these are teleported to another random circle.

Fionnlagh can use a bonus action to activate a specific effect instead of rolling.

PCs can try to decipher and control the mosaic with a DC 18 Intelligence (Arcana) check.

Mirror Shadow Clones

At initiative count 20, roll a d20. On a 15 or higher, a mirror activates.

When activated, a mirror spawns 1d4 shadow clones of random combatants.

Shadow Clone stats:

- AC equal to the original
- HP equal to half the original
- Can use one random ability of the original
- Disappear when reduced to 0 HP or after 1d4 rounds

Clones are neutral and attack the nearest creatureDestroying a mirror (AC 15, 30 HP) prevents it from spawning clones.

Vortex Wild Magic Bursts

At the end of each round, roll a d20. On an 18 or higher, the vortex releases a wild magic surge.

Use the Wild Magic Surge table from the *Player's Handbook*, or create custom effects like:

- All spells cast next round are empowered (maximum damage).
- Gravity reverses for one round.
- All creatures are teleported to random locations in the room.
- Everyone gains fly speed for one round.
- A random elemental creature appears and attacks indiscriminately.
- Fionnlagh can try to control the surge with a DC 20 Intelligence (Arcana) check.

Weakening Planar Barriers

As the battle progresses, the chance of planar incursions increases.

Every third round, roll a d20. The DC for an incursion starts at 18 and decreases by 1 each check.

When an incursion occurs, roll a d6 to determine the plane:

- **Feywild**: Pixies appear, causing mischief and confusion.
- **Shadowfell**: Shadows seep in, creating areas of magical darkness.
- **Elemental Plane of Fire**: Small fire elementals appear, igniting objects.
- **Abyss**: Minor demons materialize and attack indiscriminately.
- **Astral Plane**: Psychic echoes cause all creatures to make a DC 15 Wis save or be stunned for one round.
- **Far Realm**: Tentacles emerge from rifts, attempting to grapple creatures.

Incursions last for 1d4 rounds before the entities or effects return to their plane.

PCs with planar knowledge can attempt to close rifts (DC 17 Intelligence (Arcana) check).

Additional Considerations

These elements should activate in a staggered manner to avoid overwhelming the players all at once.

Fionnlagh should be aware of most of these effects and try to use them to his advantage.

Allow players to interact creatively with these elements (e.g., using the mirrors for surprise attacks or the mosaic for tactical positioning).

Consider having certain elements become more intense or frequent as Fionnlagh's ritual progresses.

Climactic Moments

Ritual Thresholds: At certain points in the ritual, Fionnlagh gains new abilities or the room's dangers intensify.

Artifact Overload: If too many artifacts are activated at once, they might explode, causing massive damage to everyone in the room.

Reality Warp: Near the end of the battle, Fionnlagh might partially succeed in his ritual, temporarily warping reality and transporting the battle to a surreal, ever-changing mindscape.

Scaling the Tower of Shadows Final Encounter

Beginning Players (PC levels 1-5)

Reduce all DCs by 2 (e.g., DC 15 becomes DC 13).

Entrance Hall:

- Reduce number of statues to 6.
- Simplify puzzle to 3 steps.

Armory of Corrupted Relics:

- Reduce number of animated armors to 1d4.
- Lower damage of corrupted weapons by 1 die type.

Chamber of Corrupted Nature:

- Reduce number of hazards.
- Lower damage of plant attacks to 1d8.

Ritual Chamber:

- Fionnlagh uses 3rd-5th level spells.
- Ritual has 3 stages instead of 5.
- Only 2 artifacts active.
- No legendary actions.
- Minions use CR 1-2 creatures.

Intermediate Players (PC levels 6-10)

Keep all DCs as written.

Use all encounters and mechanics as described.

Ritual Chamber:

- Fionnlagh uses 6th-8th level spells.
- Ritual has 4 stages.
- 3-4 artifacts active.

- Limited legendary actions (1-2 per round).
- Minions use CR 3-5 creatures.

Advanced Players (PC levels 11+)

Increase all DCs by 2 (e.g., DC 15 becomes DC 17).

Entrance Hall:

- Add complex magical traps.
- Increase number of statues to 15.

Armory of Corrupted Relics:

- Add more powerful cursed items.
- Animated armors use veteran or gladiator stats.

Chamber of Corrupted Nature:

- Add more mutation effects.
- Increase damage of hazards.

Ritual Chamber:

- Fionnlagh uses 9th level spells and custom spells.
- Ritual has all 5 stages with additional effects.
- All 5 artifacts active with enhanced effects.
- Full legendary actions (3-4 per round).
- Minions use CR 7+ creatures.
- Add lair actions for Fionnlagh.
- Increase frequency and intensity of environmental effects.

Denouement

Denouement

Use this denouement to replace the conclusion "The Triskelion Restored" for players who wish to enact the ritual to remove all corruption from Inis Solais and roleplay their characters taking personal part in purifying the region. This encounter serves as the triumphant conclusion to the adventure, allowing players to witness the fruits of their labor. It focuses on the emotional payoff and celebration, providing closure to the story and honoring the players' achievements.

As you crest the final hill, the village comes into view, but it's hardly recognizable from when you first arrived. The oppressive gloom that once hung over the settlement has lifted, replaced by warm, golden sunlight that bathes the thatched roofs and cobblestone streets. The withered crops in the surrounding fields have sprung back to life, their green stalks swaying gently in a fragrant breeze.

The village square, once eerily empty, now teems with life and color. Villagers, their faces bright with hope and joy, mill about, hanging festive garlands and preparing for what looks to be a grand celebration. As you approach, all eyes turn to you, and a hush falls over the crowd, filled with anticipation and gratitude.

Perform the Purification Ritual with the Unified Triskelion

Preparation

Eilidh the Druid guides the party to the center of the Village Green.

Villagers form a large circle around the PCs, holding hands.

The unified Triskelion is placed on a specially prepared altar.

Ritual Components

Three key elements are needed, representing the three aspects of the Triskelion:

- A vial of pure spring water (Life)
- A handful of soil from the village's oldest tree (Rebirth)
- A candle made from beeswax of the local hives (Death)

The Ritual Process

The PCs must each take on a role, corresponding to the Triskelion's aspects.

They form a triangle, each component in the hands of a different PC.

Eilidh the Druid instructs them to recite an incantation in unison (see below).

As they chant, they must pour/sprinkle their components onto the pieces of the Triskelion.

Incantation

English: "Three become one, balance restored, Life, death, rebirth, forevermore. Triskelion's power, hear our call, Cleanse this land, protect us all."

Irish Gaelic: "Trí ina cheann, cothromaíocht ar ais, Beatha, bás, athnuachan, go deo. Cumhacht na Trískéile, clois ár nglaoch, Glan an tír seo, cosain sinn go léir."

Phonetic Pronunciation: "Tree in-a kyown, kuh-rum-ee-ocht er ash, Ba-ha, baws, ah-noo-kun, guh jay-oh. Koo-ocht na tree-shkey-la, klish awr glee, Glan an teer shuh, kus-an sheen guh lair."

Magical Effects

The Triskelion begins to glow, its light intensifying with each verse of the incantation.

Streams of energy in gold, green, and purple emerge from the Triskelion, spiraling outward.

These energies wash over the village, visibly restoring and rejuvenating everything they touch.

Challenges

Each PC must make a DC 15 Constitution check to channel the Triskelion's power.

Failure doesn't stop the ritual but causes the PC to take 2d6 force damage from the magical strain.

The PCs must maintain concentration (as if concentrating on a spell) for the duration of the ritual.

Climax and Resolution

As the ritual reaches its peak, a burst of radiant energy explodes outward from the Triskelion.

The PCs witness the visible lifting of the curse: withered plants springing to life, sickly villagers becoming healthy, and the oppressive atmosphere dissipating.

The Triskelion, having fulfilled its purpose, separates back into its three components, their malevolent energy now purified.

The villagers erupt in cheers and celebration.

Key NPCs from the adventure approach to thank the PCs personally.

Scaling the Epilogue

Beginning Players (PC levels 1-5)

Reduce ritual DC to 13.

Magical strain damage: 1d6 force damage.

Simplify the ritual:

- Only one component needed (e.g., spring water).
- Shorter incantation.

Triskelion effects:

- Limit to immediate area around the village.
- Less dramatic visual effects.

Intermediate Players (PC levels 6-10)

Keep ritual DC at 15.

Magical strain damage: 2d6 force damage.

Use ritual as described:

- All three components.
- Full incantation.

Triskelion effects:

- Extend to the village and surrounding area.
- Full visual effects as described.

Advanced Players (PC levels 11+)

Increase ritual DC to 17.

Magical strain damage: 3d6 force damage.

Enhance the ritual:

- Add a fourth component (e.g., a personal sacrifice).
- Extend incantation with additional verses.
- Each PC must succeed on an additional check (e.g., Arcana or Religion).

Triskelion effects:

- Extend to a large region around the village.
- Add extra effects (e.g., temporary planar convergence, time distortion).

Add an optional challenge:

- Remnant of Fionnlagh's power attempts to disrupt the ritual.
- PCs must overcome this while maintaining the ritual.

Conclusions

Conclusions

The Triskelion Restored: A New Dawn for Aerilon

This conclusion wraps up the adventure, providing closure and celebrating the players' achievements. Adjust the specific details of the rewards and legacy to fit your campaign and the players' individual contributions throughout the adventure.

As the final piece of the Triskelion clicks into place, a surge of energy pulses through the unified artifact, spreading outward in waves of golden light. The oppressive darkness that has long plagued Aerilon seems to dissolve before your eyes, replaced by warm sunlight and a gentle breeze carrying the scent of blooming flowers.

The villagers emerge from their homes, their faces a mixture of awe and joy as they witness the transformation of their home. The withered crops in the fields spring back to life, trees once bare now burst with lush foliage, and the very air seems to hum with renewed vitality. As the light of the Triskelion fades, you realize that you've not just saved a village, but restored balance to a land long suffering under the weight of corruption and discord.

Reward

Each PC receives:

A substantial amount of gold (5,000 – 10,000 gp depending on player level).

A title of honor bestowed by the village elders (e.g., "Guardian of Aerilon").

Legacy

The characters' names are woven into local legend, with bards composing songs of their deeds.

A memorial is erected in the village square, depicting the heroes and the unified Triskelion.

The restored balance has far-reaching effects, with nature flourishing and magic becoming more harmonious throughout the region.

The Triskelion, now purified, becomes a sacred artifact under the protection of Aerilon, with the PCs as its honorary guardians.

A Pyrrhic Victory: The Shadow of the Triskelion Lingers

This conclusion acknowledges the players' partial success while setting up potential future conflicts. Adjust the specifics based on which apprentices survived and how much of the Triskelion remains uncollected.

The dust settles in the aftermath of your climactic battle with Fionnlagh, the Dark Sorcerer. His defeat has lifted a great weight from the land, and signs of recovery are already visible as nature begins to heal. However, a sense of unease lingers in the air, a reminder that your quest remains incomplete.

As you return to Aerilon, the villagers greet you with a mixture of gratitude and apprehension. Their faces, while no longer marked by despair, show concern for the future. The remaining pieces of the Triskelion, still scattered and in the hands of Fionnlagh's surviving apprentices, cast long shadows over your victory. You've won a critical battle, but the war for balance in these lands is far from over.

Reward

Each PC receives:

A magical item recovered from Fionnlagh's lair, bearing traces of his dark power but purified for the PCs' use.

A modest amount of gold, gathered from grateful villagers and recovered treasures (1,000 - 3,000 gp depending on player level).

Legacy

The PCs are hailed as heroes for defeating Fionnlagh, but whispers of the unfinished quest follow them.

Areas where the Triskelion pieces were recovered show signs of healing and renewed vitality.

Regions influenced by the missing pieces and surviving apprentices remain unstable, with pockets of corruption persisting.

The PCs gain allies among those who opposed Fionnlagh, but also inherit his enemies and wary factions concerned about the remaining threats.

Stories of the adventurers' deeds spread, intertwined with cautionary tales about the power still at large.

The incomplete Triskelion becomes a source of research and concern for scholars and mages, potentially leading to future quests or conflicts.

The Looming Shadow: Fionnlagh's Enduring Threat

This conclusion emphasizes the bittersweet nature of the players' victory and sets up Fionnlagh as a recurring villain. Adjust the details based on which pieces of the Triskelion were recovered and the specific outcomes of the battles with the apprentices.

As you stand amidst the remnants of your final battle, the defeated forms of Fionnlagh's apprentices lying still, a mix of triumph and unease washes over you. The land already shows signs of healing where the Triskelion pieces were recovered, vibrant life pushing through the cracks of corruption. But a chill wind carries whispers of a darkness not fully vanquished.

Returning to Aerilon, you're met with cheers from the villagers, their faces bright with hope yet etched with lingering fear. The defeat of the apprentices has brought respite, but rumors of Fionnlagh's survival cast long shadows over your victory. As you look to the horizon, you can't shake the feeling that this is but a pause in a greater conflict, with the Dark Sorcerer biding his time, plotting his return.

Reward

Each PC receives:

A substantial amount of gold, collected from the lairs of the fallen apprentices and grateful communities (3,000 - 6,000 gp depending on player level).

A title of respect from the people of Aerilon (e.g., "Apprentice Slayer" or "Shield of the Realms").

Legacy

The adventurers are celebrated as heroes for defeating the apprentices and recovering parts of the Triskelion.

Areas freed from the apprentices' influence begin to flourish, though pockets of corruption remain where Fionnlagh's power lingers.

The incomplete Triskelion becomes a closely guarded secret and object of study, its partial power used to ward off remaining dark forces.

Fionnlagh's survival becomes the stuff of fearful legend, with sightings and rumors of his activities spreading across the land.

The PCs gain powerful allies in their fight against dark forces, but also the enmity of Fionnlagh's remaining supporters.

Their actions have disrupted the balance of power in the region, leading to political and magical upheavals that may require their intervention in the future.

The unfinished nature of their quest leaves open the possibility for future adventures, with the looming threat of Fionnlagh's return and the search for the remaining Triskelion pieces.

The Fall of Hope: Darkness Triumphant

This conclusion presents a grim outcome, setting the stage for a potential follow-up campaign or a dramatic shift in your world's status quo. Be prepared to discuss with your players how they want to proceed, whether with new characters or a time-jump to continue the story.

As consciousness slowly returns, you find yourselves in the depths of Fionnlagh's dungeon, your bodies battered and spirits broken. Through the bars of your cell, you catch glimpses of a world transformed. The sky outside is perpetually dark, streaked with ominous purple lightning. The distant sounds of suffering and chaos echo through the stone corridors.

In your moments of lucidity, you hear tales of Fionnlagh's victory. With the Triskelion nearly complete in his grasp, his power has grown beyond measure. The lands you once sought to protect now writhe under his corrupting influence, as nature itself twists into nightmarish forms. Your failure weighs heavily upon you, a constant reminder of the dire consequences of your defeat.

Reward

Though traditional rewards are scarce in this bleak scenario, the PCs receive:

Connections with fellow prisoners, potentially including powerful allies who were also defeated by Fionnlagh.

A deep understanding of their enemies' strengths and weaknesses, should they ever break free.

Legacy

The PCs become legendary figures, but as cautionary tales of hubris and failure.

Songs and stories spread of their valiant but ultimately doomed struggle against Fionnlagh.

Small pockets of resistance form, inspired by the PCs' initial victories, holding out hope for their return.

The incomplete Triskelion, now in Fionnlagh's possession, becomes an object of terrifying power and the focus of any remaining opposition.

The PCs' actions, though ultimately unsuccessful, have sown seeds of rebellion that may flourish in time.

Their defeat serves as a rallying cry for a new generation of heroes, who may seek to free them and finish what they started.

Embracing the Darkness: Champions of Chaos

This conclusion dramatically alters the campaign's trajectory, potentially setting up an evil-aligned continuation. Discuss with your players how they want to proceed in this new paradigm, and be prepared to adjust your world and future adventures accordingly.

> Standing atop the highest tower of Túr na nScáth, you survey the land that now bows to your combined might. The sky churns with dark clouds, streaked with flashes of arcane lightning, a testament to the power you've embraced. Below, the once-verdant fields and forests twist into new, chaotic forms, reshape by your dark influence.
>
> Fionnlagh approaches, a pleased smile on his face as he regards you - no longer as pawns or even apprentices, but as true allies in his vision. The Triskelion, now complete and corrupted, pulses with malevolent energy in his grasp. As he speaks of the realms yet to conquer and the old order to overthrow, you feel the intoxicating rush of your newfound power. The world trembles at your feet, ready to be remade in your image.

Reward

Each PC receives a powerful, cursed artifact attuned to their specific skills and the aspect of the Triskelion they've embraced.

Vast wealth plundered from conquered lands and defeated foes (5,000 - 12,500 gp depending on player level).

Control over a significant territory within Fionnlagh's growing empire.

Legacy

The PCs become feared and reviled figures across the land, their names spoken only in hushed whispers.

Songs and tales spread of their betrayal and the fall of once-great heroes to darkness.

Nature itself warps in their presence, creating pockets of chaotic, corrupted landscapes wherever they go.

Former allies and innocents they once protected now lead resistance movements against them.

The balance of power in the world is shattered, with other nations and powerful entities scrambling to defend against Fionnlagh's empire.

Their actions inspire others to seek power through dark means, creating cults and splinter groups in their honor.

The Triskelion, now a symbol of corruption, becomes the focus of quests by those seeking to destroy it and end their reign.

Appendix

Appendix

Welcome to the Appendix of *The Triskelion Prophecy*, a comprehensive resource designed to enhance your journey through this epic adventure. Here, you'll find a wealth of information, from detailed monster stat blocks to magical items, NPC descriptions, and important pronunciations. These entries are crafted to provide Dungeon Masters and players with the necessary tools to fully immerse themselves in the rich, mythological world of *The Triskelion Prophecy*.

This section aims to not only support your gameplay but also deepen your understanding of the intricate lore and cultural elements embedded within the campaign. Whether you are looking for specific monster abilities, the history behind a magical artifact, or the correct pronunciation of an Irish Gaelic name, the Appendix serves as your go-to reference. Dive into the magical realm of *The Triskelion Prophecy* and let this guide help bring your adventures to life with greater depth and authenticity.

Scaling Monsters

Scaling Monsters

Use the following table for party size to increase the number of monsters:

Party Size	Increase number by
5-8	x 1.5
9-12	x 2
13	x 2.5

Use the following table for party level to increase the number of monsters:

Party Level	Increase number by
5-8	x 1.5
9-12	x 2
13-15	x 2.5
Level 16+	x 3.5

Now take the number for the party and the level and add the two together. For instance, if you have a party size of 5 with an average party level of 10, then you would add 1.5 + 2.5 to get 4 times the monsters. 3 creatures for a level 10 party are no challenge, especially if there are 6 or 7 PCs. Increase that to 12, and suddenly you have a challenge. Feel free to adjust as you see fit.

In addition to scaling monster numbers, many of the traps and puzzles in the game have a sliding scale that the DM can use to change the level of difficulty depending on the skillset of the characters.

Monsters

Monsters

Animated Spellbook

Small construct (grimoire guardian), unaligned

Armor Class: 17 (natural armor)

Hit Points: 17 (5d6)

Speed: 0 ft., fly 50 ft. (hover)

STR	DEX	CON	INT	WIS	CHA
12 (+1)	15 (+2)	11 (+0)	14 (+2)	7 (-2)	1 (-5)

Saving Throws: Dex +4

Skills: Arcana +4, Perception +0

Damage Immunities: poison, psychic

Condition Immunities: blinded, charmed, deafened, frightened, paralyzed, petrified, poisoned

Senses: blindsight 60 ft. (blind beyond this radius), passive Perception 10

Languages: Understands Common but can't speak

Challenge: 1/4 (50 XP)

Antimagic Susceptibility. The Animated Spellbook is incapacitated while in the area of an antimagic field. If targeted by *Dispel Magic*, the grimoire guardian must succeed on a Constitution saving throw against the caster's spell save DC or fall unconscious for 1 minute.

False Appearance. While the Animated Spellbook remains motionless on a bookshelf or table, it is indistinguishable from a normal book.

Spellcasting Focus. The Animated Spellbook can serve as a spellcasting focus for any spellcaster holding it. When used this way, the spellcaster gains a +1 bonus to spell attack rolls.

Actions

Paper Cut. *Melee Weapon Attack:* +4 to hit, reach 5 ft., one target. *Hit:* 5 (1d6 + 2) slashing damage.

Ink Spray (Recharge 5-6). The Animated Spellbook sprays magical ink in a 15-foot cone. Each creature in that area must make a DC 12 Dexterity saving throw. On a failed save, a creature takes 7 (2d6) acid damage and is blinded until the end of its next turn. On a successful save, a creature takes half as much damage and isn't blinded.

Spell Flare. The Animated Spellbook flips open to a random page and casts a cantrip (DM's choice from Wizard spell list) using its Arcana bonus as the spellcasting modifier.

Description

The Animated Spellbook appears as a large, leather-bound tome with intricate arcane symbols embossed on its cover. Its pages rustle constantly, as if blown by an unseen wind. When in motion, it floats upright, its cover acting as a shield while pages flip rapidly, occasionally releasing small bursts of arcane energy. The book's 'face' is its open pages, which seem to form expressions through the arrangement of text and magical diagrams.

Animated Spellbooks were originally created by an eccentric archmage who sought to protect his vast library from thieves and unworthy apprentices. Over time, the method of their creation spread to other powerful wizards and magical institutions. These sentient tomes not only guard magical knowledge but also serve as formidable aids in magical study and spellcasting. Some have developed distinct personalities over centuries of existence, becoming valuable companions to generations of spellcasters.

Corrupted Beast

Large monstrosity, chaotic evil

Armor Class: 14 (natural armor)

Hit Points: 37 (5d10 + 10)

Speed: 50 ft.

STR	DEX	CON	INT	WIS	CHA
17 (+3)	15 (+2)	15 (+2)	3 (-4)	12 (+1)	7 (-2)

Skills: Perception +3, Stealth +4

Damage Resistances: necrotic

Damage Vulnerabilities: radiant

Senses: darkvision 60 ft., passive Perception 13

Languages: —

Challenge: 2 (450 XP)

Keen Hearing and Smell. The beast has advantage on Wisdom (Perception) checks that rely on hearing or smell.

Pack Tactics. The beast has advantage on attack rolls against a creature if at least one of the beast's allies is within 5 feet of the creature and the ally isn't incapacitated.

Corrupting Presence. At the start of each of the beast's turns, each creature within 5 feet of it takes 2 (1d4) necrotic damage.

Actions

Bite. *Melee Weapon Attack:* +5 to hit, reach 5 ft., one target. *Hit:* 10 (2d6 + 3) piercing damage plus 2 (1d4) necrotic damage.

Howl of Despair (Recharge 5-6). The beast lets out a chilling howl. Each creature within 30 feet of the beast that can hear it must succeed on a DC 13 Wisdom saving throw or be frightened for 1 minute. A creature can repeat the saving throw at the end of each of its turns, ending the effect on itself on a success.

Description

The Corrupted Beast appears as a grotesque amalgamation of wolf and shadow. Its fur is a deep, unnatural black that seems to absorb light, with streaks of sickly purple running through it. Tendrils of dark energy constantly writhe around its form. Its eyes glow with an eerie, purple light, and wisps of black smoke curl from its mouth and nostrils. The beast's claws and teeth are oversized and jagged, dripping with a dark, oily substance.

Corrupted Beasts are the result of Maolmhuire's twisted experiments with the Life Fragment of the Triskelion. Once ordinary animals, these creatures have been infused with dark energy, transforming them into monstrous servants of evil. The corruption process is agonizing and irreversible, driving the beasts mad with pain and turning them into relentless hunters. Local legends speak of entire forests being emptied of wildlife, only for packs of these nightmarish creatures to emerge days later. The presence of Corrupted Beasts is often seen as a harbinger of greater evils, a sign that the natural order has been deeply disturbed.

Fey Skeleton

Medium undead, chaotic neutral

Armor Class: 13 (natural armor)

Hit Points: 32 (5d8 + 10)

Speed: 30 ft.

STR	DEX	CON	INT	WIS	CHA
14 (+2)	16 (+3)	15 (+2)	10 (+0)	12 (+1)	14 (+2)

Skills: Acrobatics +5, Stealth +5

Damage Vulnerabilities: bludgeoning

Damage Immunities: poison

Condition Immunities: exhaustion, poisoned

Senses: darkvision 60 ft., passive Perception 11

Languages: Understands Sylvan but can't speak

Challenge: 2 (450 XP)

Fey Essence. The skeleton is considered both undead and fey for the purposes of spells and magical effects.

Twilight Step. As a bonus action, the Fey Skeleton can teleport up to 30 feet to an unoccupied space it can see.

Magical Resistance. The Fey Skeleton has advantage on saving throws against spells and other magical effects.

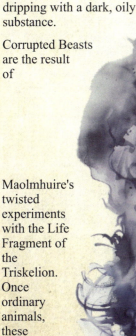

Actions

Multiattack. The Fey Skeleton makes two Spectral Blade attacks.

Spectral Blade. *Melee Weapon Attack:* +5 to hit, reach 5 ft., one target. *Hit:* 6 (1d6 + 3) slashing damage plus 3 (1d6) cold damage.

Fey Fire (Recharge 5-6). The Fey Skeleton unleashes a burst of magical fire. Each creature in a 15-foot cone must make a DC 13 Dexterity saving throw, taking 14 (4d6) fire damage on a failed save, or half as much damage on a successful one. This fire is pale blue and feels unnaturally cold.

Description

The Fey Skeleton appears as a hauntingly beautiful fusion of death and nature. Its bones are bleached white but adorned with intricate, glowing patterns that pulse with an eerie, pale light. Delicate vines and spectral wisps intertwine through its ribcage and around its limbs. The skeleton's eye sockets flicker with an otherworldly, blue-green flame, and a faint mist seems to cling to its form, giving it an ethereal appearance.

Fey Skeletons are the result of a dark ritual that binds fey spirits to mortal remains. These unholy creations retain some of their fey nature, blending the magic of the Feywild with necromantic energy. They are often created by malevolent fey lords or necromancers seeking to exploit the unique properties of fey magic. Legends speak of ancient battlefields in the borderlands between the mortal realm and the Feywild, where the bones of fallen warriors rise as Fey Skeletons during the twilight hours, forever reliving their final moments in an eternal, spectral dance.

Lucht Siúil (Traveler)

Medium undead (incorporeal), neutral

Armor Class: 13 (natural armor)

Hit Points: 66 (12d8 + 12)

Speed: 30 ft., fly 40 ft. (hover)

STR	DEX	CON	INT	WIS	CHA
10 (+0)	16 (+3)	12 (+1)	14 (+2)	16 (+3)	18 (+4)

Saving Throws: Dex +6, Wis +6, Cha +7

Skills: Perception +6, Stealth +9, Survival +6

Damage Resistances: acid, cold, fire, lightning, thunder; bludgeoning, piercing, and slashing from nonmagical attacks

Damage Immunities: necrotic, poison

Condition Immunities: charmed, exhaustion, frightened, grappled, paralyzed, petrified, poisoned, prone, restrained

Senses: darkvision 60 ft., passive Perception 16

Languages: Common, Sylvan

Challenge: 6 (2,300 XP)

Proficiency Bonus: +3

Ghostly Travel. The Lucht Siúil can move through other creatures and objects as if they were difficult terrain. They take 5 (1d10) force damage if they end their turn inside an object.

Knowledge of the Road. The Lucht Siúil have extensive knowledge of the land and can offer guidance. They have advantage on Survival checks and can cast the *Find the Path* spell once per day without requiring material components.

Vengeful Spirits. When disturbed or threatened, the Lucht Siúil can become hostile. As a bonus action, they can transform into vengeful spirits for 1 minute, gaining advantage on all attack rolls and dealing an extra 2d6 necrotic damage on each hit.

Actions

Multiattack. The Lucht Siúil make two Ghostly Touch attacks.

Ghostly Touch. *Melee Spell Attack:* +7 to hit, reach 5 ft., one target. *Hit:* 14 (4d6) necrotic damage.

Whisper of the Dead. The Lucht Siúil can use an action to whisper ancient secrets. Each creature within 30 feet that can hear the whispers must make a DC 15 Wisdom saving throw or be frightened for 1 minute. A frightened target can repeat the saving throw at the end of each of its turns, ending the effect on itself on a success.

Description

The Lucht Siúil appear as ghostly, ethereal figures cloaked in tattered, flowing robes that seem to blend with the mist and shadows around them. Their faces are partially obscured, revealing only glimmers of their eyes, which glow faintly with an otherworldly light. Moving with an eerie grace, they leave no footprints and make no sound, as if they are one with the air itself.

The Lucht Siúil, or Travelers, are the restless spirits of ancient wanderers who perished far from their homes. These spectral nomads are believed to roam the land, driven by a desire to guide and protect travelers, sharing their vast knowledge of the roads and pathways. However, their benevolence can quickly turn to vengeance if they are disturbed or threatened, manifesting as vengeful spirits that exact retribution on those who disrespect them. Tales of the Lucht Siúil often serve as cautionary stories, reminding the living to honor the dead and seek their guidance with respect and reverence. These spirits are also associated with the festival of Samhain, when the veil between the worlds is thinnest, and the Lucht Siúil are said to walk among the living once more.

Peist Dhraíochta (Magic Serpent)

Gargantuan dragon, neutral

Armor Class: 18 (natural armor)

Hit Points: 198 (12d20 + 72)

Speed: 30 ft., swim 60 ft.

STR	DEX	CON	INT	WIS	CHA
24 (+7)	18 (+4)	22 (+6)	16 (+3)	14 (+2)	20 (+5)

Saving Throws: Str +12, Dex +9, Con +11, Wis +7, Cha +10

Skills: Perception +12, Stealth +9, Arcana +8

Damage Resistances: cold, fire, lightning

Damage Immunities: acid

Senses: darkvision 120 ft., passive Perception 22

Languages: Common, Draconic, Sylvan

Challenge: 15 (13,000 XP)

Proficiency Bonus: +5

Amphibious. The Peist Dhraíochta can breathe air and water.

Legendary Resistance (3/Day). If the Peist Dhraíochta fails a saving throw, it can choose to succeed instead.

Water Jet. As an action, the Peist Dhraíochta can unleash a powerful jet of water in a 60-foot line that is 5 feet wide. Each creature in that line must make a DC 18 Strength saving throw, taking 45 (10d8) bludgeoning damage on a failed save, or half as much damage on a successful one. Creatures that fail the save are also pushed 20 feet away from the Peist Dhraíochta.

Colorful Hypnosis. The Peist Dhraíochta's scales shimmer with all the colors of the rainbow, creating a hypnotic effect. As a bonus action, it can target one creature it can see within 30 feet. The target must succeed on a DC 18 Wisdom saving throw or be charmed for 1 minute. The charmed target is incapacitated and has a speed of 0. The effect ends if the target takes damage or another creature uses an action to shake the target out of its stupor.

Treasure Guardian. The Peist Dhraíochta is fiercely protective of its hoard. It has advantage on all Wisdom (Perception) and Intelligence (Investigation) checks made to detect intruders or hidden creatures within its lair.

Actions

Multiattack. The Peist Dhraíochta makes three attacks: one with its Bite and two with its Tail.

Bite. *Melee Weapon Attack:* +12 to hit, reach 10 ft., one target. *Hit:* 21 (3d8 + 7) piercing damage plus 14 (4d6) acid damage.

Tail. *Melee Weapon Attack:* +12 to hit, reach 15 ft., one target. *Hit:* 18 (3d6 + 7) bludgeoning damage, and the target must succeed on a DC 20 Strength saving throw or be knocked prone.

Hypnotic Scales. The Peist Dhraíochta uses its Colorful Hypnosis.

Legendary Actions

The Peist Dhraíochta can take 3 legendary actions, choosing from the options below. Only one legendary action option can be used at a time and only at the end of another creature's turn. The Peist Dhraíochta regains spent legendary actions at the start of its turn.

Detect. The Peist Dhraíochta makes a Wisdom (Perception) check.

Tail Attack. The Peist Dhraíochta makes a Tail attack.

Water Surge (Costs 2 Actions). The Peist Dhraíochta creates a surge of water around it. Each creature within 20 feet of the Peist Dhraíochta must succeed on a DC 18 Strength saving throw or take 14 (4d6) bludgeoning damage and be knocked prone.

Description

The Peist Dhraíochta is a colossal serpentine creature, its scales shimmering with a mesmerizing array of colors, reminiscent of a living rainbow. These iridescent scales not only serve as an awe-inspiring spectacle but also have a hypnotic quality, capable of entrancing those who gaze upon them. The serpent's eyes are deep, swirling pools of color, adding to its otherworldly appearance. Its long, sinuous body moves with both grace and power, making it a formidable presence in any aquatic environment.

The Peist Dhraíochta, or Magic Serpent, is often depicted as a guardian of ancient treasures and secrets hidden beneath the waters of deep lakes and rivers. These mythical creatures are said to have been created by the gods to protect the sacred and powerful artifacts left behind by ancient civilizations. The shimmering scales of the Peist Dhraíochta are believed to possess magical properties, capable of both enchanting and protecting the creature. Legends tell of heroes and adventurers who sought the knowledge and riches guarded by these serpents, only to be met with the formidable challenge of overcoming their hypnotic gaze and powerful water attacks. The Peist Dhraíochta's connection to the mystical and the divine makes it a revered and feared entity in Celtic folklore.

Saoi na Coille (Sage of the Forest)

Large fey, neutral good

Armor Class: 17 (natural armor)

Hit Points: 136 (13d10 + 65)

Speed: 30 ft.

STR	DEX	CON	INT	WIS	CHA
20 (+5)	10 (+0)	20 (+5)	16 (+3)	22 (+6)	18 (+4)

Saving Throws: Str +9, Con +9, Wis +10, Cha +8

Skills: Nature +10, Perception +10, Survival +10

Damage Resistances: bludgeoning, piercing, and slashing from nonmagical attacks

Senses: darkvision 60 ft., passive Perception 20

Languages: Common, Sylvan, Druidic

Challenge: 10 (5,900 XP)

Proficiency Bonus: +4

Plant Camouflage. The Saoi na Coille has advantage on Dexterity (Stealth) checks made to hide in forested terrain.

Ancient Wisdom. The Saoi na Coille can add its Wisdom modifier to any Intelligence check it makes related to nature, history, or magic.

Speak with Beasts and Plants. The Saoi na Coille can communicate with beasts and plants as if they shared a language.

Actions

Multiattack. The Saoi na Coille makes two Branch Slam attacks.

Branch Slam. *Melee Weapon Attack:* +9 to hit, reach 10 ft., one target. *Hit:* 19 (3d8 + 6) bludgeoning damage.

Entangle. The Saoi na Coille targets a point on the ground that it can see within 60 feet. Grasping roots and vines sprout in a 20-foot square centered on that point. Each creature in the area must succeed on a DC 18 Strength saving throw or be restrained. A creature restrained by the plants can use its action to make a DC 18 Strength check, freeing itself on a success.

Healing Touch (3/Day). The Saoi na Coille touches another creature. The target magically regains 36 (6d8 + 9) hit points and is freed from any curse, disease, poison, blindness, or deafness.

Summon Forest Allies (1/Day). The Saoi na Coille summons 1d4 dryads or treants (DM's choice) that appear in unoccupied spaces within 60 feet and act as its allies for 1 hour or until they drop to 0 hit points.

Legendary Actions

The Saoi na Coille can take 3 legendary actions, choosing from the options below. Only one legendary action option can be used at a time and only at the end of another creature's turn. The Saoi na Coille regains spent legendary actions at the start of its turn.

Detect. The Saoi na Coille makes a Wisdom (Perception) check.

Root Grasp. The Saoi na Coille targets one creature it can see within 30 feet. The target must succeed on a DC 18 Strength saving throw or be restrained by roots and vines (escape DC 18).

Nature's Ward (Costs 2 Actions). The Saoi na Coille grants itself and all allied creatures within 30 feet resistance to all damage types until the start of its next turn.

Description

The Saoi na Coille is a towering, ancient being resembling a tree given life. Its bark-like skin is gnarled and weathered, covered in moss and small plants, with branches sprouting from its back and shoulders. Its eyes glow with a serene, green light, reflecting its deep connection to the forest. Vines and leaves continuously grow and move around its form, giving it a constantly shifting, verdant appearance.

The Saoi na Coille, or Sage of the Forest, is considered one of the oldest and wisest beings within the natural world. Legends tell of its creation by the ancient druids to serve as a guardian and protector of sacred groves and ancient forests. The Saoi na Coille possesses unparalleled knowledge of the natural world, and its wisdom is sought by both druids and rangers who respect the balance of nature. It can communicate with all forest creatures, from the smallest insect to the mightiest treant, and is revered for its ability to heal and protect the land it watches over. The Saoi na Coille embodies the spirit of the forest, ensuring that nature thrives and remains in harmony, making it a revered and respected entity in Celtic folklore.

Scáthannaí (Shadow Walker)

Medium undead, chaotic neutral

Armor Class: 17 (natural armor)

Hit Points: 136 (16d8 + 64)

Speed: 30 ft.

STR	DEX	CON	INT	WIS	CHA
16 (+3)	20 (+5)	18 (+4)	14 (+2)	16 (+3)	18 (+4)

Saving Throws: Dex +9, Con +8, Wis +7, Cha +8

Skills: Stealth +13, Perception +7, Arcana +6

Damage Resistances: acid, cold, fire, lightning, thunder; bludgeoning, piercing, and slashing from nonmagical attacks

Damage Immunities: necrotic, poison

Condition Immunities: charmed, exhaustion, frightened, grappled, paralyzed, petrified, poisoned, restrained

Senses: darkvision 120 ft., passive Perception 17

Languages: Common, Infernal, Sylvan

Challenge: 10 (5,900 XP)

Proficiency Bonus: +4

Shadow Stealth. While in dim light or darkness, the Scáthannaí can take the Hide action as a bonus action.

Shadow Step. As a bonus action, the Scáthannaí can teleport up to 60 feet to an unoccupied space it can see that is in dim light or darkness. It then has advantage on the first melee attack it makes before the end of its turn.

Create Shadow Portals. The Scáthannaí can create two linked portals in areas of darkness or dim light within 120 feet of each other. Each portal is a 5-foot-radius circular void of darkness. Any creature entering one portal immediately exits from the other, appearing in an unoccupied space within 5 feet of the second portal. The portals last for 1 hour or until the Scáthannaí dismisses them as a bonus action.

Shadow Tendrils. The Scáthannaí can use an action to extend tendrils of shadow in a 20-foot radius. Each creature within the area must make a DC 18 Strength saving throw or be restrained by the tendrils. A restrained creature can use its action to make a DC 18 Strength check, freeing itself on a success.

Actions

Multiattack. The Scáthannaí makes three Shadow Blade attacks.

Shadow Blade. *Melee Weapon Attack:* +9 to hit, reach 5 ft., one target. *Hit:* 17 (3d8 + 4) necrotic damage.

Shadow Tendrils. The Scáthannaí uses its Shadow Tendrils ability.

Legendary Actions

The Scáthannaí can take 3 legendary actions, choosing from the options below. Only one legendary action option can be used at a time and only at the end of another creature's turn. The Scáthannaí regains spent legendary actions at the start of its turn.

Detect. The Scáthannaí makes a Wisdom (Perception) check.

Shadow Blade Attack. The Scáthannaí makes one Shadow Blade attack.

Shadow Displacement (Costs 2 Actions). The Scáthannaí uses its Shadow Step ability.

Description

The Scáthannaí appears as a tall, humanoid figure composed entirely of shadows, its form constantly shifting and wavering as if made from living darkness. Its glowing red eyes pierce through the black void of its body, giving it an eerie, menacing presence. When it moves, it seems to glide effortlessly, merging with the shadows around it, and leaving a trail of darkness in its wake. The air around it feels cold and oppressive, as if the very light is being drained away.

The Scáthannaí, or Shadow Walker, is a mysterious and feared entity that dwells in the darkest corners of the world. These creatures are believed to be the spirits of those who have been consumed by darkness, either through malevolent deeds or tragic circumstances. Legends say that the Scáthannaí can move through shadows and darkness, creating portals that allow them to traverse great distances in an instant. They are often depicted as harbingers of doom, appearing before great calamities or to claim the souls of the wicked. The Scáthannaí's ability to manipulate shadows and its relentless pursuit of its prey have made it a subject of many cautionary tales in Celtic folklore, serving as a reminder of the thin veil between light and darkness.

Sídhe Sentinel

Small fey, neutral good

Armor Class: 16 (natural armor)

Hit Points: 65 (10d6 + 30)

Speed: 30 ft., fly 50 ft. (hover)

STR	DEX	CON	INT	WIS	CHA
12 (+1)	18 (+4)	16 (+3)	14 (+2)	16 (+3)	17 (+3)

Saving Throws: Dex +7, Wis +6

Skills: Perception +6, Stealth +7, Insight +6

Damage Resistances: bludgeoning, piercing, and slashing from nonmagical attacks

Senses: darkvision 60 ft., passive Perception 16

Languages: Common, Sylvan, telepathy 60 ft.

Challenge: 5 (1,800 XP)

Magic Resistance: The Sídhe Sentinel has advantage on saving throws against spells and other magical effects.

Fairy Dust: As a bonus action, the Sídhe Sentinel can sprinkle fairy dust on itself or an ally within 5 feet, granting advantage on the next saving throw made within 1 minute.

Shimmercloak: The Sídhe Sentinel can use a bonus action to become invisible until the start of its next turn or until it attacks or casts a spell.

Fey Connection: The Sídhe Sentinel has an empathic link with Ríona na Sí and can communicate telepathically with her at any distance while on the same plane.

Actions

Multiattack: The Sídhe Sentinel makes two Moonblade attacks.

Moonblade: *Melee Weapon Attack:* +7 to hit, reach 5 ft., one target. *Hit:* 11 (2d6 + 4) slashing damage plus 7 (2d6) radiant damage.

Fey Charm (1/Day): The Sídhe Sentinel targets one humanoid it can see within 30 feet. The target must succeed on a DC 14 Wisdom saving throw or be magically charmed for 1 minute. While charmed, the target regards the Sídhe Sentinel as a trusted friend. The charm ends early if the Sídhe Sentinel or its allies do anything harmful to the target.

Blink Step (Recharge 5-6): The Sídhe Sentinel teleports up to 30 feet to an unoccupied space it can see. For 1 round after teleporting, its movement doesn't provoke opportunity attacks.

Reactions

Protective Flare: When a creature the Sídhe Sentinel can see within 30 feet of it is hit by an attack, the Sídhe Sentinel can create a burst of blinding light. The attacker must succeed on a DC 14 Constitution saving throw or be blinded until the end of its next turn.

Description

The Sídhe Sentinel appears as a slender, ethereal humanoid standing about 3 feet tall. Its skin shimmers with an iridescent glow, and gossamer wings flutter gently behind it. The Sídhe Sentinel's eyes are entirely silver, reflecting the light around them. It wears light armor that seems to be made of interwoven moonbeams and carries a blade that glows with an inner light.

These loyal guardians are created by Ríona na Sí herself, infused with the essence of the forest and bound to her will. They are fiercely protective of their queen and the sacred spaces of Coill Draíochta. Sídhe Sentinels are known for their grace in battle and their ability to appear and disappear at will, making them formidable defenders of the fey realm.

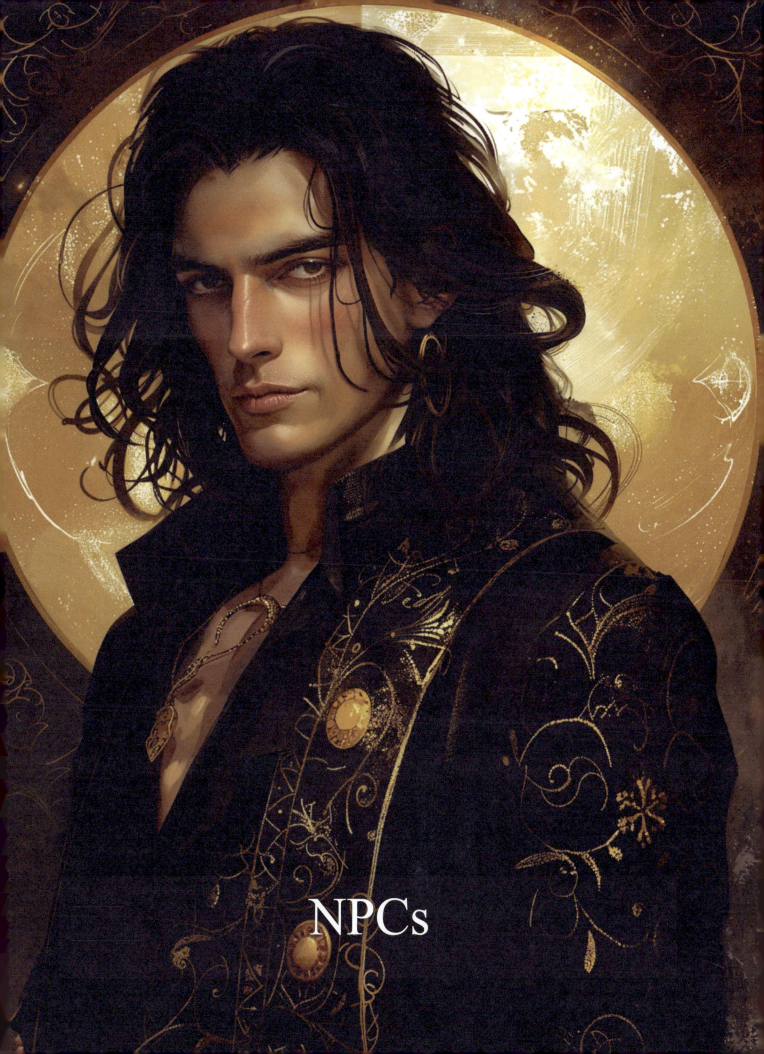

NPCs

Conall

Medium humanoid (human), chaotic evil

Armor Class: 18 (natural armor)

Hit Points: 190 (20d8 + 100)

Speed: 30 ft.

STR	DEX	CON	INT	WIS	CHA
14 (+2)	16 (+3)	20 (+5)	18 (+4)	14 (+2)	18 (+4)

Saving Throws: Con +10, Int +9, Cha +9

Skills: Arcana +9, Intimidation +9, Perception +7, Stealth +8

Damage Resistances: necrotic; bludgeoning, piercing, and slashing from nonmagical attacks

Senses: darkvision 60 ft., passive Perception 17

Languages: Common, Elvish, Infernal, Sylvan

Challenge: 13 (10,000 XP)

Proficiency Bonus: +5

Innate Spellcasting. Conall's spellcasting ability is Intelligence (spell save DC 18, +9 to hit with spell attacks). He can innately cast the following spells, requiring no material components:

- At will: Chill Touch, Mage Hand, Minor Illusion
- 3/day each: Animate Dead, Bestow Curse, Vampiric Touch
- 1/day each: Create Undead, Finger of Death, Cloudkill

Necromantic Mastery. Conall can control up to 12 undead creatures at once without needing to maintain concentration.

Undead Fortitude. If damage reduces Conall to 0 hit points, he must make a Constitution saving throw with a DC of 5 + the damage taken, unless the damage is radiant or from a critical hit. On a success, Conall drops to 1 hit point instead.

Actions

Multiattack. Conall makes two Necrotic Touch attacks.

Necrotic Touch. *Melee Spell Attack:* +9 to hit, reach 5 ft., one target. *Hit:* 18 (4d6 + 4) necrotic damage.

Deathly Wave (Recharge 5–6). Conall releases a wave of necrotic energy in a 30-foot radius. Each creature in that area must make a DC 18 Constitution saving throw, taking 45 (10d8) necrotic damage on a failed save, or half as much damage on a successful one. Undead creatures in the area are healed for half the damage dealt.

Legendary Actions

Conall can take 3 legendary actions, choosing from the options below. Only one legendary action option can be used at a time and only at the end of another creature's turn. Conall regains spent legendary actions at the start of his turn.

Detect. Conall makes a Wisdom (Perception) check.

Necrotic Touch. Conall makes one Necrotic Touch attack.

Summon Undead (Costs 2 Actions). Conall summons 1d4 skeletons or zombies in unoccupied spaces within 30 feet of him. The summoned undead obey his commands and act on the next available initiative count.

Description

Conall is a gaunt, spectral figure with sunken eyes that glow with a malevolent green light. His skin is deathly pale, stretched tightly over his bones, and he wears tattered robes that seem to billow with an unnatural wind. His presence exudes an aura of death and decay, and the ground beneath his feet seems to wither and die as he moves.

Conall grew up in the small village of Ballyvourney in County Cork, Ireland. He was known from a young age for his keen intellect and fascination with the local legends of death and the afterlife.

Tragedy struck when a devastating plague swept through Ballyvourney, claiming the lives of Conall's parents and many villagers. Grief-stricken and desperate to understand death, Conall left his home to study at a prestigious arcane academy.

There, his brilliance in necromancy quickly became apparent, as did his willingness to cross ethical boundaries. Expelled for his increasingly dark experiments, Conall wandered Ireland as an outcast, his powers growing alongside his notoriety for raising the dead.

It was during this time that Fionnlagh found him, offering Conall what no one else would: acceptance and the promise of unparalleled power over death through the Triskelion fragment. Seduced by the opportunity to further his necromantic studies without constraints, Conall eagerly became Fionnlagh's apprentice.

Now, Conall sees himself as a pioneer, pushing the boundaries between life and death. His ultimate goal, shaped by the loss of his village and nurtured by dark magic, is to create a world where death is merely a temporary state - a vision he believes can only be achieved through Fionnlagh's guidance and the Triskelion's power.

Conall wields the fragment of the Triskelion that grants him dominion over the dead. From his desolate, cursed cave, he commands an army of undead minions, spreading terror and death across the land. His mastery of necromantic magic and his relentless pursuit of power have made him a feared figure in the realm.

Eilidh the Druid

Medium fey (shapechanger: Draoi Caorach), neutral good

Armor Class: 15 (natural armor)

Hit Points: 75 (10d8 + 30)

Speed: 30 ft. (Druid form), 40 ft. (Ram form)

STR	DEX	CON	INT	WIS	CHA
16 (+3)	14 (+2)	16 (+3)	12 (+1)	18 (+4)	14 (+2)

Saving Throws: Dex +5, Wis +7, Cha +5

Skills: Nature +7, Perception +7, Survival +7

Damage Resistances: cold, fire, lightning

Senses: darkvision 60 ft., passive Perception 17

Languages: Common, Sylvan, Druidic

Challenge: 7 (2,900 XP)

Proficiency Bonus: +3

Shapechanger. The Draoi Caorach can use its action to polymorph into a large, mystical ram, or back into its true form. Its statistics, other than its AC, speed, and size, are the same in each form. Any equipment it is wearing or carrying isn't transformed. It reverts to its true form if it dies.

Nature's Wrath (Druid Form). As a bonus action, the Draoi Caorach can call upon the power of nature to enhance its spells and attacks. Its melee attacks deal an additional 1d6 force damage, and it gains advantage on attack rolls and saving throws against spells and other magical effects until the end of its next turn.

Actions

Multiattack (Druid Form). The Draoi Caorach makes two Quarterstaff attacks or casts one spell and makes one Quarterstaff attack.

Quarterstaff. *Melee Weapon Attack:* +6 to hit, reach 5 ft., one target. *Hit:* 7 (1d8 + 3) bludgeoning damage plus 3 (1d6) force damage.

Spellcasting (Druid Form). The Draoi Caorach is a 9th-level spellcaster. Its spellcasting ability is Wisdom (spell save DC 15, +7 to hit with spell attacks). It has the following druid spells prepared:

- *Cantrips (at will): Druidcraft, Guidance, Thorn Whip*
- *1st level (4 slots): Cure Wounds, Entangle, Faerie Fire*
- *2nd level (3 slots): Barkskin, Moonbeam, Spike Growth*
- *3rd level (3 slots): Call Lightning, Plant Growth, Wind Wall*
- *4th level (3 slots): Conjure Woodland Beings, Grasping Vine*
- *5th level (1 slot): Insect Plague*

Ram Charge (Ram Form). If the Draoi Caorach moves at least 20 feet straight toward a target and then hits it with a Ram attack on the same turn, the target takes an extra 10 (3d6) bludgeoning damage. If the target is a creature, it must succeed on a DC 15 Strength saving throw or be knocked prone.

Ram. *Melee Weapon Attack:* +6 to hit, reach 5 ft., one target. *Hit:* 14 (2d8 + 3) bludgeoning damage.

Description

Eilidh the Druid, in her human druid form, appears as a wise, elderly figure adorned in a flowing robe made of wool and natural elements like leaves and flowers. Her eyes are a deep, earthy brown, exuding wisdom and a profound connection to nature. When she shifts to her ram form, she transforms into a large, majestic ram with thick, white fleece and imposing, spiraled horns that shimmer with a faint magical aura.

Eilidh the Druid, also known as the Draoi Caorach, or Druid of the Sheep, is a revered shapeshifter renowned for her profound wisdom and mastery of nature magic. Legends tell of these druids serving as guardians of sacred groves and ancient knowledge, using their dual forms to protect the land and its inhabitants. In her human guise, Eilidh counsels and heals, drawing upon the earth's energy to cast powerful spells. As a mystical ram, she embodies strength and resilience, capable of fending off threats with formidable physical prowess. The Draoi Caorach is often associated with the deity Lugh, known for his versatility and mastery of multiple skills, reflecting the dual nature of this unique creature. Eilidh has foreseen the coming of the Triskelion's power and provides crucial guidance and support to those on their journey, encouraging them to seek the aid of the fey in the forest.

Eoghan na Luí (Eoghan of the Sunset)

Medium fey, neutral

Armor Class: 18 (natural armor)

Hit Points: 168 (16d8 + 96)

Speed: 30 ft.

STR	DEX	CON	INT	WIS	CHA
16 (+3)	20 (+5)	22 (+6)	18 (+4)	16 (+3)	24 (+7)

Saving Throws: Dex +10, Con +11, Cha +12

Skills: Deception +15, Insight +10, Persuasion +15, Stealth +10

Damage Resistances: psychic; bludgeoning, piercing, and slashing from nonmagical attacks

Senses: darkvision 60 ft., passive Perception 13

Languages: Common, Elvish, Sylvan

Challenge: 12 (8,400 XP)

Proficiency Bonus: +5

Master of Diplomacy. Eoghan has advantage on all Charisma (Deception) and Charisma (Persuasion) checks.

Twilight Step. As a bonus action, Eoghan can teleport up to 60 feet to an unoccupied space he can see that is in dim light or darkness.

Aura of Command. Allies within 30 feet of Eoghan have advantage on saving throws against being charmed or frightened.

Innate Spellcasting

Eoghan's innate spellcasting ability is Charisma (spell save DC 20, +12 to hit with spell attacks). He can innately cast the following spells, requiring no material components:

- *At will:* Disguise Self, Minor Illusion, Prestidigitation
- *3/day each:* Charm Person, Hold Person, Invisibility
- *1/day each:* Dominate Person, Greater Invisibility, Modify Memory

Actions

Multiattack. Eoghan makes two Shadow Blade attacks.

Shadow Blade. *Melee Weapon Attack:* +10 to hit, reach 5 ft., one target. *Hit:* 18 (3d8 + 5) psychic damage.

Sunset Glare (Recharge 5–6). Eoghan releases a burst of dazzling light. Each creature of his choice within 30 feet must make a DC 20 Constitution saving throw or be blinded for 1 minute. A blinded target can repeat the saving throw at the end of each of its turns, ending the effect on itself on a success.

Legendary Actions

Eoghan can take 3 legendary actions, choosing from the options below. Only one legendary action option can be used at a time and only at the end of another creature's turn. Eoghan regains spent legendary actions at the start of his turn.

Detect. Eoghan makes a Wisdom (Insight) check.

Shadow Blade Attack. Eoghan makes one Shadow Blade attack.

Fade into Twilight (Costs 2 Actions). Eoghan uses his Twilight Step.

Description

Eoghan na Luí is a tall, charismatic figure with dark, wavy hair that frames his sharp features. His eyes are a deep amber, glowing with cunning and intelligence. He dresses in elegant, dark clothing with hints of gold that shimmer like the setting sun, and his demeanor is both commanding and alluring, exuding an aura of authority and confidence that draws people to him.

Eoghan na Luí, the leader of Clann na Coimhthrátha, the Twilight Kin, is a master of diplomacy and manipulation. His strategic mind and persuasive skills make him a formidable opponent and a key figure in the delicate balance of Coill an Luí na Gréine, the Sunset Forest. Eoghan's ultimate goal is to further his faction's interests, often at the expense of others, but he is not without reason and can be negotiated with under the right circumstances. Eoghan embodies the concept of the liminal space between day and night, dawn and dusk, times considered magical and often associated with supernatural beings. His presence ensures that the Twilight Kin maintain their role as mediators and guardians of transitions, helping those who seek balance in their lives.

Fionnlagh, the Dark Sorcerer

Medium humanoid (human), chaotic evil

Armor Class: 19 (*Mage Armor*, Dexterity)

Hit Points: 198 (22d8 + 88)

Speed: 30 ft.

STR	DEX	CON	INT	WIS	CHA
12 (+1)	18 (+4)	18 (+4)	22 (+6)	16 (+3)	20 (+5)

Saving Throws: Int +12, Wis +9, Cha +11

Skills: Arcana +12, Deception +11, Insight +9, Perception +9

Damage Resistances: cold, fire, necrotic; bludgeoning, piercing, and slashing from nonmagical attacks

Senses: darkvision 60 ft., passive Perception 19

Languages: Common, Elvish, Infernal, Sylvan

Challenge: 14 (11,500 XP)

Proficiency Bonus: +6

Innate Spellcasting. Fionnlagh's spellcasting ability is Intelligence (spell save DC 20, +12 to hit with spell attacks). He can innately cast the following spells, requiring no material components:

- At will: *Mage Hand, Minor Illusion, Prestidigitation*
- 3/day each: *Counterspell, Dispel Magic, Fireball, Hold Person*
- 1/day each: *Dominate Person, Finger of Death, Plane Shift, True Seeing*

Magic Resistance. Fionnlagh has advantage on saving throws against spells and other magical effects.

Corrupting Presence. Any beast or plant within 60 feet of Fionnlagh becomes corrupted and hostile toward all other creatures. These creatures gain advantage on attack rolls and saving throws.

Dark Mastery. Fionnlagh can control up to 10 corrupted beasts or spirits within 1 mile of him, commanding them telepathically.

Actions

Multiattack. Fionnlagh makes three Eldritch Blast attacks.

Eldritch Blast. *Ranged Spell Attack:* +12 to hit, range 120 ft., one target. *Hit:* 12 (1d10 + 6) force damage.

Shadow Bolt. *Ranged Spell Attack:* +12 to hit, range 60 ft., one target. *Hit:* 27 (6d8) necrotic damage.

Dark Wave (Recharge 5–6). Fionnlagh releases a wave of dark energy in a 30-foot radius. Each creature of his choice within that area must make a DC 20 Constitution saving throw, taking 54 (12d8) necrotic damage on a failed save, or half as much damage on a successful one. Plants and beasts affected by this wave become corrupted if they are not already.

Legendary Actions

Fionnlagh can take 3 legendary actions, choosing from the options below. Only one legendary action option can be used at a time and only at the end of another creature's turn. Fionnlagh regains spent legendary actions at the start of his turn.

Detect. Fionnlagh makes a Wisdom (Perception) check.

Eldritch Blast. Fionnlagh makes one Eldritch Blast attack.

Corrupting Touch (Costs 2 Actions). Fionnlagh touches one creature within 5 feet of him. The target must succeed on a DC 20 Constitution saving throw or be poisoned for 1 minute. While poisoned in this way, the target is also paralyzed. The target can repeat the saving throw at the end of each of its turns, ending the effect on itself on a success.

Description

Fionnlagh is a tall, imposing figure with piercing, malevolent eyes that seem to burn with an inner fire. His hair is a deep, raven black, and his skin is unnaturally pale, giving him a ghostly appearance. He is clad in dark, flowing robes adorned with arcane symbols that glow faintly with a sinister light. His presence is both captivating and terrifying, exuding an aura of dread and power.

Fionnlagh's descent into darkness began as a quest for knowledge and power to protect his homeland. Born into a clan of druids tasked with maintaining the balance of nature, he witnessed firsthand the devastating effects of a great calamity that threw the natural world into chaos. Believing that the traditional druidic ways were insufficient to combat such threats, Fionnlagh sought out forbidden knowledge and ancient artifacts, including the legendary Triskelion. His pursuit led him to delve into dark magics and make pacts with sinister entities, each step justifying his actions as necessary for the greater good.

However, the more Fionnlagh immersed himself in shadow magic and corruption, the more his original noble intentions twisted. The power he amassed began to corrupt his mind, warping his perspective until he saw the natural order itself as flawed and in need of reshaping. Fionnlagh came to believe that only by controlling and manipulating the forces of nature and magic could true stability be achieved. This corrupted vision, combined with his ever-growing abilities, transformed him into the Dark Sorcerer he is today. Now, Fionnlagh seeks to remake the world according to his distorted ideals, viewing himself not as a villain, but as the only being capable of bringing true order to a chaotic world, no matter the cost.

Fionnlagh, the Dark Sorcerer is a malevolent figure bent on corrupting the balance of nature and harnessing the power of the Triskelion for his own dark purposes. His mastery of shadow magic and manipulation of corrupted beasts and spirits make him a formidable antagonist. Commanding a network of apprentices, Fionnlagh seeks to spread his influence and further his nefarious goals. Legends speak of his ruthless ambition and cunning, making him a feared and reviled figure in the land. His ultimate aim is to control the Triskelion's immense power, disrupting the natural order and bending the world to his will.

Maolmhuire

Medium humanoid (human), chaotic evil

Armor Class: 17 (natural armor)

Hit Points: 150 (20d8 + 60)

Speed: 30 ft.

STR	DEX	CON	INT	WIS	CHA
14 (+2)	16 (+3)	18 (+4)	20 (+5)	14 (+2)	16 (+3)

Saving Throws: Int +10, Wis +7, Cha +8

Skills: Arcana +10, Deception +8, Intimidation +8, Perception +7

Damage Resistances: necrotic; bludgeoning, piercing, and slashing from nonmagical attacks

Senses: darkvision 60 ft., passive Perception 17

Languages: Common, Infernal, Sylvan

Challenge: 10 (5,900 XP)

Proficiency Bonus: +5

Innate Spellcasting. Maolmhuire's spellcasting ability is Intelligence (spell save DC 18, +10 to hit with spell attacks). He can innately cast the following spells, requiring no material components:

- At will: Mage Hand, Minor Illusion, Prestidigitation
- 3/day each: Hold Person, Invisibility, Ray of Enfeeblement
- 1/day each: Blight, Dominate Person, Wall of Force

Dark Magic. Maolmhuire's attacks and spells deal an additional 1d6 necrotic damage.

Corruption Aura. Creatures within 10 feet of Maolmhuire have disadvantage on saving throws against being frightened or charmed.

Actions

Multiattack. Maolmhuire makes two Shadow Strike attacks.

Shadow Strike. *Melee or Ranged Spell Attack:* +10 to hit, reach 5 ft. or range 60 ft., one target. *Hit:* 13 (2d6 + 6) necrotic damage.

Dark Wave (Recharge 5–6). Maolmhuire releases a wave of dark energy in a 20-foot radius. Each creature in that area must make a DC 18 Constitution saving throw, taking 36 (8d8) necrotic damage on a failed save, or half as much damage on a successful one. Plants and beasts affected by this wave become corrupted if they are not already.

Legendary Actions

Maolmhuire can take 3 legendary actions, choosing from the options below. Only one legendary action option can be used at a time and only at the end of another creature's turn. Maolmhuire regains spent legendary actions at the start of his turn.

Detect. Maolmhuire makes a Wisdom (Perception) check.

Shadow Strike. Maolmhuire makes one Shadow Strike attack.

Corrupting Touch (Costs 2 Actions). Maolmhuire touches one creature within 5 feet of him. The target must succeed on a DC 18 Constitution saving throw or be poisoned for 1 minute. While poisoned in this way, the target is also frightened. The target can repeat the saving throw at the end of each of its turns, ending the effect on itself on a success.

Description

Maolmhuire is a menacing figure, his eyes glowing with a malevolent light. His gaunt, pale face is framed by dark, unkempt hair, and his lips often twist into a cruel smile. He is clad in tattered robes that seem to be woven from shadows, constantly shifting and swirling around him. His hands crackle with dark energy, ready to unleash his corrupting magic on those who dare to oppose him.

Maolmhuire's path to darkness began as a desperate bid for survival. Born into a poor family in a remote village plagued by harsh winters and failed harvests, he witnessed his loved ones succumb to famine and disease. Determined to never feel powerless again, Maolmhuire sought out any means to gain control over his circumstances. His search led him to ancient, forbidden texts that promised power at a terrible cost. Driven by desperation and a growing bitterness towards a world he saw as cruel and uncaring, Maolmhuire began to dabble in dark magic, slowly corrupting himself in the process.

It was in this vulnerable state that Fionnlagh found him. The Dark Sorcerer recognized the potential in Maolmhuire's raw talent and burning desire for power. Fionnlagh offered him not just knowledge and strength, but a twisted sense of purpose - a chance to reshape the world that had caused him so much pain. Seduced by the promise of never being victim to nature's whims again and blinded by his own trauma, Maolmhuire eagerly accepted Fionnlagh's offer of apprenticeship. Under Fionnlagh's tutelage, Maolmhuire's powers grew exponentially, as did his capacity for cruelty. Now, wielding the Life Fragment of the Triskelion, he sees himself as an agent of necessary change, believing that only through fear and domination can true order and security be achieved.

Maolmhuire wields dark magic to terrorize and corrupt local villages and farmsteads. Holding a fragment of the Triskelion, he uses its power to spread fear and corruption, twisting the land and its inhabitants to his will. Maolmhuire's loyalty to Fionnlagh and his mastery of dark magic make him a formidable foe, embodying the malevolence and corruption that threaten to unbalance the natural order.

Ríona na Sí (Ríona of the Fey)

Medium fey, neutral good

Armor Class: 18 (natural armor)

Hit Points: 150 (20d8 + 60)

Speed: 30 ft., fly 40 ft. (hover)

STR	DEX	CON	INT	WIS	CHA
12 (+1)	18 (+4)	16 (+3)	20 (+5)	22 (+6)	24 (+7)

Saving Throws: Dex +8, Wis +10, Cha +11

Skills: Arcana +9, Insight +10, Nature +10, Perception +10, Persuasion +11

Damage Resistances: cold, fire; bludgeoning, piercing, and slashing from nonmagical attacks

Senses: darkvision 120 ft., passive Perception 20

Languages: Common, Elvish, Sylvan

Challenge: 12 (8,400 XP)

Proficiency Bonus: +4

Innate Spellcasting. Ríona's spellcasting ability is Charisma (spell save DC 19, +11 to hit with spell attacks). She can innately cast the following spells, requiring no material components:

- *At will: Druidcraft, Detect Magic, Mage Hand*
- *3/day each: Cure Wounds (5th level), Dispel Magic, Moonbeam, Plant Growth*
- *1/day each: Greater Restoration, Heal, Sunbeam*

Magic Resistance. Ríona has advantage on saving throws against spells and other magical effects.

Nature's Aura. Friendly creatures within 30 feet of Ríona have advantage on saving throws against being frightened and charmed.

Regal Presence. Ríona can use her action to exude an aura of command. Each creature of her choice that is within 60 feet of her and aware of her must succeed on a DC 19 Wisdom saving throw or be charmed by her for 1 minute. A charmed target can repeat the saving throw at the end of each of its turns, ending the effect on itself on a success.

Actions

Multiattack. Ríona makes three Radiant Touch attacks.

Radiant Touch. *Melee Spell Attack:* +11 to hit, reach 5 ft., one target. *Hit:* 15 (3d6 + 5) radiant damage.

Guiding Bolt (Recharge 5–6). Ríona targets one creature she can see within 120 feet. The target must make a DC 19 Dexterity saving throw, taking 45 (10d8) radiant damage on a failed save, or half as much damage on a successful one. The next attack roll made against this target before the end of Ríona's next turn has advantage.

Legendary Actions

Ríona can take 3 legendary actions, choosing from the options below. Only one legendary action option can be used at a time and only at the end of another creature's turn. Ríona regains spent legendary actions at the start of her turn.

Detect. Ríona makes a Wisdom (Perception) check.

Radiant Touch. Ríona makes one Radiant Touch attack.

Mystic Shield (Costs 2 Actions). Ríona grants herself or an ally within 30 feet a +2 bonus to AC until the start of her next turn.

Description

Ríona na Sí is a tall, regal figure with long, flowing silver hair that shimmers like moonlight, giving her an ethereal and majestic appearance. Her eyes are a deep, otherworldly blue, reflecting the wisdom and depth of the ancient forest she protects. She wears a robe made of woven leaves and flowers that change with the seasons, enhancing her connection to the natural world. Her presence exudes an aura of calm and authority, commanding respect and trust from those who encounter her.

In the heart of Coill Draíochta, the Enchanted Forest, Ríona na Sí serves as both a guide and guardian, embodying the ancient magic and wisdom of this mystical place. Her profound knowledge of the Triskelion's power and the sorcerer's schemes makes her an invaluable ally to those who seek to restore balance and justice. Ríona's leadership is marked by her cautious but fair judgment, always seeking to maintain harmony within the forest. Her ability to communicate with the creatures of the forest and her deep connection to the land make her a central figure in the tales and legends based on Gaelic mythology, where she can be placed as a figure who is revered as a protector of nature and a beacon of hope.

Rivac Amretvo, the Storm Herald

Medium humanoid (human), neutral

Armor Class: 14 (natural armor)

Hit Points: 120 (16d8 + 48)

Speed: 30 ft.

STR	DEX	CON	INT	WIS	CHA
12 (+1)	14 (+2)	18 (+4)	16 (+3)	20 (+5)	12 (+1)

Saving Throws: Con +8, Wis +9, Cha +5

Skills: Nature +9, Perception +9, Survival +9

Damage Resistances: lightning, thunder

Senses: darkvision 60 ft., passive Perception 19

Languages: Common, Elvish, Sylvan

Challenge: 8 (3,900 XP)

Proficiency Bonus: +4

Innate Spellcasting. Rivac's spellcasting ability is Wisdom (spell save DC 17, +9 to hit with spell attacks). He can innately cast the following spells, requiring no material components:

- At will: Gust, Thunderclap
- 3/day each: Call Lightning, Lightning Bolt, Thunderwave
- 1/day each: Control Weather, Storm of Vengeance

Storm's Favor. Rivac has advantage on saving throws against lightning and thunder damage.

Eye of the Storm. While in a storm, Rivac can see through heavy precipitation, fog, and other weather-based obscurants without any penalties.

Actions

Multiattack. Rivac makes two Lightning Strike attacks.

Lightning Strike. *Ranged Spell Attack:* +9 to hit, range 120 ft., one target. *Hit:* 18 (4d8) lightning damage.

Thunderous Roar (Recharge 5–6). Rivac releases a burst of thunderous sound. Each creature within 20 feet of him must make a DC 17 Constitution saving throw, taking 27 (6d8) thunder damage and being pushed 10 feet away on a failed save, or half as much damage and not being pushed on a successful one.

Legendary Actions

Rivac can take 3 legendary actions, choosing from the options below. Only one legendary action option can be used at a time and only at the end of another creature's turn. Rivac regains spent legendary actions at the start of his turn.

Detect. Rivac makes a Wisdom (Perception) check.

Lightning Strike. Rivac makes one Lightning Strike attack.

Storm Call (Costs 2 Actions). Rivac calls down a bolt of lightning at a point he can see within 60 feet. Each creature within 10 feet of that point must make a DC 17 Dexterity saving throw, taking 14 (4d6) lightning damage on a failed save, or half as much damage on a successful one.

Description

Rivac is a rugged and weathered man, his skin tanned and lined from years spent braving the elements. His hair is a wild mane of silver, and his piercing blue eyes seem to hold the fury of a thousand storms. He wears simple, practical clothing suitable for a life in the wilderness, often covered with a heavy cloak that billows like storm clouds. Despite his rough appearance, his presence is calming, like the eye of a storm.

Rivac, known as the Storm Herald, is a hermit who has made his home in the storm-ravaged lands controlled by Róisín. He has spent years observing her actions and understanding the nature of her fragment's power. With a deep connection to the elements, Rivac can navigate the storms with ease, using his abilities to gather crucial information about Róisín's weaknesses. Though he prefers solitude, Rivac is willing to aid those who seek to restore balance and defeat the dark forces threatening the land.

Róisín

Medium humanoid (human), chaotic evil

Armor Class: 18 (natural armor)

Hit Points: 168 (24d8 + 72)

Speed: 30 ft.

STR	DEX	CON	INT	WIS	CHA
14 (+2)	18 (+4)	18 (+4)	16 (+3)	20 (+5)	18 (+4)

Saving Throws: Dex +9, Con +9, Wis +10

Skills: Arcana +8, Intimidation +9, Nature +10, Perception +10

Damage Resistances: lightning, thunder; bludgeoning, piercing, and slashing from nonmagical attacks

Senses: darkvision 60 ft., passive Perception 20

Languages: Common, Elvish, Sylvan

Challenge: 12 (8,400 XP)

Proficiency Bonus: +5

Innate Spellcasting. Róisín's spellcasting ability is Wisdom (spell save DC 18, +10 to hit with spell attacks). She can innately cast the following spells, requiring no material components:

- At will: *Gust, Thunderclap*
- 3/day each: *Call Lightning, Lightning Bolt, Thunderwave*
- 1/day each: *Control Weather, Storm of Vengeance, Chain Lightning*

Weather Manipulation. Róisín can use her action to create or dissipate a storm within a 1-mile radius around her. She can control the intensity and direction of the storm, causing effects such as heavy rain, strong winds, lightning strikes, and hail.

Storm Aura. A stormy aura surrounds Róisín. Creatures that start their turn within 10 feet of her take 10 (3d6) lightning damage.

Actions

Multiattack. Róisín makes two Lightning Strike attacks.

Lightning Strike. *Ranged Spell Attack:* +10 to hit, range 120 ft., one target. *Hit:* 18 (4d8) lightning damage.

Thunderclap (Recharge 5–6). Róisín creates a burst of thunderous sound. Each creature within 20 feet of her must make a DC 18 Constitution saving throw, taking 27 (6d8) thunder damage and being pushed 10 feet away on a failed save, or half as much damage and not being pushed on a successful one.

Legendary Actions

Róisín can take 3 legendary actions, choosing from the options below. Only one legendary action option can be used at a time and only at the end of another creature's turn. Róisín regains spent legendary actions at the start of her turn.

Detect. Róisín makes a Wisdom (Perception) check.

Lightning Strike. Róisín makes one Lightning Strike attack.

Storm Call (Costs 2 Actions). Róisín calls down a bolt of lightning at a point she can see within 60 feet. Each creature within 10 feet of that point must make a DC 18 Dexterity saving throw, taking 14 (4d6) lightning damage on a failed save, or half as much damage on a successful one.

Description

Róisín is a striking figure, her presence as formidable as the storms she commands. Her long, wild hair crackles with static electricity, and her piercing blue eyes flash like lightning against a backdrop of storm clouds. She wears flowing garments that seem to be woven from storm clouds, constantly shifting and billowing around her. Her very being radiates with the power of the tempest, making her an awe-inspiring and terrifying sight.

Róisín's journey to becoming Fionnlagh's apprentice began with a deep connection to nature and a desire to protect her coastal village from devastating storms. As a young druid, she showed an exceptional affinity for weather magic, often using her gifts to safeguard fishermen and warn of impending tempests. However, a catastrophic hurricane that decimated her home despite her best efforts left Róisín feeling powerless and filled with guilt. Driven by the need to gain greater control over the elements, she began to seek out more potent and dangerous forms of weather magic, gradually pushing the boundaries of natural law.

It was during her relentless pursuit of power that Fionnlagh found Róisín. The Dark Sorcerer recognized her potential and offered her the Rebirth Fragment of the Triskelion, promising her the ability to not just predict or mitigate storms, but to command them at will. Blinded by her ambition and the lingering trauma of her failure, Róisín accepted his offer, believing that absolute control over the weather was necessary to protect the world from nature's wrath. Under Fionnlagh's tutelage, her powers grew exponentially, but so did her detachment from the natural balance she once revered. Now, Róisín sees herself as nature's master rather than its steward, using her storm magic to enforce her will and Fionnlagh's vision, convinced that only through domination of the elements can true safety and order be achieved.

From her remote, storm-ravaged domain, she unleashes devastating storms to terrorize and manipulate those who cross her path. Her mastery of storm magic makes her a formidable foe, capable of bringing down entire villages with the wrath of nature.

Tadhg an Airgid (Tadhg of the Silver)

Medium fey, neutral good

Armor Class: 18 (natural armor)

Hit Points: 136 (16d8 + 64)

Speed: 30 ft.

STR	DEX	CON	INT	WIS	CHA
22 (+6)	16 (+3)	18 (+4)	14 (+2)	20 (+5)	16 (+3)

Saving Throws: Int +9, Wis +10, Cha +7

Skills: Arcana +13, History +13, Insight +10, Perception +10

Damage Resistances: psychic; bludgeoning, piercing, and slashing from nonmagical attacks

Senses: darkvision 60 ft., truesight 30 ft., passive Perception 20

Languages: Common, Elvish, Sylvan

Challenge: 11 (7,200 XP)

Proficiency Bonus: +4

Innate Spellcasting. Tadhg's spellcasting ability is Intelligence (spell save DC 19, +11 to hit with spell attacks). He can innately cast the following spells, requiring no material components:

- At will: *Detect Magic, Mage Hand, Prestidigitation*
- 3/day each: *Identify, Dispel Magic, Counterspell*
- 1/day each: *Legend Lore, True Seeing, Teleport*

Magic Resistance. Tadhg has advantage on saving throws against spells and other magical effects.

Keeper of Relics. Tadhg can identify the properties and history of any magical item with a touch, as if casting the Identify spell without expending a spell slot or material components.

Actions

Multiattack. Tadhg makes two Silver Staff attacks.

Silver Staff. *Melee Weapon Attack:* +9 to hit, reach 5 ft., one target. *Hit:* 12 (2d6 + 5) bludgeoning damage plus 7 (2d6) radiant damage.

Arcane Pulse (Recharge 5–6). Tadhg releases a burst of magical energy from his staff. Each creature in a 30-foot radius centered on him must make a DC 19 Dexterity saving throw, taking 45 (10d8) radiant damage on a failed save, or half as much damage on a successful one.

Legendary Actions

Tadhg can take 3 legendary actions, choosing from the options below. Only one legendary action option can be used at a time and only at the end of another creature's turn. Tadhg regains spent legendary actions at the start of his turn.

Detect. Tadhg makes a Wisdom (Perception) check.

Silver Staff Attack. Tadhg makes one Silver Staff attack.

Relic Shield (Costs 2 Actions). Tadhg uses the magic of his relics to create a shimmering shield around himself or an ally within 30 feet, granting a +2 bonus to AC until the start of his next turn.

Description

Tadhg an Airgid is a dignified figure with striking silver hair and a beard that glints in the light. His eyes are a piercing gray, full of knowledge and experience, reflecting the countless years he has spent safeguarding the relics of the Enchanted Forest. He wears robes adorned with intricate silver embroidery depicting ancient symbols and runes, and he often carries a staff topped with a crystal that pulses with magical energy, symbolizing his deep connection to the arcane.

Tadhg an Airgid, known as the Keeper of the Relics, is entrusted with the safekeeping and knowledge of the magical artifacts within Coill Draíochta, the Enchanted Forest. His expertise in the history and significance of these relics makes him a key figure in any quest to recover stolen artifacts. Tadhg's role extends beyond that of a custodian; he serves as a mentor, offering advice and sharing his vast knowledge to aid those who seek his wisdom. His presence ensures that the magical balance of the forest is maintained, and his guidance is sought by heroes and adventurers who face trials and seek to uncover the deeper truths of the world.

Magic Items

The Triskelion

Wondrous item, artifact (requires attunement)

The Triskelion appears as three interlocked spirals or bent human legs, crafted from an otherworldly metal that seems to shift between gold, silver, and bronze. When united, it pulses with an energy that reflects the cycle of life, death, and rebirth. The artifact can be separated into three distinct fragments, each embodying a different aspect of its power.

Properties:

Life Fragment (Creation):

- Cast *Mass Cure Wounds* and *Regenerate* once per day each.
- Cast *Conjure Celestial* (CR 4 or lower) once per day.

Death Fragment (Destruction):

- Cast *Finger of Death* and *Abi-Dalzim's Horrid Wilting* once per day each.
- Cast *Create Undead* (CR 3 or lower) once per day.

Rebirth Fragment (Transformation):

- Cast *Shapechange* and *Control Weather* once per day each.
- Cast *True Polymorph* once per day.

Unified Triskelion:

- **Restore Balance:** Once per week, perform a 1-hour ritual to remove all curses, diseases, and unnatural influences within a 1-mile radius.
- **Ultimate Control:** Once per day, combine any two abilities from the individual fragments.
- **Protection:** Gain resistance to all damage types and immunity to charm and fear effects.

Curse: Each time you use an ability of the Triskelion, you must succeed on a DC 15 Wisdom saving throw or gain one level of exhaustion. On a critical failure (roll of 1), you also gain a form of short-term madness (DM's choice).

Attunement: To attune to the Triskelion or any of its fragments, you must spend 24 hours meditating with it, experiencing visions of the cosmic cycle of life, death, and rebirth. You can attune to individual fragments or the unified Triskelion, but not both simultaneously.

Lore: The Triskelion is an artifact of immense power, its origins lost to time but deeply rooted in ancient Gaelic mythology. It's said to have been forged by the Tuatha Dé Danann at the dawn of creation to maintain the balance of the natural world. Throughout history, the Triskelion has appeared in times of great crisis, its power used to restore balance when the world teetered on the brink of chaos. However, its immense power has also drawn the attention of those who would use it for selfish or destructive purposes, leading to its division into three parts. Legends speak of the catastrophic consequences when the Triskelion falls into the wrong hands, warning of lands laid waste and the very fabric of reality torn asunder. Many believe that only a truly worthy individual, one who understands the delicate balance of nature and the responsibility that comes with such power, can safely wield the unified Triskelion.

Claidheamh Solais (Sword of Light)

Weapon (longsword), legendary (requires attunement)

This magnificent longsword features a blade adorned with intricate Celtic knotwork and glows with a radiant, golden hue. The hilt is wrapped in supple leather, and the pommel is set with a brilliant golden gem that pulses with inner light.

Properties:

- You gain a +2 bonus to attack and damage rolls made with this magic weapon.
- **Radiant Strike:** When you hit an undead or fiend with this weapon, the target takes an extra 2d8 radiant damage.
- **Light of the Ancients:** As a bonus action, you can cause the sword to shed bright light in a 30-foot radius and dim light for an additional 30 feet, or extinguish the light.
- **Healing Light:** Once per day, you can use an action to cast the *Cure Wounds* spell from the sword. The spell is cast at a level equal to your proficiency bonus. Wisdom is your spellcasting ability for this spell.

Attunement: To attune to this weapon, you must spend a short rest meditating with the sword under the light of the sun or moon. Once attuned, the sword's glow intensifies slightly in your grasp.

Lore: Claidheamh Solais is said to have been forged by ancient druids and blessed by the spirits of the forest. Legends speak of heroes wielding this blade to banish darkness and heal the land. It is believed that the sword draws its power from the very essence of light and life, making it particularly effective against creatures of darkness and undeath. Some sages theorize that Claidheamh Solais may be one of several celestial weapons created to maintain balance in the world, its radiant power a counterpoint to artifacts of shadow and decay.

Brat Draíochta (Cloak of Enchantment)

Wondrous item, very rare (requires attunement)

This flowing cloak is woven from enchanted silk that shimmers with the colors of the forest. Its hues shift subtly as it moves, ranging from deep emerald greens to soft, dappled browns. The edges of the cloak seem to blur slightly, as if not quite solid.

Properties:

- **Fey Camouflage:** While wearing this cloak, you have advantage on Dexterity (Stealth) checks. In natural environments, you can attempt to hide even when you are only lightly obscured by foliage, heavy rain, falling snow, mist, or other natural phenomena.
- **Silent Step:** Your footsteps make no sound while wearing this cloak, regardless of the surface you're moving across.
- **Nature's Embrace:** Once per day, you can use an action to cast the *Pass Without Trace* spell from the cloak, without requiring components. The spell affects you and up to 5 other creatures you choose within 30 feet of you.

Attunement: To attune to this cloak, you must spend a short rest wearing it in a natural setting, such as a forest, grove, or meadow.

Lore: The Brat Draíochta is a legendary garment said to have been worn by ancient fey lords during their sojourns in the mortal realm. Crafted by master weavers using silk infused with the essence of the Feywild, the cloak allows its wearer to move through nature as silently and unseen as the gentlest breeze. Some legends claim that wearing the cloak can grant glimpses into the Feywild itself, while others warn that extended use may slowly transform the wearer into a fey creature. The creation of such cloaks is a lost art, making each one a priceless treasure sought after by rangers, druids, and those wishing to walk unseen through the wild places of the world.

Cruach Draíochta (Cauldron of Magic)

Wondrous item, very rare (requires attunement)

This large, ancient cauldron is crafted from blackened iron and stands on three sturdy legs. Its surface is covered in intricate runes and Celtic symbols that seem to shimmer and move when viewed from the corner of the eye. The cauldron emanates a faint, magical warmth.

Properties:

- **Potion Brewing:** When you use this cauldron to brew potions, the brewing time is halved and you only need half the usual amount of ingredients.
- **Spell Catalyst:** When you cast a spell using a spell slot, you can choose to channel it through the cauldron. If you do, add one additional die to the spell's damage or healing effect. For example, a spell that normally deals 8d6 damage would instead deal 9d6 damage.
- **Rejuvenating Brew:** Once per day, you can use an action to command the cauldron to produce a magical brew. Any creature that drinks this brew regains 2d8 hit points and is cured of one of the following conditions: blinded, deafened, paralyzed, or poisoned.

Attunement: To attune to this cauldron, you must succeed on a DC 15 Intelligence (Arcana) check and then spend a short rest performing a ritual around it, burning herbs and chanting ancient druidic phrases.

Lore: The Cruach Draíochta is a legendary artifact believed to have been created by the archdruid Cathbad during the time of Cú Chulainn. It's said that the cauldron played a crucial role in many of the great tales of Irish mythology, brewing potions of heroism, concocting elixirs of prophecy, and even facilitating communication with the Otherworld. Some legends claim that the cauldron has the power to resurrect the dead, though at a terrible cost. Throughout history, the Cruach Draíochta has passed through the hands of many powerful druids and mages, each adding to its mystical properties. Its appearance often heralds great changes and epic quests, and many seek it for its power to enhance magic and create miraculous brews.

Pronunciations

Pronunciations

Irish Gaelic Name	Phonetic Pronunciation	Meaning
Aerilon	AIR-ih-lon	A constructed name meaning "land of air"
Aillte na Mara	AWL-cha na MA-ra	Cliffs of the Sea
Aillte na nDeor	AWL-cha na nyor	Cliffs of Tears
Bran Ó Ceallaigh	BRAWN oh KYAL-ee	Bran descendant of Ceallach (meaning "bright-headed")
Brat Draíochta	BRAT DREE-ukh-ta	Cloak of Enchantment
Caisleán na Taibhse	KASH-lawn na TYV-sha	Castle of the Ghost
Caoimhe	KWEE-va or KEE-va	Beautiful, gentle, precious
Ciarán an Sióg	KEER-awn an SHEE-ohg	Ciarán (meaning "little dark one") of the Fairy
Cionnaola Ó Dhonnaile	KUN-ay-la oh GON-il-yuh	Cionnaola descendant of Domhnall (meaning "ruler of the world")
Claidheamh Solais	KLYEEV SU-lish	Sword of Light
Clann na Coimhthrátha	KLAWN na KOH-hra-ha	Clan of the Twilight
Coill an Luí na Gréine	KWIL an LEE na GRAY-nya	Forest of the Setting Sun
Coill Draíochta	KWIL DREE-ukh-ta	Enchanted Forest
Conall	KON-ul	Strong wolf
Conor MacCarthaigh	KON-or mak-KAR-tee	Conor son of McCarthy (lover of horses)
Cruach Draíochta	KROO-akh DREE-ukh-ta	Cauldron of Magic
Draoi Caorach	DREE KAY-rakh	Druid of the Sheep
Droichead na Carraige	DRIH-had na KAR-ig-uh	Bridge of the Rock
Eamon O'Connell	AY-mun oh-KON-el	Eamon descendant of Conall
Eilidh	AY-lee	Light
Eilis Ní Chathasaigh	AY-lish nee KAH-ha-see	Elizabeth daughter of Cathasach (meaning "vigilant")
Eoghan na Luí	OH-in na LEE	Eoghan (meaning "born of the yew tree") of the Sunset
Fáinne na Sí	FAWN-ya na SHEE	Ring of the Fairies
Fiachra	FEE-a-kra	Raven
Fiona Ní Fágáin	FEE-na nee FAW-gawn	Fiona (meaning "fair") daughter of Fagan
Fionnlagh	FYUN-la	Fair hero
Gleann na Marbh	GLYOWN na MARV	Valley of the Dead
Inis Solais	IN-ish SUL-ish	Island of Light
Liam Ó Domhnaill	LEEM oh DOH-null	William descendant of Domhnall

Lucht Siúil	LUKHT SHOOL	Traveling People
Maolmhuire	MWEEL-vur-uh	Devotee of Mary
Moira Ní Bhraonáin	MOY-ra nee VRAY-nawn	Moira (variant of Mary) daughter of Brennan (meaning "descendant of the sorrowing one")
Nessa Ní Chléirigh	NESS-a nee KLAY-ree	Nessa (from Nas, meaning "gentle") daughter of Cleary (meaning "clerk")
Niamh an tSolais	NEEV an tuh-LIS	Niamh (meaning "bright") of the Light
Oileán na nAmhrán	IL-awn na NOW-rawn	Island of Songs
Peist Dhraíochta	PESHT GHREE-ukh-ta	Magic Serpent
Ríona na Sí	REE-na na SHEE	Ríona (Queenly) of the Fairies
Rivac Amretvo	RI-vak AM-ret-vo	Not a traditional Irish name
Róisín	ro-SHEEN	Little Rose
Saoi na Coille	SEE na KWIL-ya	Sage of the Forest
Scáthannaí	SKAW-han-ee	Shadow Walker
Seamus Ó Raghallaigh	SHAY-mus oh RYE-lee	James, descendant of Raghallach (meaning "powerful in battle")
Sídhe Sentinel	SHEE SEN-ti-nel	Fairy Mound Guardian
Siobhan Ní Shuilleabhain	shi-VAWN nee HWIL-a-vawn	Siobhan (variant of Joan) daughter of Sullivan (meaning "dark-eyed")
Sorcha Ní Bhraonáin	SOR-ka nee VRAY-nawn	Clara, daughter of Brennan
Tadhg an Airgid	TYG an AR-gid	Tadhg (meaning "poet" or "philosopher") of the Silver
Túr na nScáth	TOOR na SKAWTH	Tower of Shadows
Turlough Ó Murchadha	TUR-lock oh MUR-ka-ha	Turlough descendant of Murchadh (meaning "sea warrior")
Uaimh Chráite	OO-iv KRAW-cha	Ghost Cave

Map

Map

Thank You

Abdul Aziz Al-Kaboor

Becky-Jane

Brandon Adcock

Brian Schnapp

Cabot Aycock

C. B. Pelton

Cory O'Donnell

Craig Hackl

Captaen Rik

David Stephenson

Ed Bachner

Ian Smith

Jason Taylor

Jayson Holovacs

Justing Parker

Matthew Ceplina

Michelle McFarlin

Miron Arljung

Misty

Parker Wesley McClellan

Susannah Kervin

The Weule Bros.

Walter Brown

Wells

This work includes material taken from the System Reference Document 5.1 ("SRD 5.1") by Wizards of the Coast LLC and available at https://dnd.wizards.com/resources/systems-reference-document. The SRD 5.1 is licensed under the Creative Commons Attribution 4.0 International License available at https://creativecommons.org/licenses/by/4.0/legalcode.

Copyright © M A D / Matthew David / MAD Games 2024 - A Penny Blood Adventure